OPEN ARMS

Vince Cable is MP for Twickenham, and also served from 1997–2015. He was the Liberal Democrats' Shadow Chancellor in opposition and Deputy Leader, having previously served as Chief Economist for Shell. He was Business Secretary under the Coalition Government from 2010–2015. Cable has published three non-fiction books with Atlantic to critical acclaim: *Free Radical, The Storm* and *After the Storm*. *Open Arms* is his debut novel.

OPEN ARMS

VINCE CABLE

CORVUS

First published in hardback in Great Britain in 2017 by Corvus, an imprint of Atlantic Books Ltd.

Copyright © Vince Cable, 2017

10 9 8 7 6 5 4 3

A CIP catalogue record for this book is available from the British Library.

Hardback ISBN: 978 178 649 1718
E-book ISBN: 978 178 649 1725

Printed and bound in Great Britain by TJ International Ltd, Padstow, Cornwall

Corvus
An imprint of Atlantic Books Ltd
Ormond House
26–27 Boswell Street
London
WC1N 3JZ

www.corvus-books.co.uk

OPEN
ARMS

CHAPTER 1

THE BODY

Reuters, 7 June 2019:

Indian sources report a border incident on the Line of Control in Kashmir. Several Indian jawans (soldiers) and infiltrators were reported dead. A defence ministry spokesman said that terrorists from the militant group Lashkar-e-Taiba had been intercepted crossing the border. He warned that under India's Cold Start doctrine, Pakistan could expect a rapid military response if its government was found to be implicated.

The stinking rivulet was part bathroom, part laundry, part sewer and part rubbish tip, servicing the needs of a city within a city. But for Ravi it was an aquatic adventure playground. Those not acquainted with the sights and smells of the baasti would have grimaced at the tannery waste and turds and dead dogs of this slum. But he was endlessly absorbed by the stately progress downstream of his flotilla of boats made from twigs, cans and bottles on their way through swampland to Mumbai harbour and thence to the Indian Ocean.

That morning his mother had risen early to be ahead of the queue performing their bodily functions and washing at the stream. There was a healthy flow swollen by heavy overnight rain and Ravi's attention was caught by a bundle of clothes trapped under a fallen tree, brought down by the rainstorm. This time of year produced a rich haul of driftwood, cans and plastic bottles to augment his merchant navy. He saw the potential of fabric for his sailing ships and with the help of a stick he managed to free the clothes until they floated closer to his harbour, a broken plastic frame that had so far escaped the attention of the boys scavenging for material to recycle. As he pulled on his catch he realised that it was bulkier than a bundle of clothes, and belonged to a man. This wasn't his first corpse but this one lacked hands and feet and the gaping eyes carried, even in death, the look of terror. His scream had the early morning bathers rushing to examine his discovery.

Had Deepak Parrikar been interested in these happenings a little over a mile away he could have seen them with the help of a telescope from the top floor of Parrikar House where he was fielding an early morning round of calls.

Dharavi, with its million or more inhabitants, can claim to be Asia's largest slum and it sits wedged between a major highway to the east, serving downtown Mumbai, and the seafront residences of Mahim Bay to the west, with fashionable Bandra to the north and the even more fashionable hilly area to the south where Parrikar House was located. But it was a place of which Deepak knew little and had never visited. And of the township of thousands of slum dwellers, where Ravi and his mother lived, between Dharavi and the middle class suburb of Chembur further to the east, he knew absolutely nothing. Yet this corner of Mumbai had a distinction: the World Health Organization had designated it one of the most polluted places on earth. Such a status was earned not just by the organically rich collection of bacteria in its water courses – for which any prize would have to be shared with many other sites in the city – but by a uniquely toxic soup of airborne, inorganic matter, a blend of traffic-generated particulates and the vaporised by-products of an ancient chemical plant, which Deepak's father owned.

Deepak had long been able to filter out of his conscious-ness the sights, sounds and smells of India's poor. It had once been necessary to apologise to overseas business visitors for the unpleasantness of the drive from the airport. But a new highway, partly built on stilts across the sea from downtown Mumbai en route to the new international airport, bypassed the more sordid and congested districts. He was able to concentrate single-mindedly on his business and the web of interlocking interests that he had spun, stretching from California to Singapore via London, Munich and Tel Aviv. The only smell drifting across his desk was the perfume of his PA, 'Bunty' Bomani, bought for her on a visit to Paris and now intermingling with his own expensive aftershave. Outside the large windows the sky had cleared after the monsoon storm the previous evening and the usual cloud of dust and smoke had dissipated to reveal the endless townscape of what, on some measures, was the world's biggest city. The only sight to upset Deepak in the panoramic view was the grotesque, vulgar, multi-storey block of luxury apartments erected by one of his family's main rivals, breaching every known principle of planning, let alone aesthetic design.

'A call from your father, sir,' said Bunty. He lay back in his comfortable office chair, legs on the desk, tie askew, and in his shirtsleeves, with the jacket of his exquisite, hand-sewn suit lying on the floor. 'How's Mummy-ji?' he asked, switching to Hindi for his father's benefit. 'How's her sciatica? Have you got rid of that good-for-nothing doctor yet? Charges you the earth. Useless. Quack. Absolutely hopeless. Ancient Tamil remedies! Nonsense! I told you to try the physiotherapist at the clinic on Dr Merchant's Road.

He has sorted out a lot of our friends' back problems.' And so on, for the statutory five minutes until his father switched the conversation to politics, then business, or the other way round, since they usually came to the same thing.

'I spoke to my old friend Vikram, number three in the ruling party High Command,' Parrikar Senior explained. 'Sensible man, like the PM. Not one of these fanatics. He thanked me for our generous contribution to party funds. They know I used to back Congress and was close to Madam herself. But we are no longer outcasts. The PM likes the sound of our avionics operation, also. He may visit your factory to see India's high tech manufacturing. He understands that the country needs to develop with our overseas partners. The government knows all about the technology being developed in Pulsar, our partner company in the UK, and is keen to bring it to India. No more stupid "Swadeshi" talk about "self-sufficient" India, reinventing the wheel.'

'But Daddy-ji, where are we with this air force contract? We keep being promised. In the press ministers continue to say India has finally agreed to buy aircraft from the French – Dassault – not Eurofighter. Our British business partners are saying that India can only get access to the UK avionics technology if the air force buys Eurofighter.'

'I know. Vikram says don't believe what you read in the press. The PM understands. He has to respect procurement rules after all that fuss around the Congress party and Bofors, and other scandals. He wants clean government.

Things have to be done by the book. So it will take some time to change things. However, the British are sending a ministerial delegation to negotiate in Delhi. They may come here also to visit the factory. Check us out. The British have left Europe and want to trade with us. The PM thinks they are beggars who can't be choosers.'

The deal centred on the growing reputation of Deepak's company, in India and abroad, in the world of radar-based detection systems, used in the latest generation of jet fighters and in India's embryonic anti-missile defence shield. The company's origins lay in a century-old British firm, Smith & Smith, which had made weapons for the British Army in India. Several takeovers later it had become Pulsar but the link remained with its former Indian subsidiary, now renamed Parrikar Avionics after a burst of Indianisation by Mrs Gandhi in the 1970s. Parrikar Avionics added lustre to India's new image of sophisticated technology companies in IT, pharmaceuticals, precision engineering and aerospace. It had been built up by Deepak over the last decade. But the inspiration, as well as the capital behind it and the original acquisition of a majority stake in the clapped-out engineering plant, came from Ganesh Parrikar, his father.

Parrikar had started life as a street urchin in what was then Bombay in newly independent India. It was literally a rags to riches story. His family, landless, low caste Hindus, were starving in one of Bihar's periods of drought and, aged ten, he was packed off to a distant relative in Bombay. He never found the relative and had to survive on the streets. He did survive thanks to the kindness of strangers, a streak of ruthlessness and the immense good luck of sharing a pavement with another Bihari who was making his way in the world running errands for a developer building cheap housing for the expanding population north of downtown Bombay. Ganesh ran errands for the errand boy and acquired a tiny foothold in an industry in which he was to make his fortune. He progressed within half a century to becoming one of the city's dollar billionaires. A few years earlier his wealth would have placed him in the exclusive pantheon of India's business deities alongside the Birlas and Ambanis. But there were now dozens of billionaires, in so far as it was possible to measure wealth that was often hidden from the tax authorities and jealous relatives, dispersed internationally and embedded in family trusts of Byzantine complexity.

Ganesh Parrikar's energy, guile and unfailing instinct for property market trends and turning points were only part of his success. No one could succeed, as he had done, without being integrated into the network of corrupt officials and politicians that operated at city and state level. Nothing could be achieved without the right palms being greased. Nor could he operate without the muscle of gangsters who, for a consideration, would clear a site of unwanted occupants and ensure that rents were fully paid on time. But as a good father and patriotic Indian, Parrikar then diversified into productive and legitimate businesses to secure a legacy for his three children.

He made a berth for his eldest, Deepak. Deepak had been sent, aged thirteen, to an expensive school in England followed by engineering at Cambridge and a PhD at Imperial, and from there to Harvard Business School and several years' practical experience in the aerospace industry on the west coast of America. When he returned he was charged with building up a high-level tech business in civil and military aircraft electronics. This he had done successfully, starting with a collaboration to adapt Russian MiGs to Indian conditions and then improving quality management to become part of the supply chain of Boeing and Airbus. The company's British partner, Pulsar, was also an invaluable source of technology and marketing contacts, though the Indian offshoot was beginning to outgrow its former parent.

In truth, Parrikar Avionics made little money, though it added lustre to the family's image and India's reputation for world class manufacturing. It also advertised good corporate governance, since Deepak was a crusader for the kind of wholesome, caring, visionary company advocated by his friends in California. But the reality behind the opaque family business accounts was less wholesome: the balance sheet depended on the inflating price of land, much of it acquired by dubious means, and the cash flow was boosted by rentals from innumerable shacks of the kind occupied by Ravi and his family.

Inspector Mankad was settling into a pile of paperwork, which flapped in the gusts of air from the fan on his desk, when the call came in that a body had been found in suspicious circumstances. He was required immediately. He groaned. The pile of paper would continue to grow and the call also required venturing out into the muggy, oppressive heat until another monsoon downpour gave some relief. A possible murder in one of the most squalid, fetid, overcrowded and volatile of Mumbai's innumerable patches of slumland was not a glamorous assignment.

He straightened out his khaki uniform in front of a small mirror that nestled among his display of family photos; twirled his impressively long moustache modelled on a heroic Bollywood crime fighter; tightened his belt a notch or two to disguise a little better his prodigious paunch; and collected his even more overweight assistant, Sergeant Ghokale, to head for the waiting jeep. Both carried revolvers but they were ancient and probably didn't work. Rather, the officers' badge of authority and legitimate force was a thick bamboo cane, the lathi stick, which, from colonial times, had been used to intimidate crowds and dispense instant justice to troublemakers.

When they arrived at the scene of the crime, Inspector Mankad and Sergeant Ghokale pushed their way confidently through the swelling crowd towards the inanimate lump by the edge of the stream, now covered by a dirty cloth. The faces were suspicious, fearful: poor people who knew all about police beatings and extortion.

They parted meekly for the officers, whose peaked caps radiated authority and whose stomachs, bulging over their belts, suggested a prosperous career in law enforcement.

The four-year-old Ravi who had made the discovery pointed to the body and Sergeant Ghokale tried to ingratiate himself with the crowd by patting the child on the head and hailing him as a budding policeman. But no one understood his Marathi language. So he turned to his superior officer, and said, after a very quick inspection of the mutilated, bullet-ridden corpse, 'Sahib, gang killing. One less goonda to chase.'

'I don't know the face,' replied his boss. 'I know all their mugshots. Nice clothes. Businessman? Maybe a money man; managing their loot? Look in his pockets.'

Sergeant Ghokale did as he was told. Inspector Mankad was a good boss, shared out any pickings, looked after his team. Ghokale fought back nausea from the stench around him and expertly picked his way over the wet, bloodstained clothes. 'Nothing, Sahib. Clean. No ID.'

This could be awkward. Gang killing of unknown businessman. Kidnapping? Extortion? No one had been reported missing that fitted this man, as far as Mankad knew. He had survived and flourished in the Maharashtra police by bagging a regular crop of minor villains; generously sharing out any glory and financial rewards with superiors and subordinates; and knowing which cases to avoid, the political ones. Mankad calculated the risks. Gangland killings were dangerous. The top villains had friends in the state assembly and administration. Cases were mysteriously terminated. Police officers who showed too much curiosity could find themselves transferred to some fly-blown, poverty stricken country district. Now, with new faces after state elections, was especially dangerous. Mankad would have to be very careful.

But he was also a professional police officer. He may have played the game of brown envelopes and learnt how to swim in the shark infested seas of police politics. But he also had a medal for gallantry, and several highly commended awards, for doing his duty confronting armed criminals and protecting his team. He loathed the idea of gangsters going free.

As the officers moved to leave, Sergeant Ghokale grabbed hold of Ravi's father who was standing protectively next to his celebrity son. 'You. Witness. Come with me. Make statement.' The man cowered and pleaded with the police officer not to take him: 'Know nothing, Sahib.' His Telugu language was totally incomprehensible to the policeman but the ripple of anger through the crowd gave the officer pause. They knew what would happen. The man would be taken to the police station, beaten and detained. His family would lose their meagre income: the two hundred rupees (three dollars) a day he earned from dangerous and exhausting labour on a building site, whenever there was work available. They would be told they needed to pay for food at the police station, to stop the beatings and then to stop a false statement being filed and then again to get him released. Every last rupee, and the limit of what the money lender would advance, would be squeezed out of them. And if they didn't pay he would be charged as an accessory to the murder and the police station would be able to maintain its impressive hundred per cent clearup rate for serious crime. Either way, the family would be destroyed and return to the bottom of the ladder, back into the extreme poverty from which they had just begun to ascend.

The tension was broken by a bark of command: 'Ghokale. Leave it. We have work to do.'

As the officers retreated to their jeep, Mankad took a long look at the site. He tried to ignore the flies, the stench from the sewage pit and the curious crowd of children who were following them. He let his police training take over. One thing he noticed out of the ordinary was the pukka building on elevated land a quarter of a mile away, upstream from where the body had been found. Parked outside was a smart SUV that was unlikely to belong to the slum dwellers. And the flags flying from the building belonged to an extreme Hindu nationalist outfit that, in the heyday of its founder, ran the city and was blamed for much of the sectarian violence that plagued Mumbai. It was still a considerable political force where its cadres, operating from branch offices like the building nearby, were able to whip up communal feelings against outsiders: southerners, especially Tamils; northerners; Muslims. But all power corrupts and the pursuit of ethnic purity had long since taken second place to the spoils of extortion, smuggling, prostitution and other flourishing rackets. Mankad ordered Ghokale to drive the jeep a little further to make a note of the SUV's registration number. But not too close.

CHAPTER 2

THE CANDIDATE

One year earlier: August 2018

Kate Thompson yawned with relief. The annual summer fete had produced record takings. Over five thousand pounds. The elderly ladies who made up the backbone of the Surrey Heights Conservative Association clucked with satisfaction. They disagreed, however, as to whether the big money spinner had been Kate's Indian textiles, heavily discounted from her shop, or Stella's cupcakes. The former verdict would align them with the glamorous wife of the local party's sugar daddy. Loyalty to the latter would protect them from being flayed by the malicious, razor-edged tongue of the longstanding local party agent.

Appearances defined these respective factions. Kate was exceptionally tall, with long, comfortably unruly and naturally blonde hair; proud of her well-honed physique;

and always shown to advantage in fashionable and expensive clothes. Stella's army of elderly volunteers, with permed grey and white hair, were uniformly attired in dresses that reflected M&S fashions of a decade earlier.

Kate had never really felt she belonged to or understood the party, though her matching blue outfit and diligent work for The Cause might suggest otherwise. Her well-heeled, middle class parents – her late father had been a successful surgeon; her mother a pillar of the WI – had always voted Tory out of habit, though their broadly liberal views had sat uncomfortably with the content of their morning *Telegraph*. Kate had actually voted for Tony Blair in the noughties and at the last general election had turned up at the polling station sporting a large blue rosette and voted for the Lib Dem who seemed so much more interesting than the useless local MP. She had been further alienated by the Brexit vote, which she regarded as a disaster, one caused in part by the likes of Stella terrifying the pensioners of Surrey Heights by telling them that eighty million Turks were on their way. But a competent Prime Minister had arrived just in time to keep her in the party.

Still, she asked herself why on earth she was spending time here rather than with her daughters, her friends or her business. She had a seriously rich husband and what were rich husbands for if not to sign large cheques? His annual cheque to the association was worth at least ten times the amounts raised at this fundraiser, which had been planned over three months with as much detail as the Normandy landings. Unfortunately, he also had a tendency to treat his trophy wife as part of his successful property portfolio and had volunteered Kate's services to the association without her knowledge or approval, leading to a considerable row in a marriage increasingly characterised by lows rather than highs.

Kate realised that money wasn't really the point. The event was all about bonding, and nothing bonded the activists together more closely, short of an election, than gossip. An audible buzz rose and fell as Stella moved around like a bumble bee sucking nectar on its journey from stall to stall, while also injecting a little poison along the way. Stella was over fifty, blue rinse and twinset in imitation of her idol. She had a fathomless collection of stories from the highest sources – 'absolutely true' – about gay orgies, paedophile rings and fraud involving everybody she disliked. Kate had a firm policy of not being bitchy about other women, but those with acute hearing would have heard her mutter: 'What an absolute cow.'

This year Stella was almost out of control, such was the pitch of her excitement. The rumour mill was working flat out, fed by the story that the veteran MP, Sir Terence Watts, was about to step down. His appearances in the constituency were infrequent and embarrassing. Today he had opened the fete, not an onerous feat, but had muffed his lines, got the name of the village wrong and thanked the wrong hostess for the loan of her beautiful garden. Perhaps he was distracted by the recent press revelations that he had seriously overclaimed for his parliamentary expenses, including three properties, one in Jamaica. He would be unlikely to survive the weekend.

Kate had never understood how he had managed to cling on like a limpet through a quarter of a century of inactivity. Her husband explained that the whips valued his uncritical loyalty and many older voters liked his military bearing and beautifully tailored three-piece suit worn in all weathers. Moreover, Stella had provided him with a formidable Praetorian Guard. Her devotion may have been grounded in an ancient passion but he was also the source of her local power. Now her loyalties had moved on and she was telling her geriatric army that the party of Mrs Thatcher, with the new female PM, needed more mature women MPs and fewer 'bright young men'. Her profile of the ideal MP fitted herself perfectly. But had she been better at interpreting body language she would have realised that her enthusiasm was not widely shared.

The name on everyone's lips was Jonathan Thompson, Kate's husband: very rich, very handsome in a louche way, clever, capable, personable and well connected, a man who would inexorably rise to the top. Knowing her husband better than the party faithful, Kate could have added to the list of his attributes an insatiable appetite for serial philandering, a major deficit in emotional intelligence, and political convictions that mainly centred on the sanctity of his private property, particularly the parts of the property market that generated his fortune. She had, however, learnt to balance the bad with the good. But when she heard herself being addressed as the MP presumptive's wife, something inside her rebelled.

She flushed with annoyance and struggled to concentrate against the competing claims of fussy customers, securing change for depleting floats, polite repartee and approaching rain clouds. Although she had never publicly articulated the thought, she had long felt that she would be a far better MP than many of the men she saw, and encountered, trying to do the job, not least the useless Sir Terence. The material comforts of life with Jonathan and family duties had dulled her ambition. But there was an ambitious woman waiting to emerge and this afternoon had stirred up what she had long suppressed. Her incoherent thoughts were crystallised when she was approached by one of the few local Conservatives she actually liked. Len Cooper was a long-serving county councillor, now the leader of the council. He was highly competent, unpretentious and modest: a successful local businessman in the building trade who believed in public service and practised it. They enjoyed a good friendship, uncomplicated by any emotional undertones. Her only discomfort was that at six foot without heels she towered over his small and totally spherical body. This didn't seem to faze him; he was a man comfortable in his own skin and especially comfortable in the company of his equally spherical wife, Doris. As they started to talk they soon got around to the runners and riders and the short odds being offered on Jonathan. Len Cooper was non-committal but, after a long pause, said: 'I am surprised that you haven't considered standing yourself.' Since Len didn't do flattery, she took the comment seriously and was pleased as it reinforced a thought that had already crossed her mind.

It hadn't crossed the mind of her husband, however. They had a rare evening at home together that night, as the girls were staying with family friends while competing in a gymkhana. Over dinner he set out the pros and cons of his own candidacy and various alternative scenarios in none of which Kate featured. He saw himself as the ideal candidate but had done the maths. They had three daughters at expensive schools; horses and paddock; a 'cottage' (actually a small château) in Burgundy; Kate's Land Rover and his Maserati; the annual pilgrimage to the ski slopes at Klosters; membership of an exclusive golf club; and that was after cutting out some of the luxuries. An MP's salary would reduce them to wretched poverty if he was forced into being a full-time MP – as the party High Command was now demanding – and to hand over the property business to his partners. Kate reminded him of the contribution she made from the profits on her business and could see a 'p' word forming on his lips – 'pin money' or 'peanuts' – before he stopped himself. He had a better idea: 'The High Command is keen to find a bright young man. Ex-Oxford. Special adviser to the Foreign Secretary.

The next David Cameron. Surrey Heights would be perfect.'
He – and possibly the High Command – seemed not to have
noticed that posh boys were no longer the darlings of local
constituency associations.

By now Kate was becoming seriously irritated. 'If you
don't want the seat, why are you spending your money
and my time bailing out the local Tories?' she asked.

He thought for a while, hurt by his wife's cynicism.
'Because I care. The Labour Party has been taken over by
Marxist-Leninist revolutionaries. If they get into power at
the next election our heads will be on spikes. They hate
us. The politics of envy.'

Kate shared the more conventional view reflected in the
polls that the chances of Labour winning were roughly
comparable to Elvis Presley being found on Mars. But this
passionate outburst reminded her that while she and her
husband agreed on some things – Remain being one –
they disagreed on most others. She was privately relieved
that her husband wasn't going to be her next MP.

She then braced herself for a difficult exchange.

'It may surprise you, Jonathan, but my name also came
up in the chatter this afternoon.'

'Who from?'

'Never mind who. It did. And I am thinking about it.'

She knew him well enough to know that the words
'don't be ridiculous, woman' were forming in his mind,
but he knew her well enough not to utter them. He opted
for soft soap instead.

'You are a brilliant mother. Don't the girls need our continued attention?' (But apparently not his!) 'Your business is doing well. Are you going to let it go?' (This from someone who prided himself on not getting out of bed for a business deal worth under a million pounds.) And then the coup de grâce: 'We have had our differences but you have been a wonderfully supportive wife. I need you.' She cursed her lack of foresight in not having set up a tape recorder.

She kept going. 'The children are no longer babies. There is a commuter train from the station down the road. I have a plan for my business. I can cope. And it might help you with your business to have an MP for a wife, close to the centre of power.'

He grunted in acknowledgement. 'OK, you have a point. Let's think about it.' With that he disappeared to attend to his emails. Kate called after him: 'I take that as a "yes". Thank you, Jonathan.' There was no reply. The 'thank you' was sincere. She would win the hearts and minds of the local association only as part of a happy, smiling family. And she would need Jonathan's money.

The following morning, she rang Len Cooper. 'I have been thinking about your suggestion. The answer is positive. Jonathan isn't wild about it but he's on board.' Len expressed no surprise but took her through the practicalities. First, shortlisting by the executive committee. He would speak to Stella and assure her that her job was safe, but insist that she drop her ridiculous candidacy.

He would tell HQ that after a quarter of a century of an absentee MP there had to be a strong local candidate. The 'next Cameron' should try elsewhere. And could they suggest a few other names of aspiring MPs who wanted experience of a selection meeting? 'Then you have the hustings meeting in front of three or four hundred members. It will be a bit of an ordeal. Our Brexit militants will be out in force. You must put on a good show, but I know you will. A few of us will prep you properly.'

Reassured, Kate started to think about what she was letting herself in for. The girls were not babies, but not adults either. She had firmly resisted pressure from Jonathan to pack them off to a 'character building' boarding school (like his). She took mothering seriously, and it showed; the girls were close to each other and to her. Kate assembled them when they had returned from the gymkhana and had calmed down after telling her about their heroics in the saddle. When she explained her plans their faces lit up with excitement and they were soon texting their friends to tell them Mum was going to be the next Prime Minister. A good start.

Then there was her business: the product of twenty years' hard work and a lot of emotional investment. On the surface it was just a fancy clothes and fabrics shop on the high street specialising in high-end Indian fashion. But it also housed a strongly growing internet sales operation. And behind it all was a small army of Indian suppliers: maybe a hundred women, mainly widows, whose livelihoods depended on being able to sell their beautiful, handcrafted embroidery to Yummy Mummies in Surrey. But as a Yummy Mummy herself she understood the market better than her competitors. Jonathan had been dismissive early on, seeing her shop as a hobby business to keep her out of mischief. But to be fair to him, he had put up some cash to help her acquire the freehold. And he had pulled some effective strings when an inflexible local bank manager tried to put her out of business during the credit crunch.

It had all started when she went off to India aged eighteen, with her girlfriend, Sasha, to 'see the world' in a gap year between leaving St Paul's Girls' School and going on to study medieval history at Oxford. Her parents were nervous but reassured that they were travelling as a pair. Shortly after arriving in India Sasha was laid low by Delhi Belly, which turned out to be a severe case of amoebic dysentery, and flew back home. Kate lied to her parents and told them she had teamed up with another girl and would stay. The truth was that she was utterly captivated by India. Walking around Old Delhi constantly assailed by new sounds, sights and smells, she felt as if a door was opening up to an utterly different world she needed to explore.

Kate's academically stretching but chaste education at St Paul's had equipped her with an impressive understanding of dynastic politics in the Plantagenet era but hadn't educated her in the various species of predatory men. In Delhi's coffee shops, in Connaught Circus frequented by Westerners, she bumped into a friendly Australian, Jack (or as she discovered later, he had contrived to bump into her). He was seriously scruffy with a tangled beard and unkempt long black hair and clearly hadn't washed for some time. But beneath the grime he had an open, welcoming smile and a reassuring, generous manner. He listened sympathetically to her anxieties and adventures and offered – without, he hastened to add, any obligations – to let her tag along with him. Travelling would be safer. He explained that he was in search of true enlightenment, discovering his transcendental soul, and was finding in the poverty of India a genuine richness of spirit. His spiel was thoroughly convincing and Kate was entranced.

Needless to say, his search for enlightenment soon led to her bed, in the cheap and dirty hotels they passed through along the Gangetic plain. The experience was neither physically nor emotionally satisfying but Kate was persuaded that she was getting ever closer to her inner being. He also introduced her to pot, which made her violently sick and provided none of the mystical wonders she had read about. They finally parted company when he took her to an ashram presided over by a naked sadhu, His Holiness the Guru Aditya, who preached the renunciation of bodily needs but actively solicited sexual favours and money from his Western acolytes. Kate fled back to Delhi, alone.

She could hardly wait to get on the next plane home. But before leaving she headed into Delhi's profusion of handicraft emporia to buy presents for family and friends. She was attracted to a modest stall offering exquisitely embroidered garments and furnishings – at modest fixed prices. She spent her remaining money and, as she left, the owner, Anjuli, ran after her in some distress explaining that she had accidentally overcharged. This novel experience led to a conversation and an invitation to visit her workshop, a room off an alley nearby, where a dozen women worked, barely pausing to greet her. An idea began to form that was later to become the basis for Kate's business. The pair exchanged addresses; Kate placed an advance order for goods to sell to her friends; they worked out how she could send the money to India. Two decades later, she had established a flourishing high street and internet business on the back of Anjuli's crafts, which never failed in quality, quantity or delivery. They won other customers including a leading UK fashion brand. And when Kate had last seen Anjuli she was a little greyer but, by now, a leading social entrepreneur whose network of cooperatives was an obligatory feature of development agency reports. Together they had achieved something. Kate was now ready to hand the running of her business to others and move on to a new challenge.

The Conservative Association hired a large hall to accommodate the five hundred members who wanted to attend the selection hustings. Kate had never spoken to a big meeting before and was extremely nervous despite intensive preparation and the presence of Jonathan and her daughters in the front row. She sensed that the meeting was cheering her on, though some of the questions were hostile. 'What are you going to do about immigration?' '… standing room only… overcrowded island… swamped' etc. She struggled to reconcile these questions with the local village of five thousand souls whose immigrant population consisted of Mr Shah and his family at the post office and the largely invisible owner of the Chinese restaurant. She had been advised, however, not to appear too condescending but to show, at least, a willingness to listen to heartfelt concerns. Her unsound social liberalism on gay marriage lost a few votes. But it didn't matter. She was overwhelmingly adopted on the first ballot.

Three months later the party machine swung into action for the general election, which the Prime Minister called early when her Brexit programme ran into serious trouble in parliament and before rising unemployment dented her popularity. Since the constituency had returned Conservatives with massive majorities, even in 1945 and 1997, there was little basis for anxiety.

Kate was required only to put in a few days' work shaking hands and being photographed. The Tory machine did the rest. The sole ripple of controversy in the campaign was her initial refusal to put her family in front of the cameras when she worried that this old-fashioned public display of traditional family values might prove a hostage to fortune. Stella led the opposition, arguing that the members would not countenance such a display of metropolitan liberalism so soon after the demise of Sir Terence.

Such interest as her campaign excited centred on her appearance. Her height and figure would have qualified her to be a professional model. Her face was very handsome rather than conventionally beautiful, and with her naturally blonde hair, she had the classical good looks of a well-bred, upper middle class English family whence she came. All of this would have been reserved for the electors of Surrey Heights, had an earnest Labour shadow minister not chosen to enliven the election campaign with an attack on the 'objectification of women' by the right-wing media deterring talented young women from coming forward into public life. The press, which had been bored to death by the opposition leader's lectures on the evils of capitalism, at last had a serious subject to get their teeth into. The *Sun* retaliated with a headline and two-page spread. Prominently featured was a photo of Kate taken half a lifetime earlier when she had tried modelling in her gap year, posing in a minimalist bikini. She was one of several 'Gorgeous Girls' who would be banished to an appalling Gulag if Manchester's Madame Mao and her Loony Left Labour friends got within a million miles of Downing Street. Kate was rather relieved that the *Sun* was not more widely read in Surrey Heights.

⁂

8 June 2019

Air conditioning was an essential of life for Deepak Parrikar. Without it, office and home were intolerable. For his father it was an uncomfortable, alien distraction. His small office, downtown in the bazaar area around the old fort, relied on a noisy overhead fan. Bits of paper flapped under their weights as the fan revolved – that is, when it worked, downtown Mumbai being subject to 'brownouts' from time to time, the symptom of India's creaking infrastructure. And the noise of the fan was competing with the cacophony outside: the rattling, squeaking, banging and scraping of vehicles being loaded and unloaded; the constant hooting of horns by moped, motorcycle and car drivers and, in a deeper register, from the boats plying the harbour; the barking of dogs; the cawing of crows; the plaintive whining of the beggars; and the shouting of street hawkers and hustlers. The senses were further assaulted by a heady cocktail of smells: richly scented garlands on the wall, diesel fumes, rotting food in the street, cooking oil, human waste, spices.

None of this could be heard or smelt in Parrikar House but this was where Parrikar Senior preferred to work. It wasn't sentiment that kept him there. It was here, and in the chai shop on the corner, that his network of informers and confidants, business contacts and friendly officials could slip in and out quietly, like a colony of ants ferrying gossip, rumours and inside knowledge back to the nest. The stock exchange, the bullion market and the municipal offices were all nearby. Here he could keep up with, or ahead of, the markets in which he operated.

This morning, one of Parrikar Senior's oldest associates was in his office: Mukund Das, flustered and sweating profusely in a safari suit that was at least one size too small.

'We have a problem, Parrikar Sahib. Our Mr Patel has gone missing. He didn't come home yesterday evening.'

'Girlfriend?'

'More serious, Sahib. A few days ago he had a visit from a couple of goondas. I recognised them: shooters; the Sheikh's men. People we don't mess with. Trouble. I asked what they had come about. Patel said: "Nothing. The usual shit. I told them to fuck themselves." He didn't want to say more. But I knew the reason: these goondas want protection to cover potential "accidents" on the site. We normally pay. No problem. But not Patel. He has high principles. Then, next day, he said he had had late night calls. Some goondas threatening him. He was frightened, very shaken. He planned to come and talk to you. Now he has gone. Mrs Patel telephoned to say he did not come home last night.'

The mystery did not last long. Parrikar Senior's PA brought in the morning newspapers. On the front page of *Bharat Bombay* was a picture of a body. Unmistakably Mr Patel.

'Exclusive' is a valid claim for Mayfair's Elizabethan Hotel. It is tucked away down a quiet, cobbled mews and never advertises, relying instead on a reputation for tasteful luxury and absolute discretion of the kind demanded by those among the world's super-rich and powerful who prefer to stay out of the limelight. These qualities were especially valued by the Chairman of Global Analysis and Research when he needed to convene a meeting of his directors.

He was sprawled across a soft leather armchair in a private room in the bowels of the hotel sipping occasionally at the large tumbler of neat whisky beside him and giving his captive audience of three the benefits of his geopolitical world view. The lecture was delivered in the slowest of Cajun drawls and he could have been chewing the cud on the verandah of his eighteenth-century French mansion overlooking the swamp-lands of Louisiana. But his associates were careful not to let their attention wander too far. The Chairman's brain moved a lot quicker than his speech. And there were crocodiles in his swamp.

'Good news, colleagues. History is on our side. Good friends of our company are now in charge in the US and Russia. Islamic terrorists are in retreat. More and more customers are queuing up for our anti-missile technology and we are now the dominant supplier in parts of that market. Our external shareholders are delighted with the thirty per cent return we are giving them. And I hope you are all pleased with the size of your Cayman accounts. Let us drink to the future of Global.' There was a growl of approval and glasses clinked.

'Now, let us get down to business. Reports on our next project, please. Admiral?'

'I am lining up the British company we have researched. No problems. My contacts in government will play ball.'

The Chairman paused, sensing overconfidence and seeing that the Admiral was rather flushed. He had brought class and an impressive contacts list to the company. But he was too fond of rum.

'Are you sure? I need to be sure.'

After an awkward silence, the burly, crew-cut Orlov spoke up for his old friend. 'The Admiral always delivers. Ever since we worked together in St Petersburg twenty-five years ago he has been as good as his word. And he is the only Britisher I have met who can drink Russians under the table.' His belly-laugh proved infectious.

The Chairman swallowed his doubts. Orlov was a thug. But a reliable thug. And a man with almost unprecedented access to his old KGB chum in the Kremlin.

One member of the group remained silent and unsmiling. Dr Sanjivi Desai was slowly making his way through his favourite tipple: apple juice. He was a small man with a neat moustache, greying hair, a look of great intensity and a beautifully tailored suit of Indian design. His English was impeccable with slight Indian cadences and traces of an American accent. 'There are uniquely promising opportunities in India. A competent government aligned with our values. Badly in need of what we have to offer.'

The Chairman had known Desai for a long time and trusted his judgement. 'Good. Let us know how you get on.

'Now, I have some news of my own. On medical advice I have decided to appoint a deputy Chair. Another American. Colonel Schwarz is recently retired from the Pentagon. Their top man on anti-missile defence. Close to the Trump people. A find. None of us are indispensable, including me.'

CHAPTER 3

THE GUARD

Twitter, 8 June 2019:

President Trump's tweet after the regular six-monthly meeting between the Presidents of the US and the Russian Federation:

'Good meeting with #Putin. Sorted #Europe and #MiddleEast. Biggest nuclear war risk India and Pakistan. nice people. #SAD!'

The dead of night was very dead. For the night watchman, sitting in a cubicle outside the front entrance of the factory, the challenge was to stay awake and carry out the few tasks he was paid the minimum wage to perform. In the months since Mehmet had been given the night shift outside the Pulsar factory he had seen a variety of urban foxes and stray dogs, two tramps, an illegal fly tipper and several couples doing what couples do in the back of cars when they think they are alone in a quiet corner of a sleeping industrial estate away from the neon lights. Silence was broken only by the distant hum of the M1.

It was a job nonetheless. Not quite the intellectual stimulus of his earlier job as professor of mathematics at the Eritrean Institute of Technology. But he was grateful to have been allowed to stay and work in the UK after he had escaped the mindless carnage on the battlefields separating Ethiopia and his native Eritrea and, then, as a disabled war veteran, and known dissident, had abandoned a harsh and insecure life under the dictatorship. As he surveyed the nocturnal tranquillity of the estate he endlessly replayed in his mind the events that had led him to this life of safety and excruciating boredom.

After being conscripted into the army and surviving a pointless war that left a hundred thousand dead on both sides, there followed a long trek, familiar to asylum seekers from the Horn of Africa, through Sudan and Egypt, the journey on a leaking, dangerously overcrowded boat across the Mediterranean followed by the trek to Calais, a month's agonising wait in the Jungle and, after numerous attempts, entering the UK clinging to the chassis of a lorry. He had then been accepted as a refugee seeking asylum.

Tedium and poor wages were now a small price to pay for freedom. Eventually he would get his Indefinite Leave to Remain and he had sketched out a long term route map, requalifying through the Open University, teaching and being reunited with his family.

Little was asked of him at work beyond monitoring CCTV footage of the perimeter, protected by a formidable fence with razor wire. He was also to check that the premises were empty before switching off the main lights and locking the entrance at 10pm. Occasionally research staff stayed late and he was to ensure that they were signed out and accounted for. The purpose of the factory was never explained to him – the supervisor had simply said Pulsar did 'hush-hush' things, something to do with the military. There was a secure area from which he was barred – only accessible by lift to a small number of pass holders. In an emergency he had access to a panic button; back-up security staff would arrive within five minutes. In his six months, alternating shifts with a Nigerian, it had not been needed.

At 2am that night he needed the toilet, which was beside the reception area. As he left the building he spotted a faint light under one of the doors to the main building: torchlight perhaps? He unlocked and opened the door. There was a brief, faint scuffling sound and then silence and darkness. Mehmet looked carefully in all the rooms accessible from the door. But nothing. He rechecked the ledger. No one officially in the building. He kept a careful eye on the building until morning – but no one appeared. He signed off in the morning: 'Investigated possible intruder but no one found. Decided not to raise alarm.' He looked back through the log book and saw that Osogo, the Nigerian, had made a similar note a few weeks earlier. He asked to speak to the head of security, who laughed it off: 'Ghosts! You Africans have a very vivid imagination.' Mehmet resented the security chief's patronising manner and the rather phoney bonhomie he had displayed since their first meeting at the job interview. But he was not going to compromise his job or his immigration status by picking a quarrel. So he smiled deferentially, agreeing that Africans were indeed people with small brains and childlike fears.

***

While Mehmet left after his night duty and his encounter with ghosts, the CEO, Calum Mackie, was already in his office, preparing for an early morning call, looking over the papers from his safe first, and checking the relevant emails.

Mackie was a technological genius whose world-beating research in ultra-high frequency radio waves had found both commercially profitable and militarily useful applications. He had taken over Smith & Smith, the once great manufacturer of military equipment, when it ran aground. Renamed Pulsar, it retained a highly skilled workforce, some valuable patents and an excellent network of export outlets and overseas investments dating from the days of Empire. Calum rebuilt the business, strengthened by his inventions, and over the last ten years massively expanded exports to NATO countries and others for which he could get export licences. Like other successful British technology companies, his had struggled to raise capital to expand and he had been tempted to sell out to US competitors who were only too keen to get their hands on his technology. Indeed, the MOD was very anxious that the latest smart adaptations to his aircraft-borne missiles did not fall into the wrong hands. Fortunately for their peace of mind, and his, he had secured some American private equity investors who were willing to commit substantial sums, long term, without interfering, on expectation of exceptionally good returns, which he had, so far, delivered.

On the other end of the phone was his well-established link to government: Rear Admiral Jeremy Robertson-Smith, a military hero, UK plc's arms salesman extraordinaire and now a freelance consultant operating on the blurred boundaries of business and state. A legend promoting UK defence sales (much of it made by his former employer), his fingerprints were all over a decade of successful defence deals, and many British companies, including Pulsar, were in his debt (as he was not slow to remind them).

His soubriquet, the Red Admiral, appeared to have originated during a secondment by the MOD, via NATO, to help the Yeltsin government sort out the chaos in the former Soviet navy whose formidable military assets, some of them highly dangerous, were rusting in port or being stolen. The Red Admiral ensured that the equipment was put out of harm's way and managed, in two years of operating out of St Petersburg, to negotiate some lucrative deals including one that saw India, through a brilliant official called Desai, who was familiar with Soviet kit, acquiring a state of the art aircraft carrier and other vessels on the cheap. The Russians ensured that the Red Admiral was well rewarded, a fact not reported to HMRC or the MOD.

'Things are now moving fast,' said the Red Admiral. 'My friends in government have already sounded you out on a possible collaboration with India. I have been asked to brief you on the big picture. We both know some of the key players. The deal is this: the UK is still trying to prise the Indians away from Dassault, their chosen bidder for a new fighter. We are offering the Eurofighter. I don't need to tell you that there are thousands of jobs in the UK supply chain if we can swing it. What the Indians really want is your little toy, the MRP3, strapped onto the wings.'

'Why the MRP3?' Mackie asked. 'There are other airborne missile systems.'

'They know that. The reason you are the key is this technology you have developed for using high frequency electromagnetic waves for simulating the after-effects of a nuclear blast, when all electronic systems are disabled within a radius of several miles. They believe that if the pulsar mechanism can be incorporated into the MRP3 it can be used to disable missiles in flight. You see where I am going?'

'Sure.'

'The Indian military establishment has nightmares worrying about extremists getting their hands on Pakistani nuclear weapons and firing them off at Indian cities. India has a powerful second strike capability, which is an effective deterrent to rational military men and politicians in Islamabad. But a deterrent can't work with people who belong to a death cult. India is desperate for an anti-missile shield of the kind the US has, and Israel. They have done a lot of work already and have good lines into Washington and Tel Aviv. They have been trying for almost a decade to develop an anti-missile defence system to cover, at least, Delhi and Mumbai. They have tested an interceptor missile – the Prithic – several times and it works for high altitude ballistic missiles. But critics think it will take another decade, perhaps longer, to develop a half-effective system with all the paraphernalia of ground radar, telecommunications and data links. Meanwhile, the Pakistanis are acquiring M-11 missiles from China and the technology to help fool anti-missile defences. The Indian government is getting anxious. They are already talking to the Israelis about purchasing their successful David's Sling system and the present lot don't have hang-ups about dealing with Israel.

'Britain isn't big in this whole area of anti-missile defence. But we have you. And you in turn have your Indian partners, Parrikar Avionics, which makes the issue of getting access so much easier. And preliminary discussions between our military attachés in Delhi and the Indians suggest that they are very – repeat very – interested.

'Their boffins think your technology could help them cut corners. Very smart people. But they need our help. The Americans are keen that we should offer it. Trump's people see the Indians as "good guys" taking on militant Islam and the Chinese too. The PM is keen as well. The post-Brexit export drive. And as a sweetener the Indians are dropping hints that if we give them access to the technology they want, they will also take off our hands the second of those bloody aircraft carriers that Gordon Brown ordered and we can't find any use for.'

Calum was used to the Red Admiral's style: orders from the bridge; debate not encouraged. But he had to intervene. 'Look, this is way beyond my pay grade. I'm just a wee techie. You're getting carried away, man. There is a vast amount of work to be done, testing, refining, software development.'

'Well, you can divvy up the work with your Indian opposite numbers. I believe they are very smart.'

'Well, may be, may be. Don't forget I have a company to run and investors who won't want me straying outwith our core business activities. They don't know much about India – believe it involves a lot of dirty politics. Religious headbangers. Backhanders flying everywhere. They have been trying to encourage me to sell off our investment in Parrikar Avionics. And, to be frank, I am tempted. So far it hasn't made us much money.'

'Surely they understand that India is a coming power. We have to be there. And their best people are world class. Anyway, think about it, Calum. We want to send a delegation to India, soon, led by a minister, to talk to the key people about this package. You are essential. I believe the Indians have been told you are coming.'

'You bastard, Jeremy!'

'Yes, but my friends also keep you in business, Calum. Sorry! But I had to drop that in.'

'OK, but the detail, and the money, has to be right.'

After the call Mackie felt a sense of relief. Notwithstanding the bluster, the company's order book was dangerously low. Defence cuts in the UK and USA had hurt. He had lain awake at night for weeks, preparing himself for difficult conversations with shareholders and the workforce. Maybe he was now off the hook.

His thoughts switched to how the workforce could absorb a big new contract on a very tight schedule. Calum Mackie was a gifted inventor and scientist and a shrewd businessman. But people management was not his thing. His private life was reclusive and monastic – bed, work, bed, work. He hated face to face confrontation and had no feel for the subtleties of personal relationships. He preferred to operate at one remove from his staff, working through the very small number of people whom he trusted and who could penetrate his moods and his accent. He was also, privately, a committed socialist from his Clydeside days, a Labour donor and a believer in trade unions.

Pulsar worked as a harmonious, flexible unit because of the close, symbiotic relationship – the personal chemistry – between the boss and the Unite chief shop steward, a charismatic, ambitious, thirty-year-old senior technician called Steve Grant. They had a shared experience of the University of Life, having both left school at sixteen to work, and a similar set of political ideals. But physically they were very different. Calum was small, wiry, tense – a chain smoker – and he regarded clothing as a necessary chore, rarely dressing, even in the office, in anything other than torn jeans and a hoodie. Steve was tall, well proportioned, smart, carefully manicured and, outside of work overalls, as expensively dressed as his wages and family commitments would allow. Appearances were so deceptive that a casual visitor might think Steve the boss and Calum the office boy. And cynics at the factory would say that appearances weren't so deceptive after all.

If Calum's American shareholders knew quite how much the firm relied on a former militant and, now, aspiring Labour politician to deliver their dividends, they would have run for the exit. But they didn't. And any questions about the labour force could be answered with an impressive roll call of achievements: a decade without a strike; cooperation over part-time working in the depths of the financial crisis; new shift patterns; Japanese-style quality control led by the workers. All approved by the shop stewards' committee at their weekly meeting behind the Red Lion.

***

Steve, the architect of this industrial relations miracle, prepared to leave home, as usual, at 7am. Recently divorced, the quiet of the morning without his kids was something he still hadn't got used to. Arriving at work, he was summoned from the shop floor to the CEO's office for an urgent meeting of the management team, which he attended as the workforce representative. To get there he had to pass through the finance and office services department, the only part of the building where women were visible in any numbers; elsewhere, the traditions of British engineering ensured that women were to be found only in advanced stages of undress on the calendars on the walls. The women in finance had launched a feminist counter-offensive in the form of a calendar with a generously endowed black male model whose masculinity was only partly concealed by a hand performing the role of a fig leaf. The ringleaders, Sam, Sharon and Cilla, styled themselves the Three Witches, and enlivened the office with cheerful banter about their exploits with booze and sex on a Saturday night and on the annual pilgrimage to Magaluf. They were not as dumb as they appeared, however. They had respectable accounting qualifications and more than once they had rescued Calum Mackie from the consequences of his rather cavalier approach to company accounts. The fourth member of the finance team, Shaida Khan, differed from her colleagues in her stunning looks and a detachment that may have been aloofness or shyness and was probably both. She differed too in seniority. She had arrived at the company four years earlier as a graduate trainee but had quickly established her exceptional talent, leading to a recent promotion, which meant that she now had an office of her own.

Shaida's father, Ashgar Khan, was a key member of Pulsar's engineering team, an important man in both Unite and the borough Labour Party where his ability to mobilise many of the town's Kashmiri Muslims had been crucial to Steve Grant's rapid ascent in the local party. Indeed, Steve had made sure that his daughter had got the trainee job. Mr Khan rarely talked about personal matters and had never before asked Steve for a favour but he had felt he had to explain his painful dilemma, torn between his role as a model British citizen – with an OBE for his contribution to community relations in the town – and the demands of his Islamic faith and the traditions of the Kashmiri district from where many of the local community originated. 'I want my daughter to have an education, to have a career. She is too young for marriage, children. Shaida is becoming a proper accountant. She passes her professional exams and learns here also. Maybe she will be chief finance officer in a company like this. Inshallah!' A quiet word with Calum Mackie and Steve had delivered. Four years later she was indeed chief finance officer.

Steve's interest in his protégé had evolved from the professional. The more he saw of her the more he contrasted his messy and unsatisfying domestic life – a bitter divorce from his childhood sweetheart and the mother of his three young children – with the potential offered by this Asian princess of his fantasies. The fantasy was fuelled by her habit of wearing expensive-looking but traditional clothes with a Muslim headscarf, though everything else about her – her speech, her animated eyes, her poise, her walk – suggested a thoroughly confident, modern woman. The antennae of the Three Witches had picked up the vibrations and he had to endure the embarrassment of loud comments whenever he passed through: 'Your fan club's arrived, Shaida', or, 'Sorry, lover boy, can't you see she's busy'. Shaida always worked on in her office and showed no sign of welcoming the attention.

⋙⋙⋙⋙⋙⋙⋙⋙⋘⋘⋘⋘⋘⋘⋘⋘

That day the chief finance officer had swept into the car park very early, maintaining her record of being first to work. Her diligence and capacity for hard work were major factors in her promotion. She made her way to her office, a glass room in the middle of an open plan office: sufficiently public to see and be seen; sufficiently private not to be overheard when she had a confidential conversation. It was tidy: methodical, like her life, with clearly defined priorities and no loose ends. Her personal filing system separated out family, then career, then self, in that order.

She adored her father, who worked on a high precision machine tool in the factory workshop and was now approaching retirement. Only one of Shaida's three brothers was still at home, Mohammed, a troubled young man who had fallen into bad company at school, had never managed to find a proper job after graduating in 'business studies' and who hung around with groups of Pakistani and Somali men consuming cannabis and qat. Shaida's escalating salary had enabled her family to move to a smarter detached house in a largely middle class, white, area of town, which had separated Mohammed from his friends somewhat, but increased her mother's isolation. Shaida was the emotional, as well as financial, prop that kept the family together.

Regarded as a confirmed spinster by her extended family who expected their womenfolk to produce babies at regular intervals after the age of fifteen, Shaida was sufficiently acclimatised to the British society into which she had been born to see that at twenty-five she had plenty of time to find a settled, loving relationship of her own and the family that might follow it. Meantime, she would enjoy being single.

She noticed that Steve was also in the outer office, for no very obvious reason. She didn't mind. She found him engaging and attractive; and he talked intelligently and interestingly about the politics in which he was involved, refreshingly different from the speak-your-weight machines she saw on television, trotting out the party line. She wasn't very political, but curious: voted Lib Dem as a compromise between her father's tribal loyalty to Labour and her own more business-minded and liberal instincts. She could see, however, that Steve didn't view her as a political project. He was obviously besotted with her and she enjoyed the sense of power she derived from being an inaccessible, goddess figure. In a different context he would have been a good date. If only he knew.

<hr />

At 10am Calum convened a meeting of the executive team, who arrived in his office in a state of trepidation. They knew how bad the financial position was and were expecting gallows humour from the boss following a tale of woe from the chief finance officer who, at her first meeting, had chilled them all to the bone with her forensic analysis of the near insolvency of the company.

The problem lay in the inherent riskiness of the business: the need to spend large sums on R&D to keep ahead of the field technologically, based on Calum's hunches and nods and winks from the MOD. At the same time orders were unpredictable, based on the passing enthusiasms of politicians for fancy new toys, the more or less austere disposition of other politicians who approved controversial arms export licences, and the mood of the Treasury. Calum's genius, his patient long term investors and a helping hand from the Red Admiral had kept the company afloat. But the faces that morning anticipated bad news, particularly the recently appointed head of security, Justin Starling. But to their collective relief, Calum was in an expansive mood.

'Guys, the Indian contract is happening. Could keep us in business for years. Just heard the good news from the Red Admiral who, as you know, has been a valuable friend to us and is close to the action even if no longer in government. But it is a big project. It will stretch us to the limit on both the research and production side. And, of course, this is very hush-hush.'

Starling's scepticism was clear. 'I know this is a sensitive issue', he said, looking directly at Shaida, 'but I can't be the only person in this room who is worried about taking on a highly confidential Indian military contract when we have a largely Muslim, and Kashmiri, workforce. I know the workers who need to be involved have been security cleared but… politics…'

He was met by an embarrassed silence and Shaida felt a rising sense of anger that her loyalty was being questioned.

This wasn't the first time Starling had crossed her; she had discovered that he objected to her promotion. She would have been angrier still if she had known that Starling himself was a dubious appointment; there had been unexplained holes in his CV and Calum had accepted him only after receiving a glowing recommendation from the Red Admiral based on his work at the MOD.

Steve came to the rescue. 'I have absolute confidence in my workmates. They have always been committed to this company. They are good, hard-working British people whatever their origins. They will cheer for Pakistan at the Oval like Irish and Scots sports fans do for their countries when they play England: that doesn't make them disloyal. Mr Starling – who has only recently joined the company – may not be aware that we have done business with the likes of Israel, Egypt and India before. Politics didn't come into it.'

'I hope you are right,' Starling snapped back. But Calum wanted to press on with other news.

'You all know how much I love politicians, especially Tories. Well, it seems that as our importance to the country is being recognised – at last – we are getting a ministerial visit.'

'Who is he?'

'It's a she.'

Kate's early parliamentary career was as anonymous as her arrival in Westminster. She was underwhelmed by parliament and parliament was underwhelmed by her. She got off to a reasonable start with an early, workmanlike speech generously praising Sir Terence's skeletal contributions to the local community, as custom demanded, and, for the benefit of the local press, promising to die in the last ditch fending off the horrors that disturbed her Conservative voters, notably a long mooted social housing scheme and fracking, which was improbable given the local geology, but aroused deep fears. She was momentarily buoyed by the praise lavished on her speech until it was pointed out that convention demanded it. She settled into the rhythm of parliamentary life, asking questions now and then, speaking very occasionally in debates to an empty chamber late at night, voting with the government on every sub-clause of obscure pieces of legislation, and signing lots of letters to constituents reassuring them that she was on their side fighting human rights abuses in North Korea and Iran, opposing the docking of dogs' tails and supporting the ban on fox hunting.

One morning she received a request – which amounted to a summons – to visit the chief whip in his office. She was curious, since in her year or so in parliament she had never defied the party whip, had an exemplary attendance record and responded willingly to requests to sit through the excruciating tedium of hours in primary and secondary legislative committees on the off-chance that the depleted and demoralised opposition might call a vote. She had even stooped so low as to ask obsequious questions, handed out by the whip's office, inviting ministers to acknowledge the government's brilliant record. She persuaded herself that she was not naturally so craven but merely wanted time to understand the arcane mysteries of parliament, to work out whom to trust and to build up a reputation locally for being 'loyal, conscientious and competent': adjectives that Stella was now deploying on her behalf. At some point she was determined to rebel against what she saw as the ghastly, male-dominated, pompous, antiquated, inefficient, ineffectual, dysfunctional club. But not yet.

Her sense of irrelevance and impotence reached its peak during the 'coup'. A few months earlier the Prime Minister had called an unnecessary and disastrous election, losing seats and credibility. There was a growing sense of drift around the Brexit negotiations and the new influx of militant Brexiteers had limited patience and little gratitude. The so-called 52 Group of Tory MPs and their friends in the press demanded change. Kate ignored the plotting and was unprepared for the terse announcement that the PM had resigned on 'health grounds'. Parliament went on much as before. But there was a subtle change: the boys were back in charge.

All these thoughts churned in her brain as she walked across the modern hub of parliament – Portcullis House –

with its controlled environment and indoor trees, through into the cold, stone passages that led to Speaker's Court and then to the corridor behind the Speaker's Chair and alongside the library. There was a distinctive, and reassuring, aroma of wood polish and dusty books with an occasional whiff of yesterday's dinner from the kitchens below. At that time in the morning the place was largely empty except for gnome-like figures, the clerks, who scuttled quietly in and out of offices. Then, down to the Members' Lobby, where a politically balanced selection of busts of twentieth-century giants – Lloyd George, Attlee, Churchill and Thatcher – looked down on the pygmies beneath them.

The whips' offices led off from the lobby and Kate had previously ventured inside her own only to collect messages. Now she was shown into the inner sanctum: the chief whip's office. She took in at first glance the walls covered in press cartoons that lampooned the chief whip but also advertised his importance; a capacious drinks cabinet, open and clearly in frequent use; and various pieces of expensive communications equipment that were covered in dust and obviously not used. And then she turned her attention to the large, ruddy, friendly face behind the mahogany desk. His skills in managing political power had become legendary: a survivor; a servant of three Prime Ministers; a totally uncompromising loyalist to the Prime Minister of the day until the time came to switch sides. His power was his knowledge. He knew far more about the strengths and especially the weaknesses of the four hundred-odd MPs in his charge than any of them imagined.

Kate's political apprenticeship labouring quietly in the parliamentary salt mines had not gone unnoticed. The chief whip had already put a question mark against the name of many of her contemporaries for displaying excessive independence of mind or unseemly haste to climb up the greasy pole or backing the wrong side in the coup. Kate Thompson's record was unblemished. Tom Appleby was a Devon farmer who understood human nature almost as well as his beloved horses. This Kate Thompson was a goer, a smart filly who would do as she was told, sail over the fences and manage the heavy going. A good-looker too. His political hero, John Major, would have approved. He explained he had called her in for a friendly chat after being asked by the PM to put up a list of promotable talent, with attractive women as a priority.

'I won't bullshit you,' he said. 'There are a lot more talented, hard-working and worthwhile people in this place than you.' Tough love was his preferred method of breaking in promising ponies. 'Some of your colleagues would give their right arm for a chance to be the lowest form of ministerial pond life. I have dozens of them banging on my door every day begging for jobs, even to be an unpaid parliamentary private secretary—'

She butted in: 'Chief Whip, I don't know why you have called me in but I am not complaining about lack of promotion. I'm still getting to know how this place works.'

'Not so fast. That was just my way of introducing you to some good news. You are in favour. Don't want it to go to your head. Let me explain. The PM is rattled by constant criticism that there aren't enough women in serious jobs in the government. The coup, deposing a respected woman Prime Minister, has left us open to the charge that we have a problem with women. To be very frank with you, he wants some photogenic women around him – and you are near the top of the eye candy league table… at least on our side of the House.'

'Chief Whip, Tom—'

'Sorry, I am just being straight with you. You probably think I am some kind of Neanderthal man. But that's the way it is. All those people who read the *Mail* and the *Express*, and vote for you, are more interested in how you look than what you say. I am sure I don't need to tell you that. Where I am concerned you have a spotless record. That is why I put you forward. No more, no less. I also saw that excellent interview you gave on *Newsnight*; you stuck to the line and didn't screw up, unlike that birdbrain we put up three months ago, now on her way out.

'That's it. Just a friendly word of advice. A lot of MPs will hate your guts for jumping the queue. Be careful. Watch your back. And don't waste your chance.'

She thanked the chief whip and fought back a powerful urge to puncture his self-importance and his obvious pleasure at dishing out patronage by declining his offer.

The chief whip's head of office told her to go immediately to the Prime Minister's parliamentary suite where he was waiting.

It all happened very quickly. She was ushered into the gloomy set of rooms behind the Speaker's Chair by one of the young men in the outer office. The PM looked up from the papers on his desk but clearly did not recognise her and thought she was a civil servant who had come to brief him. The speaking note in front of him put him right. He gestured to her to sit down and she had a few seconds to take in the famous face in front of her, more lined than revealed on television or in Prime Minister's Questions, but otherwise undistinguished and unmemorable.

'Kate, thank you so much for making time to come and see me. You have made such an impact since you came into the House. The tea room' (which he never visited) 'is singing your praises. Your *Newsnight* interview has become a legend – I have suggested that we use it as a master class for training wannabee MPs. How about it?'

She nodded appreciatively – feeling that although the PM was a notorious flatterer, and she was susceptible to flattery, he was getting beyond parody.

'And an entrepreneur too! Too many bloody researchers, communications consultants and special advisers. Don't you agree?' She agreed. But not too enthusiastically since she recalled that he had been all three in his time.

'I have given a lot of thought to this and have decided to fast-track you to Minister of State level. Trade. Should suit you with your outstanding business background. And deep knowledge of India. Priceless. One of our main challenges, post-Brexit, will be to land an ambitious trade agreement with the big non-EU economies. As you know, the negotiations we launched last year are coming to a climax. We are not getting much change out of the EU so we absolutely must deliver on our promises to open up other markets to British exporters. India is top of our list. But it's proving very, very difficult. We need someone who can unlock the vast potential there. You are just the person.'

Kate desperately wanted to shrink these ludicrously inflated expectations. But she could see he was in transmit, not receive, mode. She also noticed that he had a problem looking her in the eye and was gazing anywhere but. He seemed to be one of those men who struggled to engage with self-confident, attractive women. Then she remembered all those stories from years back about young men in Turkish baths and made a connection with the good-looking young men in the outer office. 'Stop it, Kate,' she said to herself. 'This is the Prime Minister.' And he was, as far as was publicly known, in a long and happy, if childless, marriage.

'Best of luck. I expect great things from you. Don't let me down. The big trade deal with India. It could be your legacy – and mine. But I will leave it to your new boss, Jim, to brief you.' A wave of the hand ended the interview.

Kate set off to start her new job as Big Ben was striking noon and ducked and weaved through the traffic, walking across the front of Westminster Abbey to where she thought the department lay. She had been offered a car by one of the PM's young men but felt the idea of taking a lift in bright sunshine for a two-hundred-yard journey was beyond parody of the ministerial lifestyle. She wasn't yet the Prime Minister, or the Queen. Leaving nothing to chance, however, the young man had arranged for her to be met by her private secretary as soon as she arrived. Unfortunately, things did not go well. She soon realised that her hazy idea of where the department lay, somewhere behind the Abbey and Methodist Central Hall, led her to the Department for Work and Pensions where baffled receptionists sought to help a lost Minister of State they hadn't expected or even heard of.

Eventually she found the right department and an extremely agitated private secretary who looked as if he was about to call the police missing persons' line. 'Sorry, I got lost in the London maze, I'm just a country bumpkin. Next time I'll take a compass.'

He didn't do humour. 'Minister, I would advise you, in future, to stick to the recognised route if you insist on not utilising the ministerial car. My name is Edwin Thoroughgood. I am your private secretary.'

She groaned inwardly at the thought of being looked after by this young fogey who was emaciated and stooped and acted as if he already had one foot in an old folks' home. His spotty and unhealthily grey face hinted at a life spent in front of a computer screen. She thought he resembled a hermit released from a lifetime of monastic contemplation who had just been confronted by his worst nightmare: a woman with attitude. The journey to the top floor took place in silence and his eyes sought refuge in the lift carpet. When they reached the ministerial corridor she was led through an expanse of open plan offices with adjacent rooms for three ministers of state and three parliamentary under-secretaries and their staff. All were regarded as unexceptional ministerial ballast, except for the most junior, a hereditary peer who owned much of Scotland but was here to promote food and drink exports, especially spirits. The Secretary of State had a grander office with a view.

Kate's office was smart, bright and functional but horribly disfigured by a dark, brooding, giant oil painting in the style of Landseer featuring a large stag and slavering bloodhounds: no doubt a masterpiece but utterly incongruous in this setting. Kate's first executive decision was to instruct Edwin to get rid of it.

'But, Minister, these things are not straightforward. There is a process. I will, however, speak to someone from the government art collection to investigate the possibility of making a change. Your predecessor, I should say, loved the painting and he was a man of good taste.'

'Please, Edwin, just get rid of it. Now.' This relationship was not going to last long.

When Mehmet sat down in his cabin for the night shift he had largely forgotten the episode two weeks ago when he sensed, or perhaps imagined, an intruder in the factory. Nothing untoward had happened since.

He had enrolled for an Open University course and had learnt to divide his attention between the CCTV monitors, the entrance area of the factory and maths problems that he found easy but at least kept his brain alive. At 3am there was absolutely nothing to disturb the peace. He set off for the entrance area for his mid-shift visit to the toilet. He had discovered that splashing water on his face helped him to keep his concentration, and the short walk was a welcome break from the tedium.

It was, however, very dark, no moon, and he had a tremor of anxiety leaving the secure cocoon of his cabin. As he unlocked the front doors, he thought he heard a sound from the inside of the building. Then silence. He decided to open the main door that led to the design office, which in turn opened out into the main production area of the factory. The office was in semi-darkness, as it should have been, but he noticed a fading glow on one of the PC screens and, nearby, the illuminated panel of the lift showed it to be in use. The lift led to the basement, the secret area to which he had no access.

He knew that something untoward was going on: someone had been using a computer and had taken refuge in the basement to which only a dozen or so high-level staff had access. He made a note of the terminal that had been in use and returned to his cabin. Perhaps someone had put in some overtime and had hidden when they heard him entering, perhaps believing him to be an intruder? That didn't seem likely. But if a senior, trusted, member of staff was engaged in something subversive inside the building, he had little or no concrete evidence. Anyway, would he be believed, an asylum seeker from Africa paid a minimum wage to sit in a hut outside? Back in his cabin he watched the monitors carefully but no one emerged from the building. When the shift ended and the first workers arrived in the morning he had a dilemma about what to put in his security report. His first report of a suspected intruder had been laughed off. This time they would think he was a fantasist or a troublemaker. But, if something was going on, and if it was exposed, why hadn't the security guard reported what he had seen?

Steve arrived for work as usual. He used to look forward to a day on the machine where his carefully honed skills made him an outstandingly productive worker. But these days his mind wandered. His work schedule would be broken up by a union meeting on the new shift patterns proposed by management and he had to prepare himself for a difficult evening meeting he was chairing at the council on budget cuts.

He had, as it happened, arrived early and on an impulse decided to make the detour through the finance department. He realised he was being ridiculous but the prospect of seeing Shaida Khan was a bigger draw than a chat before work with the lads about the weekend football results.

The room was empty except for Shaida, seemingly engrossed in work in her glass cubicle. No Witches. He couldn't hide under the comfort blanket of their office banter. He couldn't easily retreat. And he had no good reason to be there. But this was an opportunity to have the conversation he had rehearsed for some time.

The object of his fantasies was well aware that Steve was in the background. She had designed her office in such a way that through reflections in the glass she effectively had 360-degree vision. Forewarned she had time to prepare her defences against someone whose demeanour did not suggest that he anticipated a seminar in accounting. She had developed a Miss Brisk persona to impose her authority on such occasions. She turned sharply.

'Good morning. Are you here to discuss the group finances?'

'Well, actually, we've seen a fair bit of each other at meetings but I've never really introduced myself properly – I'm Steve, Grant.'

'I know exactly who you are, Steve. My dad told me

about you. Actually he is a fan of yours – he seems to think you may be a Labour Prime Minister someday. And I believe you helped secure my job. I guess I'm indebted to you… Unless there is anything else? It's a busy day and I need to get on with my work.'

Thoroughly discombobulated, he struggled to continue. He realised he had never chatted up a woman before; not beyond politics and union business. With his ex-wife he had never had to. But those big brown eyes seemed to send a different, more welcoming, message than the abrupt voice. 'Er… how do you like it here? These girls here… maybe not your cup of tea?'

'What do you mean? They are lovely. Trouble is, you men think "these girls" are only interested in shagging and booze. They're usually having you all on. Sam, the cheeky one who goes on about black blokes, spends her spare time looking after her disabled sister. Sharon, the tall one, came top in the region in her professional exams. And Cilla is seriously competitive at Taekwondo. They're kind and good fun and we have an excellent team.'

'Sorry, I didn't realise. They wind up the lads on the shop floor no end.' He started to look nervously at the clock and the stairs behind him. It was now or never. 'But you… do you fancy a drink sometime?'

'You mean you want to take me out on a date?'

'Yes… but… only…'

'Ah, the "but"… I don't want to be snide, but this conversation is quite inappropriate. We both have senior roles in this company and our relationship is professional. Besides, I am the only Asian woman here and you're a well-known face. Word gets around. And you are a bit obvious, you know, fancying me.'

He looked desperately crushed and she judged that he was a sensitive man who wasn't used to this situation. So she decided to soften the blow.

'Let me explain. My mum and dad want me to have my freedom. But even they want to line up the right kind of husband for me. They have kept the family together despite all the bad things that happen here. Somehow I have to find a way to do my own thing without breaking their hearts. That means I stay clear of trouble. This is work, not a dating agency. Do you get it?'

He mumbled a 'yes', not having expected the rebuff or the eloquent speech that she must surely have prepared in her mind. And she hadn't finished.

'So, there is no question of a date. But if you want to be a friend as well as a colleague, I have an idea. My brother and his friends are worrying my family. Radicalisation and all that. They won't talk seriously to us. My dad and I have tried to talk politics to them but they won't listen. They think the Muslim councillors in the town are a joke. Just operating a vote bank for Labour. They see you as different. They might listen to you. Will you come and chat to them?'

He didn't get a chance to say more than yes, to say what he felt: utterly besotted but with a deeper undercurrent of anxiety. There was a scramble up the stairs and Sharon emerged first: 'Ah, caught in the act!' He made himself scarce, muttering something about being on his way to see the boss.

On Steve's way to the shop floor he reflected on how he had got into this situation. He remembered the events – eight years ago? – that were the making of him, thanks to Mr Khan, but could have been a disaster. He was then a headstrong, ambitious shop-floor worker in his early twenties who had already built up a following in the union and the party. People loved the way he spoke, with the accent and idiom of his working class contemporaries but with the fluency and vocabulary of those clever, educated people who seemed to run everything including working class organisations.

One day, Calum called in the union reps for a 'frank chat'. The company was 'up the creek without a paddle', as he put it. The financial crisis was in full swing. Orders had dried up. Banks had turned nasty: wanted their money back, pronto. Big defence cuts in the US and the UK had killed the goose that laid the golden eggs for defence contractors. Over half the workforce would have to go – then, five hundred people – plus subcontractors. The rest could stay to finish contracts or do maintenance work. 'Sorry, guys, I did my best.'

But the guys didn't think much of his best. Steve, the militant, started to capture the mood of his mates and dominated the discussions in the canteen. He demanded a strike to force the management to think again by putting the rest of the business at risk. He could also see that in the absence of a strong workers' response the labour force would fracture along racial lines. Not too many years ago Pulsar, like many industrial companies, operated a colour bar confining Asian newcomers to unskilled jobs and it had taken a strong stand by the Asian workers, led by Mr Khan, to break it. But the shared jokes and sex magazines in the canteen created a fragile illusion of solidarity. Now the mood was turning ugly again with rumours that 'the Pakis' were being favoured (or discriminated against according to the audience) and BNP leaflets were circulating in the factory.

After a particularly bitter meeting, Mr Khan took Steve aside and proposed a Plan B; what was, in effect, a pay cut to save the plant and the jobs. The company would have a year to drum up some new business with a guarantee of earlier worker bonuses if profits returned. He had done the maths and it worked. Steve immediately grasped that something along these lines was necessary; he could see that militancy was no answer to this particular crisis and had no wish to become a doomed Arthur Scargill figure. When he sounded out the workforce there was support on the basis that this was the least bad option.

Mr Khan was able to mobilise the Asian workers and a branch meeting agreed, on a show of hands, to present the plan to management. Calum was relieved and promptly rang his leading investors who were so impressed that they agreed to put in more cash. Then a stroke of luck: a competitor had gone bust, couldn't deliver and Pulsar was asked to fulfil its outstanding contracts.

Soon the word got around and reached the ears of government ministers and union bosses that, in the depths of a plunging economy, here was a turnaround story, under union leadership: flexible but hard-headed, pragmatic but tough. A model for British industry. The TV cameras and print journalists needed an articulate spokesman and they found it in Steve, while Mr Khan retreated into the background, his natural modesty reinforced by his reluctance to use his heavily accented English. The local, then the national, Labour Party seized upon the new Messiah: a genuinely working class moderniser; a union man but not a Luddite, articulate but not a party wordsmith, recycling half-understood ideas from textbooks; a man who talked about 'British working families' from experience and not as if they were a tribe in Papua New Guinea.

In the years that followed Steve had progressed, and believed he now had the choice of a safe seat in parliament or progression to the leadership of his union. He had remained close to Mr Khan who could help mobilise the ethnic vote in party and council elections. He had reciprocated where possible and had cemented the friendship by prevailing upon Calum to take Ms Khan into the company, ignoring the CVs of dozens of other applicants for the job. Now he was hopelessly, and dangerously, in love with Mr Khan's daughter.

There was no way that Shaida could show any sign of reciprocating these feelings. But she had definitely taken a liking to Steve Grant, who, she had noticed, was pleasant looking and, when out of his overalls, snappily dressed. Had he been an aspiring US politician his tall, slim, athletic physique and flashing smile would have been a passport to success. But in both the industrial and political wings of the Labour Movement good looks, of men and women, were regarded with deep suspicion: indicating vanity or narcissism or, worse, a sign of reversion to the days of the traitor Blair when image and the ability to cut a dash in the Tory press enjoyed more weight than socialist substance. Shaida had so far taken little notice of such matters. But this morning's conversation had stimulated her interest. And she could see how a carefully managed friendship could be of value to them both.

CHAPTER 4

THE MINISTER

The Hindu, 23 June 2019:

The Indian government has announced that it has successfully completed the ninth test of its anti-missile defence programme. A spokesman stated that the test has been a success and that the government is on track with its plan for a missile shield for Mumbai and Delhi. However, Rtd Major-General Aggarwal of a Delhi defence think-tank cast doubt on the success of the tests and said that, with current technology, India is 'many years' away from a successful missile shield.

After a few days in the job, Kate had her first meeting with the Secretary of State who had just returned from his overseas visit drumming up business for the UK. James (Jim) Chambers was a big man: physically, politically and commercially. The Prime Minister had climbed to power on his shoulders and depended heavily on him. Out of favour under the PM's predecessor, he had come back with a vengeance to head up post-Brexit trade promotion and negotiations and was, in effect if not in name, the deputy Prime Minister. His voice had a twang of Geordie, which gave him that touch of northern authenticity so prized in his party for its scarcity value.

He was also very wealthy, a self-made millionaire many times over. Precisely how he had made his millions was the subject of numerous pieces at the back of *Private Eye*: the consumer credit company that fleeced hapless purchasers who hadn't read the small print carefully enough; the insurance claim after a conveniently timed warehouse fire; the lucrative land deal involving MOD property that could, plausibly, have only been achieved with the help of an inside source. But the mud didn't stick. He was now a TV guru on business; widely admired for his support for children's charities; while his generous donations to the Conservative Party and individual MPs had bought him political influence and, now, power.

Although several inches shorter than his new ministerial colleague, his big, shaven, bull-like head and powerful physique established a dominant presence in the room, but he was charming and solicitous, anxious to make her feel at home. His piercing blue eyes sought hers and held her gaze: a man thoroughly confident with women, as suggested by his reputation. 'Well, Kate, settling in all right?' he chortled. 'How are your Overheads?' When she looked blank, failing to get his joke, he explained that 'Overheads' was his word for civil servants. 'You and I are wealth creators. We are the profit line in UK plc's P&L. They, the public sector, consume the wealth: the debit side. We mustn't let them forget it.' The civil servant in the room, his principal private secretary, looked into the middle distance pretending not to hear, having been on the receiving end of this 'joke' many times before.

For Kate, this unorthodox introduction gave her an opportunity to broach the first awkwardness she had encountered in the department. 'Actually, I do have a problem on that front. Can we have a private word?' Jim indicated to his principal private secretary that she should leave. 'I would be grateful for your help in reshuffling my private office, Secretary of State.'

'I prefer you to call me Jim.'

'Jim, if I am to do this job I need to work with people whom I trust and have confidence in...' She explained her problem without mentioning Edwin's appearance and irritating manner: a private secretary who seemed to be devoted to her predecessor, an obscure man of mind-numbing mediocrity but who did exactly as he was told. The private secretary's style, she explained, was to advise his minister that everything he – now she – wished to do was fraught with legal, financial, reputational, organisational or presentational risk. If the case for action was overwhelming, he would invoke the Doctrine of Unripe Time to argue that the Minister should delay making a decision: 'The longer you delay, Minister, the more facts you will have on which to base your decision. Now is too soon.'

'I cannot work with this man,' she explained. 'His deputy isn't any better. He spends his time gazing at my chest and then rushes to open the door for me or help me to sit down. Where do they get these people from?'

'Kate. Absolutely right. That's what I like to hear. No nonsense. I will speak to the chief Overhead and ask him to line up some genuine talent for you. But I also want to talk to you about something else: this India thing. The PM wants you to go out there. Big deal for your first job. He thinks you will charm them. I have asked the team to come up to brief you, if you are ready.'

The civil servants trooped in: Parsons, the permanent secretary; Caroline, the principal private secretary, parked on a sofa behind the meeting table; a fierce-looking, grey-haired lady from the MOD whose label read 'Ms Kidlington'; a tall distinguished man with a military bearing who was introduced as 'the Admiral: he advises me and the Defence Secretary'; and a man in his forties who announced himself as 'Liam – security'.

'Right, ladies and gentlemen. Our new Minister, Kate Thompson, has been asked by the PM to go to India to advance the discussions on the arms contract. She doesn't need to know too much detail. The High Commissioner will fill her in and hold her hand when she gets there. But she needs to know roughly what this is about – why it matters – and what her role is. In general, she has to look beautiful – not difficult I'd say! – and speak as little as possible. But it is a bit more than that. Ms Kidlington?'

Ms Kidlington started to read from her notes, which, Kate observed, were worryingly long. 'Minister, years of patient negotiation have got us almost to the point of agreement. But the Indians are difficult negotiators and their coalition politics is complex. Buying arms from Britain, and the USA, goes against the grain with a lot of nationalist MPs and with the lefties in their parliament. But Delhi is committed to it because there is a crucial piece of equipment and associated software only we can offer them.

'Put simply, the Indians are frightened – and under-standably so – about the possibility of a Pakistan nuclear attack. They have a deterrent that could blow Pakistan to smithereens several times over. But that isn't protection against a first strike, launched by a rogue element, such as religious fundamentalists. The Indians have a "no first use" strategy as we had with the Soviets. But the Pakistanis have been unwilling to reciprocate.

'We – and they – think the risk is low but it is sufficient to build a defensive shield as best they can. Now we hear the Chinese are "giving" Pakistan an upgrade to their missile. Remember President Reagan and Star Wars? That was over thirty years ago. Technology has moved on. A shield, or a partial shield, is now possible, though the use of decoys means that missile defence is at best partial. Nonetheless, the US has a system mainly to counter rogue states like North Korea. So have the Israelis, and others are being developed. It turns out that one of the key pieces of kit is a machine that destroys the navigation systems of missiles, and aircraft, in flight. Correctly deployed it could stop, or at least minimise, a nuclear attack. Are you with me?'

Ms Kidlington paused and looked around to ensure that her lecture was still being followed. She sought to engage with Kate's eyes in order better to communicate her passion. Experience had taught her that ministers were, in general, rather ignorant about these high-level security issues and not very interested.

'Now, the bad news – the British company that has developed this technology is run by a maverick Scottish socialist, from an industrial estate north of London. His company is called Pulsar. He is a loose cannon but a genius. Frankly, MOD would prefer a more orthodox supplier but he always delivers on time and on budget, and he is British. The Indians would much prefer to deal with a recognised name, a BAE Systems or a Rolls-Royce. The American Defense Department and MOD will vouch for Mackie, but the Indians want more reassurances. We understand that, since this is a sensitive subject. They don't want the wrong kind of publicity.

'The clinching argument for Pulsar is that as a result of an old Indian connection, they have a part-owned Indian partner called Parrikar Avionics, which will make sure the technology is transferred to India and stays there. The Indians won't take our stuff off the shelf. We have done some due diligence. Family company. Old man Parrikar, the founder, is a bit of a scoundrel, but the son, Deepak, who runs the avionics company, is squeaky clean – which we need under our anti-bribery legislation.'

'Bloody Coalition government. Bloody Liberals,' broke in the Secretary of State. 'They brought in this anti-corruption crusade, crippling our businesses. Politically correct nonsense. My friends tell me they can't even buy their overseas customers a drink or they'll be sent to Wormwood Scrubs for twenty-five years.'

'Secretary of State,' interrupted the permanent secretary, who was used to his political master getting the bit between his teeth and galloping over the horizon, 'I am sure the Minister would like to know a little more about her role.'

'Yes, of course.' Chambers took over the briefing, deciding that Ms Kidlington had already had a long enough innings. 'Kate, the Indians need to be convinced that we are fully committed – politically – to this technology transfer stuff and have got a firm grip on the British supplier. If the PM or myself were spending time hobnobbing with modest-sized companies, questions might be asked about what they do. We don't want that: don't want to stir up the

Pakistanis or the arms trade protesters for that matter. A middle ranking minister will do fine. Our chaps will give you a bit of a boost in the Indian media – rising star; the next Mrs T; all that – and push to get you in to see the Indian PM. I have asked the Admiral, here, to join your party. He knows the background and is well connected in India.

'And you will like Parrikar Junior. Very handsome – one magazine called him the Indian George Clooney – not that I look at other men, unlike some I could mention. Ha.' The permanent secretary desperately tried to hide his laughter in a grotesque rictus, knowing that it would not do to appreciate a joke at the expense of the Prime Minister but equally understanding that it was career-enhancing to be amused by the Secretary of State's sense of humour.

'So Kate, smile sweetly and don't do anything I wouldn't do. And impress them with your knowledge of India. As well as your business connections, I understand you travelled around the country many years ago.'

Kate's heart sank. This was definitely not on her CV. She had erased it from her memory. That appalling Australian, whom she had fallen for. His story about spiritual enlightenment that seemed so plausible at the time. The ashram… Oh my God! They know it all!

The hitherto silent Liam interjected: 'We have you down as travelling there for four months during your gap year.'

'Actually, I spent most of my time in India on the hotel loo with amoebic dysentery. Didn't see or do much. Best ignored.' Everyone smiled understandingly.

She left the meeting rather dazed. She had never before been entrusted with confidences beyond her girlfriends' love affairs or her husband's rather obscure business deals. Now there were Star Wars, spooks and an Indian George Clooney. And people who seemed to know everything about her, even things she had managed to forget. Try as hard as she could to be calm and sensible she looked forward to this mission with a mixture of excitement and grave apprehension.

CHAPTER 5

BHARAT BOMBAY

BBC World Service, 30 June 2019:

The Pakistani Prime Minister, Imran Khan, has reshuffled his cabinet, introducing three ministers closely aligned to religious parties. They include a junior defence minister who is reputed to have been a volunteer with Al Qaeda-linked anti-Assad forces in Syria and to have been involved in training Kashmiri rebels. The Indian press has reacted furiously to a 'terrorist sympathiser' having a key position in the Pakistan government.

Inspector Mankad sat in a corner of his favourite café munching Mumbai street food and drinking mango lassi.

He liked to spend time here clearing his mind. The police station was not conducive to quiet reflection: a hive of activity, most of it not very productive.

The case of Mr Vijay Patel troubled him. He had found lots of leads and he knew he would have no difficulty finding the people who had committed the grisly murder. But he knew that there was a lot more behind the men who pulled the trigger and disfigured the corpse. They were almost certainly hired hands, minor criminals who would carry out a 'job' for a few thousand rupees. The issue was who was paying them and why.

One of his first interviews had been with the 'slumlord', the unofficial head of the community where the body was found. Within twenty-four hours of the body's discovery, Mankad's slumlord had been able to provide details of how a vehicle had arrived at the ultra-nationalist group's hut in the early hours of the morning and a group of men had emerged, one with a sack over his head. There had been muffled cries from the hut, shots were heard and shortly afterwards a heavy object, presumably the body, had been dragged outside and thrown into the stream then flowing strongly after a monsoon storm.

Mankad sent a detective, disguised as a scavenger, to nose around the site when the hut was empty and he observed footmarks and blood stains that were consistent with the account. Mankad also pulled rank to enable one of his officers to go through the records of the traffic department where the SUV could be traced back to a brother of the Corporator who was, in turn, a known associate of a powerful member of the Maharashtra Legislative Assembly. This was exactly the kind of connection that set the alarm bells ringing in Mankad's head. Especially as the killers had made few serious efforts to dispose of the body or cover their tracks: either they wanted to be traced or calculated that the police would not pursue the case.

Separate enquiries established that Vijay Patel was a law abiding project manager who had acquired a reputation for refusing to pay protection money and was widely regarded as an innocent abroad in the construction industry: unlikely to survive long. More confusingly, Patel worked for Parrikar Senior, a well-known property developer whose reputation as a survivor did not encompass innocence.

What Mankad really wanted was a good look at the Parrikar connection. Something odd there. Old man Parrikar had a reputation for being very shrewd and for keeping out of the limelight. There was a juicy scandal somewhere.

In a darkened corner of the lounge of a five star hotel in Mumbai a thin, ascetic, prematurely grey and distinguished-looking Indian was trying to direct a rambling conversation with one of his country's political class. The object of his attention was a very large, fleshy, supremely self-confident man sinking contentedly into the soft furnishings, his discursive wanderings fuelled by the bottle of whisky in front of him.

Desai preferred water. He despised such people utterly: the crude corruption advertised by the gold necklace and Swiss watch; the political promiscuity (the man had arrived at his present destination via four other parties); the bovine slow-wittedness overlaying animal cunning; the vulgarity and absence of elementary manners. But Desai had learnt to hide his contempt for such people; they could be useful. And this man was a powerful political figure in the city and the state. He was well connected to the criminal underworld that controlled much of the money on which political parties depended and had invaluable intelligence networks.

Desai had flown down from Delhi to meet this man encouraged by his associates in the intelligence and security community. They had picked up reports of heightened Pakistani activity leading, perhaps, to another major terror raid. In all probability they would try to use the gang networks, especially those with loose, ancestral ties to Pakistan. Money trumped religion in this murky world, but 'conviction criminals' were particularly dangerous and not all were under lock and key. And Desai had his own private interests to pursue.

When the politician was three quarters of his way through the bottle, Desai judged that this was the time to raise sensitive issues. 'One group that worries the government in Delhi is the criminal group around the so-called Sheikh. His brother was involved in the 2008 terrorist raid on Mumbai. We need your help in dealing with him.'

'And why should I do this? I am now a senior, respected member of the state administration. I don't get involved with such people.'

Desai rolled his eyes, suppressing his irritation that the man felt it necessary to pretend. 'Our Prime Minister has specifically asked for your cooperation and I know we can rely on you. I am not a politician; merely an adviser. But I know that the ruling party will look after you and your associates in the Assembly.'

'This Sheikh: not a problem.'

'Not a problem?'

'He cooperates with my friends these days.'

'I need more than that.'

'You don't need to know more. He is under control. Leave the details to me.'

'I understand that he is close to old man Parrikar, no?'

'No more. The old man is finished.'

'What about the son? We worry about him.'

'He is clean. Not involved in goonda business.'

'We think he is unreliable. National security concerns.'

'What're you saying? Do you want the help of my friends? My friends are expensive.'

'We can pay… I think we understand one another.'

The politician celebrated his understanding with a loud

belch, which echoed above the gentle cadences of the hotel's Muzak, and then drained the whisky bottle before demanding another.

Desai congratulated himself on a job done. He reflected on the juggling of patriotism, politics and personal enrichment in which he also indulged, though in a more cerebral and sophisticated way than this nasty piece of Mumbai low life.

CHAPTER 6

THE VISIT

The Statesman, 1 July 2019:

The Indian Defence Minister made a speech yesterday telling the Pakistani government 'not to mess with India'. Mr Subramanian Iyer is a recent appointment, the former Chief Minister of Rajasthan and known to have been active in the nationalist R.S.S., like other prominent members of the government: a 'hard liner' on communal matters and on relations with Pakistan. Mr Iyer referred to a recent escalation of incidents on the Line of Control and blamed this on a 'more aggressive anti-Indian stance by the Pakistani High Command'. He expressed particular concern over the delivery to Pakistan of M-11 missiles from China as 'an aggressive move'. He said: 'India is ready. There will be no weakness.'

Kate and her entourage touched down in Mumbai in the early afternoon. She hadn't slept much but had dutifully immersed herself in the encyclopaedic briefs prepared by the department and the High Commission, tried to memorise the bewildering collection of names of ministers and other VIPs she would meet, rehearsed a few words of Hindi and taken to heart the long list of 'elephant traps' and 'subjects to avoid'. She had even boned up on the current test series – India versus Australia – as part of her planned small talk, suppressing her memories of the mind-numbing tedium of days spent at the Oval when her husband wanted her to help chat up clients in the hospitality suite. She felt greatly reassured now that she had, in Susan, her new private secretary, a bright and warm-hearted young woman who had understood, on first acquaintance, that her job was to bring solutions rather than problems. Any tricky questions could be left to the High Commissioner. There was also the Red Admiral, whose role she couldn't quite work out and whose status as a 'consultant' somehow enabled him to travel first class while she, her civil servants and business delegation were more modestly seated.

She was whisked through the VIP arrivals and within minutes was in the High Commission Jaguar whose sporty exterior disguised the armour plating, evident only when it became necessary to open the unnaturally heavy doors. She had hoped to soak up some of the atmosphere of India; she had never been to Mumbai and was keen to explore it. But she was unable to take in very much, flashing through the suburbs with a motorcycle escort and trying, with the help of High Commission staff, to do some last minute cramming for her first meeting in the Arctic air conditioned business suite of the Taj.

It was all happening very fast: a blur of faces and voices. But she was able to take on board that a meeting had been fixed with the Indian PM, to the pleasant surprise of the High Commissioner whose extensive schmoozing with the PM's advisers and staff at his residence had paid off – or so he thought, being blissfully unaware of the role played behind the scenes by the Red Admiral and his contacts. They would all fly up to Delhi tomorrow, the only time the PM was free, double up with a call on the Defence Minister and come back to Mumbai for the rest of the visit. She protested, mildly, about the time pressures, and the onset of jet lag, but it was gently pointed out that our PM had recently 'done' India in a day and then China in a day; her two and a half days for Delhi and Mumbai was really quite leisurely.

There was to be an evening reception for her business delegation to meet the Mumbai business community: then, yes, she could change and have thirty minutes to herself and work on her address to the gathering. But first there was official business, a formal meeting chaired by her Indian opposite number. In the official hierarchy he was a junior trade minister, a very small fish in the Indian political ocean. He had been given the job to placate a sub-caste with a lot of votes in an important state and knew nothing whatever about trade, or the UK, or any of the subjects on the agenda.

In the absence of content or controversy the meeting finished very early and, after elaborate exchanges of goodwill and thanks for an invaluable discussion, most of the participants disappeared rapidly to be early in the queue for food. The High Commissioner saw the opportunity to effect an introduction between Kate and Deepak Parrikar. Her brief told her she could usefully exchange a few pleasantries, which she had memorised from her 'line to take' drawn up by officials who assumed she had never met anyone from India before: the weather in London (awful); the test score (eight wickets by Ashwin); the state of Anglo-Indian relations (excellent as always); our common history (but avoid controversy) and other inanities. Mr Parrikar was largely unknown to the High Commission having avoided social events and being closer to the Americans. The father was known to be the power behind the family company and spoke little English.

The pleasantries weren't needed. Her carefully rehearsed Namaste was aborted by the offer of a handshake. He cut short her halting introduction. He seemed to know everything about her: Oxford friends, most of the British Cabinet, her husband's business partners, all on a Christian name basis. When she had recovered from the welcoming blast she started to appraise the man described as the Indian

George Clooney. He wasn't remotely like him but extremely handsome nonetheless: tall, with very dark, almost black, skin that highlighted his large, dazzling smile; enormous brown eyes radiating warmth, engagement and sympathy.

Disregarding the private secretaries and various flunkeys hovering around the room, he took her by the elbow to the window. They looked down on the Gateway of India where the King Emperor had alighted over a century earlier and, to the right, the entrance to the Taj.

'I wanted you to see this before we sit down and talk about the deal and the equipment your country is selling us through the two linked companies, one of which I own. That, over there, is the old India when white-skinned people ruled over us and when India had its own hierarchy of privilege that for centuries confined my ancestors to the dirtiest and most menial tasks. I am from the new India where businesses like the one my father built up have broken through and where we increasingly have technology as advanced as yours.

'And over there,' he continued, pointing to the hotel entrance, 'is a symbol of the main threat to this new India. Back in 2008 a group of Islamic militants, organised by Pakistani intelligence, and helped by one of the Mumbai mafia clans, stormed the hotel. Hostages were taken. Many people were killed in cold blood – a hundred and twenty-five. This was Mumbai's 9/11.

'Our enemies are also uncomfortably close-by. We have fought four major wars since you lot left India, three against Pakistan. We face two nuclear powers, allied against us, one an almost-failed state close to being overrun by jihadis who would happily take us to Paradise with them so they can enjoy screwing all those virgins to eternity. Sorry, I am not being politically correct, am I? But I am telling you what most Indians feel.'

Kate leaned towards him, fascinated by the frank explanations which were so different to the usual political correctness.

'I believe in Indian democracy, secularism, religious tolerance – I don't do religion myself – but I recently broke the habit of a lifetime and voted for the lot we have in power at the moment. There's a lot of religious nonsense, but they are also about making the country strong. That is why I am here, and why you are here. I'm sorry,' he apologised again, 'I wanted you to understand my position before we started talking about technical and business things.'

'Don't apologise,' Kate replied. 'I am not here to judge. I have been to India a few times but I am always overwhelmed by the scale and variety of the place. I simply don't know enough about your country to have a sensible answer. I just have a job to do.' But his outburst had flicked a switch inside her. She was used to charming, handsome, articulate men, to being pursued and flattered by them and to diverting any incipient feelings into harmless channels. But this passion and intensity was new, and troubling; and also very attractive.

She knew she should stick to her – excruciating – brief and its 'line to take'. But curiosity –and something stronger – took over. 'You obviously know more about me than I know about you. I don't like to be at such a disadvantage. So tell me more about your family and yourself.'

The coughing and spluttering behind them was becoming uncomfortable, from those who had overheard snatches, like the Red Admiral who had somehow crept up to within hearing distance, or who simply wanted to get on with proceedings. The High Commissioner himself stepped forward to take the two into a side room where there was a discussion with the business delegation about their itinerary and a visit to the Parrikar factory. Kate struggled for a while to keep pace with the detail and was clearly flagging, but encouragement from the big brown eyes across the table kept her going until she was able to make a dignified exit to enjoy the promised thirty minutes of rest and recuperation. She saw the same pair of eyes following her to the door.

In another part of the city, altogether less salubrious than the environs of the Taj, there was an unexpected and unwanted visitor to the office of Deepak Parrikar's father. He arrived in a black Mercedes with darkened windows. Out stepped an elderly but distinguished-looking bearded man in dark glasses wearing the white cap and gown of someone who had recently left prayers at the mosque.

The Sheikh had been visiting his friend for half a century but the frequency of the visits had declined as the trajectories of their businesses had diverged. The borderline between legitimate business and organised crime was very unclear in Mumbai but Parrikar had leaned, albeit uncertainly, towards the former and the Sheikh to the latter. Parrikar had drawn the line at narcotics and guns while the Sheikh and his brothers had embraced them, accumulating great wealth and a fearsome but unsavoury reputation in the process. The family now mainly operated out of the Gulf, of necessity in the case of one of the Sheikh's brothers who, reputedly, had financed and provisioned the terrorist raid on the Taj and was high on India's 'most wanted' list.

The Sheikh had not been invited but, then, the length and depth of their friendship had always transcended formality. When he entered his friend's office, there was a chill beneath the effusive welcome and customary exchange of family news. Parrikar was acutely aware that the visit, if witnessed, would attract curiosity and criticism and he worried that the Sheikh, knowing that perfectly well, had decided to come regardless.

They conversed in the street patois of their joint upbringing, a mixture of Marathi and Hindi. When they had exhausted the pleasantries, the Sheikh got to the point. 'Brother, I hear that you are having troubles with the Versova development. There are some bad, bad people in the city these days; not the respect we once had. Greed has taken over. When we were working together there was much less violence. Shocking what happened to your project man.'

'Yes. Patel. You have good sources.'

'I read the press. But nothing much happens without my being told. My friends say that Patel was not paying what had to be paid for services. Showing lack of respect.'

'Patel was a good man. An honest man. My son wanted him to rise in the business.'

'So what are you doing about this killing?'

'The police...'

'That pile of turds is useless. We both know that CID stands for "Criminals in Disguise". If they know anything they will be involved.'

'You would know, my friend.'

'Come, let us not play with each other. I can help you. I can stop this.'

'There is a price, no?'

'There is no price. We are old friends. We trust each other. I want to see your business make good money. Like mine. Otherwise the gangsters get to run this city.'

'And?'

'I have a small favour to ask. A very small favour.'

'How much?'

The Sheikh shifted in his seat. 'This isn't about money. I have a nephew, a very well-qualified engineer. First class degree. PhD in America. He is ideal for your son's company. But he is a good Muslim and we know what will happen: the security people will find reasons for losing his application. Can you please speak to your son?'

'My son doesn't work like this. No caste or cousins. No backhanders. Professional hiring, and security vetting. The new India, like the West.'

But the Sheikh knew that his old friend belonged to the old India, not the new. There was a long pause and then the Sheikh started to leave. 'Thank you, my friend, I know that you will try to please me. I know we can work together again.'

He was right. Parrikar and he had grown apart but deeper bonds united them. They owed each other their lives. Parrikar had given the Sheikh's family sanctuary a quarter of a century earlier when religious fanatics ran amok in the streets of Mumbai and Muslims were being hacked and beaten to death. Many years earlier, in a violent skirmish between street children, the young Parrikar had been surrounded by knife-wielding teenagers from the Sheikh's clan. The Sheikh had pulled him to safety, then protected him and become a partner in crime and property development.

The few seconds between the Sheikh leaving the building and entering his chauffeur driven limousine was enough for a mobile phone, held by a young man standing in the shopfront opposite, to capture the event for his newspaper. And he wasn't the only person to observe and monitor the visit. India's counter-terrorism team, having received maximum cooperation from the local gangsters in the wake of Desai's meeting at the five star hotel, were also represented in the crowd outside the office.

⬥⬥⬥⬥⬥⬥⬥⬥⬥⬥⬥⬥⬥⬥⬥⬥⬥

Parrikar slept badly after the Sheikh's visit. He saw trouble ahead. The ground was shifting underneath him. The old certainties were going. Parrikar had been trying to manoeuvre from his original, less legal and decidedly underground, business into a professional legacy for his children. But the question of how to complete the transition increasingly preoccupied him. He had never explained to his children the complex accounting behind the Mumbai operations, much of which did not exist on paper, let alone on computers. Had they known how much of their shiny factories and luxury condominiums had been financed on the back of Mumbai slum dwellers and revenue defrauding scams they would have been seriously alarmed. But the Patel murder, and the unsolicited visit from the Sheikh, had now persuaded him to open up rather more to his family. Breakfast with Deepak was to be the start.

They sat outside the family bungalow set in extensive gardens where fountains played and peacocks flaunted their plumage on the carefully manicured lawns tended by a small army of servants. The setting, along the ridge of Malabar Hill looking down on Chowpatty beach, framed the most expensive real estate between Hong Kong and Monaco and it was one of Parrikar's early business coups to have acquired it cheaply.

Starting with elaborate, convoluted, childhood reminiscences to ease himself in, he soon lost Deepak's attention, which was torn between the exchange rate risk on the Pulsar contract, the stunning British Minister he had met the previous evening and the cricket commentary from Melbourne emanating from the servants' quarters. His multi-channel reverie was interrupted when his father started to talk about the disappearance and murder of Patel. Deepak had identified him as a talent but they were in different areas of the Parrikar empire. They hadn't been in touch for several weeks and Patel had given no indication of the pressures he was under. The murder hadn't been reported in the English language newspapers and none of Deepak's staff had known enough to brief him on the murky goings on in the Mumbai underworld.

His father described, haltingly, some of the background, skirting around the problems that Patel had created for himself by his attempts to be honest. He was, he said, being blackmailed by a man who knew of some irregularities in the business – without divulging the long, unedifying, history of collaboration with the Sheikh. He had initially ignored the blackmail. Patel had been the casualty. Of course the matter was now with the police but Deepak needed to understand that the blackmailer could no longer be ignored and was making fresh demands, including the posting of a 'nephew' in Deepak's factory. Otherwise more killings could follow.

Deepak took the news calmly. While he had never probed his father's dealings too closely, he had long since realised that Daddy-ji didn't belong to the Mother Teresa school of ethical business. The fact that his father had made moral compromises in his rise from poverty did not diminish Deepak's love and respect for him. He just didn't want or need to know the gory details.

'Daddy-ji, you have got to look after your staff and your family first of all. No heroics. No need to take risks. I will take on this young man. I will keep a close eye on him. But not obviously. We will make it look as if you are complying with demands. You will have to make sure your project people do what is needed to keep out of trouble.'

'Thanks, son. I knew you would understand. Things are changing in India. It isn't easy to find your way. These politicians talk about "clean hands" and pass new laws on corruption. Then they increase "commission". The goondas and the politicians are the same. And some are involved in this Muslim terrorism. Maybe even this "nephew"?'

'We can handle that. In our technology business there are always people snooping and spying. We know and we manage the risks. This country is corrupt and incompetent in lots of ways, like the clowns in the police, but high tech businesses like mine know what they are doing. Don't worry about it. Just tell your gangster friend that you will do as he asks. And that I am playing ball. And then, please, get out of this dirty property business as soon as you can.'

The old man listened for a while, and then tears appeared in his eyes. There was a long silence broken only by the cawing of the crows along the hill where the Parsees had their Tower of Silence, where the birds disposed of the flesh of the dead.

⬛⬛⬛⬛⬛⬛⬛⬛⬛⬛⬛⬛

Shaida arranged to meet Steve, with her brother, in the old part of town where she had grown up and where most of the town's Muslims lived. She hoped he would better understand the environment in which Mo and his friends were now being radicalised, though she was aware that online recruitment was just as important as peer pressure. Indeed, in one of their angry exchanges at home he had admitted surfing the internet for material on 'our fighters'. This revelation made her desperate to find a sympathetic third party who could help her stop her brother drifting towards disaster. Mo had agreed, reluctantly, to come along.

Even as one of the town's civic leaders, Steve was unfamiliar with this area and struggled to find the café. The district was full of cheap terrace housing once occupied by the white working class, who had been moved to council housing or fled to a different part of town – the one he represented – to escape the Pakistani influx. Despite being a fully paid-up multi-culturalist Steve felt uncomfortable, the only white face in the street where many women were shrouded in black, some with veils, and many of the older men had dyed orange beards, flat woollen hats and the loose pyjamas of their homeland. The café, he had been told, was in the middle of a shopping arcade. He wandered, fascinated, past halal butchers, kebab restaurants, shops selling gold jewellery and fashionable but religiously sanctioned women's clothes, newsagents advertising cheap flights to Lahore and cheap phone calls anywhere and open-air greengrocers with stalls overflowing with coriander and ginger, onions and garlic, okra and brinjal, mangoes and papayas.

Eventually he found the café, brilliantly lit by neon lights, with shiny Formica tables and a large picture of Mecca advertising the owner's Haj. A table of five young men was waiting for him, with Shaida who was, conspicuously, the only woman in the place. At the other tables, men stopped their conversation when he entered and looked suspiciously at the group he joined.

Shaida introduced them: Mo, Ibrahim, Ikram, Abdullah and Rafaaq ('Tubby'). Her brother Mo looked sullen and suspicious and completed the stereotype of a disaffected Muslim youth by sporting a beard and a white cap advertising his devotional commitment. The others were more welcoming but shy and polite, and, unlike Mo, they wore Western dress and were clean shaven. The conversation was halting and uncomfortable at first, but they were determined to tell their stories. All very similar: second generation – fathers factory workers, school at the local comprehensive, aspirational families pushing them to get good grades. Then degree courses at unfashionable universities within commuting distance from home, in subjects their families had judged to be useful and leading to good careers: accounting, business studies, law. But now frustration: no jobs, apart from pizza delivery or serving in cafés, scrounging for tips, or doing something menial in a distant relative's shop.

Steve responded: 'Young people everywhere are struggling to get into work. The local council and the union do what they can. The Labour Party has been campaigning against these zero hours contracts and dead-end jobs and to get this Tory government to invest in jobs for young people.' It sounded lame and tediously party political and he knew it. He dared to glance at Shaida for support – she had a proper job – but she was signalling detachment and was clearly on the side of the young men.

Mo, who had retreated into taciturn contempt, spoke at last. 'The trouble is, you people don't respect us. If I put in for a job with "Mohammed" on the application it goes straight in the bin, or they hit the delete key. You know that. Why give us all this crap about "jobs for young people"?'

Steve took a different tack. 'All I can say is that at our company – where Shaida and your dad work – we have no discrimination. One third black and Asian. Management and shop floor. But you need a proper trade like electrical or mechanical engineering. Did they never tell you that at school?'

Mo shifted the angle of attack. 'What exactly do you do at Pulsar? I hear you make weapons – is that right?'

Steve looked nervously at Shaida.

'Sure. Among other things. We supply the armed forces. Do you have a problem with that?'

'I have a problem with killing Muslims.'

'We don't.'

'Israel?'

'No.'

'India?'

'I don't know anything about that.'

'What a joke! I can't believe we know more than you do. Everyone in town is talking about this big contract coming your way.'

The conversation was taking a turn Steve hadn't anticipated and was becoming seriously awkward. Shaida's eyes were fixed firmly in the middle distance as if to disclaim responsibility for having lit the fuse that had led to this explosion.

The mild-mannered Tubby tried to help out, steering the conversation on to less controversial topics, and the ways that Steve could realistically help. When the time came for Steve to go, Abdullah asked if he would come back, perhaps to see a bigger group. 'There's a meeting room in the cultural centre behind the mosque. Would you be happy coming there?' It was agreed but, before Steve left, Abdullah asked if they could have a group photo. Even Mo was persuaded to shuffle into the corner of the picture. Shaida mumbled a 'thank you' to Steve on his way out and flashed a smile, her first of the evening.

Despite the smile Steve felt some unease as he left. The meeting had shaken some of his earlier belief that the good community relations enjoyed in the factory were reflected more widely in the town. The Asian councillors in his group had always exuded a breezy self-confidence, telling their colleagues that they had 'their own people' safely tied up. Their comfortable majorities seemed to bear this out. Or so he'd thought.

Kate touched down at Mumbai for the second time in three days, returning from Delhi for another round of meetings before leaving for London. Jet lag and constant travel were playing havoc with her metabolism; night and day fused into a vague, timeless, sleepy blur. But she had a warm feeling of satisfaction from a programme that seemed to be going well and the prospect of meeting again the anonymous texter who had sent the message 'You were brilliant' after her first round of meetings in Mumbai. She had a shrewd suspicion who it was and her cynical side dismissed it as the work of a charmer who was employing the technique of telling a woman how clever she is rather than how pretty. But it had aroused her interest, whatever the motivation.

The schedule of meetings had included a brief visit to the Indian PM, a rare honour for a minister some way below Cabinet rank. There were platitudes all round but the important thing was that the meeting had happened, and favourable reference made to the prospective arms contract. She had caught in his eyes a glint of the political steel that had taken him from poverty and a career starting as a tea boy to leadership of the world's biggest democracy. He had in turn been fascinated by the article in a leading Indian daily – and planted by the High Commissioner through a friendly journalist – describing her as the rising star of British politics.

There was, however, one aspect of the meeting that troubled her, and the High Commissioner even more so. The Prime Minister anticipated all of her questions and interventions and, when discussion turned to the potential contract and collaboration and the capabilities of the technology to be supplied from the UK, he seemed to know considerably more than was in the public domain. She and the High Commissioner both noticed that as he discussed these subjects he periodically turned to the thin, ascetic-looking man behind him as if for confirmation that he was on the right track.

An alert first secretary who sat at the back of the meeting had identified him as Sanjivi Desai, who had been a prominent member of the National Security Adviser's team in the days of the previous BJP administration. He was, apparently, known at the time as brilliant but ideological. Desai had since left India for a university in the USA. There he had electrified the foreign policy community with an academic article that argued the case for nuclear weapons as part of an offensive military strategy rather than simply for deterrence. The article had since been largely forgotten and India had adopted a 'no first use' strategy (while Pakistan had not). The High Commission team was clearly taken aback by Desai's resurrection but unable to cast more light on it.

Back in Mumbai the ministerial party would stay in a hotel near the international airport for the early morning flight back to London. For the rest of the day, they would travel to the Parrikar factory, located in the city outskirts, for an inspection visit.

Kate hadn't been a minister long enough to have seen many factories and her vision of an Indian factory was that it would be – well – Indian: noisy, dirty and teeming with people. Parrikar Avionics proved to be as far from that world as it was possible to be: full of computer controlled machines and robots; industrious, uniformed staff busying themselves purposefully; a factory floor so clean you could have eaten off it; a quiet hum permitting normal conversation; and odourless beyond the smell of fresh paint. It resembled what she imagined factories to be like in Japan or Germany.

She tried to restart the conversation with Deepak that had been cut off at the hotel.

'I believe you are an engineer by training.'

'Was. Now I try, not very successfully, to make money.'

'Can't help you there. I am a medieval historian.'

'I know. But a good way to understand politics.'

Throughout the visit Deepak stayed by her side, attentive and efficient but conveying nothing in his conversation or body language to suggest any interest beyond professional correctness. On her return to the hotel Kate was left wondering whether she had read too much into the first encounter and into that anonymous text. But, shortly after arriving back at the hotel, another text arrived: 'Farewell dinner? 8pm? Car outside. Black Bentley. D.' She had a 'wash up' with her officials and her business delegation but persuaded herself, without a great deal of resistance, that the national interest might be better served by getting to know Mr Parrikar a little better. She explained her change of plan to Susan, who reacted with customary aplomb, though the upward movement of her eyebrows managed to convey the message 'Lucky you. But be careful.'

After a bath and change of clothes, she took the lift to the hotel lobby a few minutes after 8pm. The black Bentley was waiting at the entrance. The chauffeur sped off into the night, arriving after a rather hair-raising drive at an expansive villa with a luxuriant garden. Deepak Parrikar was waiting at the door to greet her.

'This is the company's VIP guest house,' he explained. 'I stay here when I am at the factory. Sorry about the air of mystery. I thought you might prefer a private dinner here instead of the hotel restaurant with all your hangers-on.' If she had any reservations, it was too late. And, anyway, she hadn't.

He had obviously made discreet enquiries about her dietary tastes – she was an enthusiast for good North Indian cooking – and she was served the best, most subtle Mughal meal she had ever tasted: gently spiced lamb in biryani with almonds and sultanas, with aubergine and dal accompaniments. Conversation flowed.

'A little bird told me that you were quite a celebrity at Oxford. Much sought after. Modelling too.'

'Yes. I enjoyed myself. But don't believe everything you read in newspapers. How about you? And don't tell me you spent your years in London and the States in a self-denying monastic order.'

They flirted with their eyes, trying not to catch the attention of the uniformed staff serving the meal, as they talked about the visit – the deal was agreed bar the formalities, was his assessment – and went on to their large overlapping circles of friends and his favourite haunts in London. When the servants had cleared away the meal and retreated to their quarters she broached the subject that they had hitherto skirted around. 'You haven't mentioned Mrs Parrikar. I believe there is a Mrs Parrikar?'

'Yes, there is. Her name is Rose. She spends most of her time in Delhi. She is a very talented writer and does a lot of scripts for Doordarshan, like your BBC. And our children are there, with Rose and my mother-in-law. Perhaps you should tell me about Mr Thompson.'

'Where to start? You know his background: inherited wealth, property market and all that.'

'Yes, I do know all about that. I also heard that he had… or has?… quite a reputation.'

She hadn't expected to get into the intimacies quite so soon. Or so easily. But why not? she told herself. 'Let's just say that we have an excellent partnership, a grown-up marriage. Stable. Solid. We adore our girls and provide them with a good family life. We know each other's strengths and weaknesses and don't let the weaknesses get in the way.'

'Sounds interesting.'

Kate hesitated. She welcomed an invitation to take their after-dinner coffee to the veranda, listening to the unfamiliar racket of cicadas in the garden. She decided to take the plunge. 'He has a roving eye,' she answered candidly. 'Always has. At the beginning I retaliated a few times when I wanted to get even. But it made me feel guilty. And I didn't like the men much. So I have a lot to be satisfied about and leave romance to my girlfriends. And you?'

'Similar. I did the rounds in London and Harvard. A lot of nice girls but nothing special. When I came back here my energies went into building up the business that my father had asked me to run. Then – this is India – my family and friends started agitating about marriage. Late twenties and still a bachelor: a problem in danger of becoming a scandal. My parents started asking about suitable girls: a degree from a reputable college; wheaten complexion; preferably a virgin (but this is difficult to guarantee these days); a dowry (but we are rich enough not to be greedy).'

Kate was intrigued. 'I thought dowries were old hat in the Indian middle classes.'

'Among the highly educated, maybe, but not otherwise. Anyway, the real problem was to marry into a "good family", Indian-speak for caste. The people my parents mix with are mostly banias – merchants, traders. My father's parents rub along with them in the business world but when it comes to marriage they made it clear that for all our money we were not socially acceptable. My ancestors are Dalits, "untouchables". In the USA, our family's climb from rags to riches would be celebrated as the American Dream. But, here, it is a guilty secret.

'Eventually I met a beautiful Christian girl from the south – Rose – who didn't have any hang-ups about caste, or colour – she is as black as me. She was attracted, I don't doubt, to the family wealth, and perhaps even to me. We married quietly in a Christian church: no dowry; no astrologers; just a few friends and family.'

Kate was glad that she had taken their conversation into their private lives, realising that it had brought them closer. She was grateful too that he didn't crowd her, engaging her only with his eyes. They talked late into the night.

She hadn't talked so freely to a man for a long time and she was encouraged by his easy, natural, candour. She knew she was very attracted to him and sensed that the feeling was shared.

It seemed easier to stay than go. The packing and the final debrief could wait until the morning. But Kate forced herself to think clearly. She felt herself to be on the threshold of a serious affair and it would send the wrong signal to rush into it impetuously. Without the need for an explanation he seemed to read her mind and speedily summoned the driver when she, regretfully, indicated her wish to leave. Confident that she had done the right thing, she felt able to show something of her feelings.

The lingering kiss on the doorstep was not, however, as private as the two of them believed. The *Bharat Bombay* team had been staking out the guest house as well as the offices downtown since they had been tipped off that Deepak was staying there, and a mystery guest had been reported arriving some hours earlier and still hadn't left. The photographer was every bit as skilled and well equipped as his paparazzi cousins in Europe; there was adequate lighting in the porch area and he captured the moment for posterity.

Nor was he the only curious observer of the guest house. If the Minister had been naïve enough to imagine that her departure from the hotel had gone unnoticed, she underestimated the resources and resourcefulness of both British and Indian security and intelligence services. By the time Kate had arrived back at the hotel sometime after 2am, a report was on the desks of the British and Indian National Security Advisers recommending that their political masters might wish to be aware of this blemish on an otherwise flawless visit.

CHAPTER 7

THE RETURN

The Times of India, 2 July 2019:

Lok Sabha has passed legislation applying across India the cow protection law piloted in Haryana in 2016. Cow slaughter is now punishable by up to ten years in prison. A new Cow Protection police force has been established to enforce the law. Members of the ruling party argued in debate that those who refused to observe the taboo on eating beef should leave India.

Steve's second meeting with Shaida's friends took place in the cultural centre at the back of the town's main mosque, though Shaida waited outside. Steve had been to the mosque before, campaigning at election time, but he had not been the centre of attention and, this time, he felt much more self-conscious.

Looking around the room Steve saw mainly friendly, welcoming faces, but there was a small cluster that included Shaida's brother, Mo, who sat separately, dressed traditionally and affected an air of disapproval and rejection. The earlier discussion had forearmed Steve with many of their concerns and arguments, so he felt altogether better prepared. Different members of the group rehearsed their grievances – jobs, the police, Islamophobia – and he felt confident enough to throw back some challenges to them: why were no women present? Did they unequivocally condemn the sadistic cruelty of some extremist organisations? One of Mo's group tried to take him down the foreign policy route but this was outside his comfort zone. Steve contented himself with acknowledging that the Blair government had made a terrible blunder over the Iraq war and this had done great damage to the country's reputation and the party's standing with Muslims. This earned him a round of applause, and he hoped it would provide him with an exit route from the meeting. It didn't.

There was an awkward silence, only broken when one of Mo's group, dressed in a long white robe and cap, launched into a bitter and angry tirade. 'Do you know how many Muslims are assaulted and spat at, in this town that your party runs and claims is some kind of multi-cultural paradise? Did you know that women have their headscarves torn off? Called "Paki prostitutes" in front of their children? Many, many cases. But not reported.'

There was a growl of support in the room. Steve was feeling very much on the defensive and wondering how he had got into the position as a figurehead for the police, the council, the Labour Party and the other establishment bodies that these young people saw either as the enemy or as hypocritical neutrals. Sensing the weakness of Steve's position, Mo tried to raise the ante. 'What you people don't realise is that we are on the receiving end of constant biased coverage in the media. Muslims are always a threat; always to blame. We all know the reasons, don't we, boys? It's all those Jews, innit, controlling everything.'

There was a hushed silence. He had overstepped the mark, no doubt deliberately, to provoke Steve into trying too hard to be one of the boys.

'You mean all those Jews like Sadiq Khan, Mo Farah, Moeen Ali and Sajid Javid,' Steve replied.

The laughter drained the tension away. 'Serves you right, you idiot, Mo,' someone called out. Even Mo felt the need to retreat a little.

'We are not getting at you personally. At least you listen to us. But you need to take on board that some in our community are close to breaking point.'

Then, as usual, a group photo for social media. He was gratified that Mo's group – which had become a little friendlier – edged themselves into the centre of the picture, alongside him. As Steve left, Shaida nodded acknowledgement at the door and prepared to go home with her brother. Tubby, who saw himself as some kind of bodyguard and protégé of Steve, ran after him, anxious to pass on information. 'I've overheard some talk. People in the community know about this Indian contract. Some of them see everything as India versus Pakistan. They are saying this is like Blair and Bush attacking Iraq: a war on Muslims. They want to make trouble.' This report left Steve more troubled than the fire-eating rhetoric of the young radicals. There were hundreds of jobs – including his own – on the line.

As they left the mosque complex, Steve saw another incident that alarmed him. There was an angry altercation between a powerfully built, bearded man who looked like a cleric, and a few of his supporters who were confronting a larger group trying to prevent them entering the mosque. There was no violence but voices were raised in anger and, whatever the language being used, it was abundantly clear that the bearded cleric was unwelcome.

Tubby was reluctant to talk but, after being pressed, he explained that the cleric was a well-known radical. 'What the government calls a hate preacher,' he explained. 'He has never advocated terrorism and isn't in one of the banned groups like Al Muhajiroun. But he praises the "martyrs" who have gone to Syria and Afghanistan and demands stronger action by the local mosques against "backsliders", especially "loose women", and people who fraternise with "kafirs". Like us,' he added, giggling nervously. 'He has a growing local following. But the local mosque committees don't want trouble; so they've banned him from preaching here.'

As they walked away, Steve noticed police officers at a discreet distance and in the next street a couple of vans full of police in riot gear. One of the policemen stopped him. 'Evening, sir. I trust you and... your friend are not having any problems?'

'No, officer, we're fine.'

'OK, just checking.'

⬚⬚⬚⬚⬚⬚⬚⬚⬚⬚⬚⬚⬚

On her return to London, Kate was on a high. The department, her personal team, No. 10, the High Commission all pronounced the visit a great success. No gaffes. Everyone was impressed by her grasp of the issues and her diplomatic skills. There were no obstacles remaining to the signing of a big defence contract of which Pulsar/Parrikar was part. It only remained to secure a high-level VIP visit that would be a fitting context. And she was also able to enjoy the warm glow of reflecting on her night out and her new friend, which brought into relief the lack of emotional and physical pleasures in her married life.

India receded into the background of departmental priorities. The routine work of a department minister came to the fore. She longed for the weekend, to catch up with family news and sleep. But there was one more obstacle to negotiate: the weekly advice surgery on Friday evening. Several Tory and Labour MPs had strongly warned against such diligence. 'You only encourage the nutters and troublemakers' was the gist of their distilled wisdom. MPs in marginal seats and Liberal Democrats – she was told – set great store by surgeries but she didn't need to bother; perhaps once a month for form's sake. She decided to ignore the advice, much to the fury of Stella who would have to attend, make notes and draft letters.

Kate valued the surgeries. She learnt a lot about people and their problems, which she had been shielded from in the election campaign and throughout her protected upbringing. She came to realise that in her very prosperous constituency there was a lot of financial distress, and real poverty, made all the worse by isolation and lack of neighbourly support. And there was a growing undercurrent of anxiety about rising unemployment. Last week had produced a sad family who could have stepped out of *Jude the Obscure* and for whom everything that could go wrong had gone wrong: redundancy, repossession, children with special needs. Then there was an export salesman who couldn't travel because his passport had been mislaid somewhere in the Home Office and had lost his job; a mentally ill alcoholic who couldn't get treatment for either condition until the other had first been cured; and a hopelessly overcrowded family whom the council had deemed 'intentionally homeless' after refusing to move to a corner of a council estate infested by drug dealers. She did her best for all of them but knew that these were mostly hopeless cases.

The desperate were randomly interspersed with the self-important and selfish. This week there was a delegation protesting over the decision of the local council to grant planning permission for a large home extension, wanted by a local teacher to house his expanding family ('loss of light', 'traffic congestion', 'parking problems', 'out of character'). She explained with difficulty that planning law did not encompass their concerns about 'loss of property value'.

Then, in came a young woman with a child who had obvious learning difficulties, bearing flowers and a box of chocolates: 'I just wanted to say thank you. Freddie has got the special school you helped us find.' Kate struggled to remember how she had performed this miracle, but eventually it all came back. A struggling single mum with three children: one physically and another mentally handicapped. She remembered, with a twinge of shame, how she had initially fallen back on her stereotypical assumptions about struggling single mothers. Several fathers? Actually, no: one father, a lovely man who had been killed in an industrial accident. On benefits? Actually, no: she was working but, thanks to a recalculation of her tax credits, could no longer afford proper childcare and was having to juggle babysitters. Dependency culture? Actually, no: whenever she had spare time she helped the old lady next door. Having heard all this, Kate had written a very supportive letter to the head of the county's educational and social services departments. Maybe it had helped. Something gave way inside her when she was offered the flowers and chocolates. She burst into tears, to the embarrassment of Stella, sitting beside her, and the dismay of her constituent who left quickly, worrying about what she had done to upset this important woman.

Kate then had to recompose herself for her last visitors: a delegation from the Churches Together of Surrey Heights. Stella was convinced that they were here to deliver a blast of holy wrath after Kate's last vote in support of gay adoption. Kate was prepared to tough this one out: she had never understood what all the fuss was about. She herself preferred men to women, having tried both, but had no problem with other people's preferences. But, no, this was not what worried them.

The delegation was led by a large and cheerful young woman with a dog collar and improbably red cheeks who bore a more than passing resemblance to the Vicar of Dibley. She introduced herself and her team, saying: 'We have come to talk to you about the arms trade. We want you to use your influence in government to stop the sale of weapons to governments that abuse human rights.'

She had a long, prepared speech and Kate did her best to listen politely. But the room was overcrowded and stuffy, she was tired and desperate to get away. She looked conspicuously at her watch but the vicar and her followers had been preparing for the visit for weeks and had no intention of going quickly or quietly. Kate tried to escape.

'I have a lot of sympathy,' she explained, 'but I am new in the job and this is not my area of responsibility. And there are strict rules and processes governing arms exports.'

'But we read in the press that you have just been to India. Promoting arms exports. Shouldn't the Indians be spending their money on fighting malnutrition and illiteracy?'

'Yes. They also have a democratic government with real security concerns. And shouldn't we also be concerned about British workers and their jobs?'

An earnest member of the delegation launched into scripture –'swords into ploughshares' – and Kate could see that she could not win an argument based on textual analysis of the Bible. She managed to summon a graceful smile. 'I know how much this means to you,' she responded. 'I admire your Christian spirit. I will dig out some facts on the arms trade with India and send them to you to discuss at our next meeting.'

Stella looked aghast at this prospect. 'Time wasting *Guardian* readers. They will never vote for you whatever you say,' she muttered after the delegation had left offering Kate their prayers.

<hr />

Iqbal Aziz drove his 500cc Bajaj motorcycle confidently to the entrance of the Parrikar Avionics factory. In his pocket he was carrying a letter from the head of human resources explaining that a vacancy had appeared that fitted his engineering qualifications perfectly. Please would he present himself and, subject to the necessary checks, take up a job that was waiting for him in the R&D unit?

His journey there had started a few weeks earlier. He had been at his desk in a secretive defence research institution near Islamabad. He received a summons to see the legendary General Rashid: battlefield hero, now mastermind of Pakistan's covert operations overseas and head of the Inter-Services Intelligence agency ISI. The General got quickly to the point: 'We have a job for you. India. Mumbai. Give you a chance to meet your extended family.'

This wasn't the first job the researcher had been asked to do. On business and academic visits to the US and Saudi Arabia he had been asked to obtain classified information in his field of radar linked to missile technology, beyond the limit of what their governments would release officially. Unlike most agents he had the advantage of knowing exactly what he was looking for and what was useful.

He had shown himself adept at recruiting local helpers and mastering the technologies of copying, miniaturising, storing and transmitting sensitive data. His research superiors and his handlers at ISI were both delighted with his progress: he was destined for higher things that no longer involved risky trips in the field. But here was a big job that, with his family networks and travel experience in India, he was ideally qualified to carry out.

The briefing was specific: 'There is a defence industry installation on the outskirts of Mumbai that we want to know more about. We think it is developing technology linked to their missile defence system. We need to know where the Indians have got to. The firm, Parrikar Avionics, works on the programme – we think – with a British firm and British government backing. We want you to get inside their R&D department and find out what you can.'

Several weeks later he was in India staying with cousins whose family had remained behind at Partition. They were encouraged to believe that he was a bona fide visitor with a valid Indian passport.

Aziz manoeuvred his bike to the allocated parking area amid hundreds of other Indian made mopeds and motorcycles. He had a good look around and assessed the level of vigilance. Security was visible but not oppressive. No one had checked the panniers on his bike. The man at the gate had looked at his letter but appeared to be reading it upside down. Not very impressive. The perimeter fence was high but scalable. There were a few CCTV cameras but to his knowledgeable eye there were too few and they were badly positioned. Compared to the US military industrial establishments he had visited, or even back home, it all seemed rather sloppy.

He followed the signs to the security office to submit his papers and obtain a pass. When he entered the office he was told to wait in a queue and, after fifteen minutes, was invited into a small cubicle to sit opposite a bald overweight man who was sweating profusely in his tight uniform. Behind him sat a man introduced as his assistant who was reading the sports pages of a Mumbai newspaper. The overweight man laboriously and slowly took Iqbal through the details of his original application form, checking dates and places and ensuring that all the certificates and references were in place. The questioning was thorough but pedestrian: a box-ticking exercise of the kind perfected in subcontinental bureaucracies. Iqbal panicked at one point when it was noticed that the date on one of the certificates didn't tally with the date he had cited in his CV; but this was a genuine mistake and the man grumpily accepted it. After almost an hour he was pronounced security cleared and sent off to have his photo taken for a pass.

In fact, the interrogator was far from slow but an extremely sharp, US trained head of security. And his 'assistant' had flown down from Delhi for the interview, from Indian counter-intelligence. They were both well aware that Iqbal Aziz was not who he said he was and that his CV was largely a fabrication. He was Hussein Malik who had first appeared on the radar screens of intelligence agencies almost a decade earlier when he was pursuing his PhD at Stanford, as an overseas student from Pakistan. He had showed an unusual degree of interest in some of the avionics technology being developed at that time and in the heightened post 9/11 security his curiosity was noted, especially when he later reappeared at academic conferences and business negotiations, placing him near some very sensitive material.

But he was not caught doing anything untoward and went back home to a research establishment linked to the Pakistan military where the CIA kept close tabs on him, and, at one point, tried to recruit him. Subsequently he travelled widely to conferences dealing with avionics technology, and the interest of several intelligence agencies was aroused by the fact that he sometimes travelled with a false identity. There were several visits to India on an Indian passport that the Indian authorities had monitored but not aborted, hoping to find out what he was up to. Then, a few weeks ago, he had been spotted in Dubai and, after a series of flight changes, had ended up in Mumbai, staying with what appeared to be distant extended family.

The man from Delhi felt that he and his colleague had, so far, successfully hoodwinked Iqbal Aziz. No hint had been given that the watcher was being watched. He patted himself on the back for winning the argument in Delhi against those who questioned his recommendation to let Aziz into the country and into the factory in the hope he would lead them to a network of subversive contacts working for the enemy.

CHAPTER 8

TRISHUL

Press reports, Moscow, 5 July 2019:

President Putin paid a short informal visit to India, his third. He told a press conference that Russia 'wanted to restore the excellent relations between the two countries that prevailed before the break-up of the Soviet Union'. The Indian Prime Minister, receiving him in Delhi, agreed that there was common ground in suppressing Islamic terrorism in the region. Russia will also press for India to become a permanent member of the UN Security Council and President Putin referred, without giving details, to a 'sharing of competences' in relation to nuclear technology.

Kate was in the office bright and early on Monday, refreshed after a family weekend spending time with her daughters. She was beginning to enjoy her new life and the office worked smoothly now that her excellent private secretary had established an efficient, but pleasant, routine. Susan was a find.

This morning Susan came in with some highly confidential papers. 'Kate, I'm supposed to check that you have read these papers and then take them away. Not to be left lying around,' she announced. This was Kate's first exposure to papers marked 'Top Secret' and she was mildly titillated at the thought. Fascinated, she plunged into the first document. To her amazement it was a broadly accurate account and analysis of her India visit as presented to the Pakistan Security Council. They knew all about Pulsar and Parrikar Avionics and why they were important. Someone had risked their neck for this – or whatever part of the anatomy the Pakistan authorities severed when they uncovered secret agents.

There was, however, one sentence in the report that caused her to stop and reread it several times. Her head span as she grasped the significance of what she was reading: the Pakistan intelligence assessment of the kit to be provided by Pulsar was that it would destabilise the nuclear balance by giving India the potential to knock out the electronics of any Pakistani nuclear retaliation.

'This is the opposite of what I was told,' she said to Susan.

'It isn't my job to comment on policy,' Susan replied, 'but it may explain why my equivalent in the Foreign Office was anxious that you should see the report.'

'So, what should I do?' Kate asked.

'My strong advice is to say and do nothing at this stage. You are new to the job and so am I. You can raise the matter with the Secretary of State or even the Prime Minister, but you need more than an uncorroborated opinion by an unnamed Pakistani analyst.'

Kate read a less confidential paper by the Foreign Office Research Department piecing together press and other published reports from India and Pakistan that, individually, were of no great significance and none of which had made it into mainstream Western media, but taken together led the analyst to conclude that the 'threat level' had been raised a notch or two to just short of red. Indian sources reported increased numbers of crossings of the Line of Control into Kashmir by Kashmiri separatist militant groups allegedly backed by Pakistan. Substantial numbers of Indian soldiers and infiltrators were reported dead. The Cabinet reshuffles in both India's and Pakistan's governments had brought forward ministers who were more aggressively hostile to their neighbour and with strong links to religious fundamentalists.

And a leading Pakistani newspaper, *Dawn*, reported that the Pakistan Defence Minister had flown to Beijing to discuss the deteriorating security situation in the subcontinent and to seek Chinese support for countering 'illegal' Indian encroachments on Pakistani air space. He further announced that he had authorised a military exercise in the Sind desert near the Indian border, saying: 'We need to be prepared for all contingencies.'

None of this had been flagged up as a problem to Kate during her visit to India. It had all been 'business as usual'. But clearly it wasn't.

<hr/>

Calum called in his management team and union reps for a meeting in the boardroom.

'Good news, bad news,' he began. 'Good news: the Indian contract looks as if it is now in the bag. Due diligence has raised no problems. Our investors are happy. I have some wee financial details to sort out. Not a problem. Thanks for helping me to get the project ready for launch.

'Now, the bad news. The ministerial visit in a few days' time – it's Kate Thompson, the Minister of State who led the recent delegation to India. Bright and tipped for higher things. But you know what I think about politicians, especially Tories.

'Anyway, we have no choice. If we want MOD work in future, we have to be very nice to Mrs Thompson. Keeping Whitehall sweet. The deal is: low-key event, modest publicity – local press, regional TV only – everyone on their best behaviour; a few apprentices on parade; leave the rest to me.'

When Calum's meeting dispersed, Steve made a point of walking back with Shaida. She gave not the slightest sign of intimacy and Steve felt as if their extramural meetings had never happened. What was it all for? A beautiful young woman had taken advantage of his infatuation to pursue a personal agenda whose ultimate purpose was obscure. He had done as she asked. Now what?

She must have been reading his thoughts. As they walked through the finance department he was given a broad smile and a long look at those open, big, brown eyes rather than the usual cool detachment. He felt the gentlest of touches on his elbow.

'Thank you very much for what you did the other day,' she said. 'I can assure you it was appreciated. You may not realise how much it means to most of those lads to let off steam. They are impressionable. They have now discovered you. Last week it was Russell Brand. Before that George Galloway, Osama bin Laden – the lot. Most of them have the attention span of a goldfish but if you can help keep them out of trouble that's great.

'Mo is more serious, though. My dad and I have been really worried about my brother. Completely unable to get through to him. He blanks us or gives us an Islamist rant. But he was impressed by you and said so. It is very difficult. I felt stronger, knowing I have a friend.' After quickly checking that they were not observed, she gave him a peck on the cheek and then disappeared into her office.

Steve knew that he should be in Calum's office passing on the warning that there were elements in the community who had picked up on the India connection. But in the warm afterglow of this encounter his attention wandered.

———

Deepak Parrikar had inherited enough of his father's guile to be no pushover in detailed negotiations. Like Calum, he was ultimately dependent for business on the goodwill of his government. But he was capable of wriggling like an eel to squeeze a few more lakh rupees out of a contract. Now he was pushing up against the limits of patience of the babus in Delhi. He received a very testy phone call from the PM's office making it clear that if he wanted to avoid annoying the Prime Minister, personally, he should be on the next available flight to London to sort out any remaining difficulties. Before he went to pack a suitcase he had time to send a text.

Kate was in her office signing papers when her mobile registered a new message. She normally ignored them. She had got used to the endless stream of messages from the whip's office instructing the government payroll to vote on some obscure piece of legislation. This time she reached for the phone. Boredom? Instinct? It was from a D in Mumbai: 'Coming London tomorrow. Hilton, Park

Lane. Fancy nightcap?' Pleasant thoughts came flooding back. Yes, she would very much like to see D again. But how? This was home turf. She wasn't exactly famous but recognised around the Westminster village. The private office controlled her diary. She had an MP's flat in Kennington and her family were used to her absences during the week. But, no, there were other MPs in the block. Arriving late at night with a handsome Indian would be tea room, then press, chatter the next day. But, of course, she could go to his hotel. Use a taxi not the ministerial car. No one could be surprised to see a minister turning up for an evening reception at the Hilton… or leaving after a business breakfast. A few minutes later she replied: 'D, love to meet. Your hotel? K.'

Inspector Mankad arrived ten minutes early for his rendezvous at Rita's Sunshine Bar as was his habit. He would always check out the places where he had confidential meetings. Mumbai could be a dangerous place for police officers on their own in unfamiliar areas. Mankad was a long way from his parish so the risks were fewer. But it paid to be careful. The bar was unexceptional and unmemorable, which was how Mankad liked his rendezvous locations.

The crime reporter from *Bharat Bombay* arrived on time and after a few preliminaries they thanked each other. The journalist had enjoyed a prestigious splash and Mankad had been able to keep alive a murder enquiry that his supervisors would otherwise have sat on, fearing the consequences of tackling politically influential gangsters. But they were still no closer to finding out who was behind the killing of Vijay Patel.

The journalist explained that the paper was planning a big piece on the Parrikars. A story built around their dynastic succession was falling into place. The glamorous, charming, modernising, Westernised son and the grizzled old man, with a colourful past, losing his grip. Now there was the British VIP girlfriend – a blurred picture but just about usable – and the proof of a connection with the Sheikh's family with its unsavoury links to the underworld and, at one remove, Pakistani terrorist operations. And there were lots of stories of the old man's earlier life that could be reheated: the brutal clearing of the slum dwellers from desirable sites; an infamous scam involving adulterated cement; the Backbay Reclamation corruption scandal; the numerous unpunished breaches of building and planning regulations. All of this was being run past the lawyers. And the editor, whose vision of the paper was light entertainment for the commuting masses, still had to be persuaded that this foray into investigative journalism wasn't going to result in his experiencing the fate of Mr Patel.

The policeman listened quietly. He could see the attractions of shaking the tree. But he couldn't see where the murder case was leading. His network of informers had all repeated the gossip in the bazaars that Patel had been killed by a couple of thugs from the Sheikh's clan. And the motive was Patel's refusal to pay extortion money. But something didn't add up. Parrikar and the Sheikh had been close associates and – in the one piece of useful intelligence the Inspector had gleaned from his press contact – they had been in touch again very recently. Yet an execution of this kind would have been sanctioned from the top.

And he had just heard that the body of one of the suspected killers had been found on one of the city's rubbish tips.

As he left work, Steve was surprised to find Shaida waiting for him with her younger brother, looking sheepish and carefully studying the ground in front of him: 'Can we talk? It's important,' she said. She led the way to a patch of ground where staff came out to have their snacks in summer and kick a football around.

Once settled on a bench she explained: 'My darling brother here has a problem. Mo, tell him!' Mo wouldn't say anything so she filled in the awkward silence. 'I found him, last night, by accident, watching a disgusting video on his laptop. Not hard core. I know all about that. Sex starved boys do it. Not a problem. But this was much worse. It was from one of the jihadi groups showing what they do to their prisoners. We talked afterwards and Mo said he was given it on a memory stick by one of his friends who was at the last meeting you spoke to. Eventually the truth came out. This young man – Zuffar – is trying to organise a group to "do something for the jihad". Bombing. Or killing a policeman. Trying to get Mo involved. Come. Speak up.' Still not a word. 'We need your advice, Steve. Perhaps your help. Mo doesn't want to go along with his friends, though he agrees with a lot of their ideas and seems emotionally dependent on them. He won't shop them to the police and I worry that if the police find out they will detain him, and my dad and I could be at risk of losing our jobs. We can't tell our parents; they would go spare.'

Steve was too numb to give a reply. And Mo was no closer to communicating directly. There was a long, embarrassed silence. Eventually Steve mumbled a semi-coherent response. 'Look, I'll have to think about it. I don't have any instant wisdom. My instincts are that we have to find a way of getting the intelligence to the authorities without incriminating Mo or dragging in your family. But I don't know people in that world. The only police officer I know is the sergeant in charge of my ward community team. Or there is the security man – Starling – at Pulsar, but I don't really know him from Adam.' Shaida looked at him pleadingly. For the first time he saw not a beautiful Asian princess or a desirable woman but a frightened, vulnerable person trapped between the conflicting loyalties to her family and the country of which she was a part.

On the evening following the Pulsar staff meeting, one of the attendees prepared for a long night at the office. His usual routine was to arrive for the day by public transport so there would be no car left in the car park after the factory closed. At the end of the day he would check out, wait in the toilets near the entrance to the works and then slip quietly back inside. He had access to all parts of the building including the secret basement and so could work quickly, undisturbed, through the night, copying discs and logging into the terminals for which he had been able to obtain the access codes and passwords. He didn't understand much about the material he was acquiring but he didn't need to and his customers were well pleased with his fishing expeditions.

The nights were long but he had a makeshift bed in the basement, and by carefully timing his visits to the washroom he could be fresh, shaved and ready for work in the morning. This arrangement had worked perfectly for months, with the exception of the two nights when the night watchman had shown a worrying degree of initiative and curiosity. The scare hadn't had lasting consequences and he had a plan to eliminate the risk in future.

This evening would be tricky, however. There had been no forewarning of the staff meeting and its contents required quick action on his part. Unfortunately, he had come to work by car that day and would therefore have to cover his tracks by driving the car somewhere else and returning after dark. He knew of a back entrance, had access to a key and knew how to disable the alarm before it could go off. He did have the easier option of sending out his messages from his laptop at home but his instructions were never to leave traces of his activities on his own machine: a pristine back-up system would be his alibi if questions were ever asked about data leakage and disloyal emails. Besides, he had come to enjoy his nocturnal adventures.

As Mehmet approached the end of his shift but well before staff started to arrive for work, he needed to visit the washroom at the factory entrance. As he washed his hands and prepared to leave he noticed that one of the cubicles behind him was 'engaged'. On his way out he gave a push to the door but it was clearly locked. There was no sound, or sign, of occupation. As he left the washroom and then the building, he decided to watch the washroom entrance for a while, remaining concealed behind a pillar. A part of him reached for a rational, innocent, explanation. He also realised that if there were a less innocent explanation, he might well not be thanked for revealing it. After ten minutes he decided to return to his cabin and forget about the incident. Just as he was about to end his shift he saw a movement from the washroom. Someone he recognised emerged carrying a washbag and, after looking around furtively, disappeared into the body of the factory. Mehmet hadn't been seen, he hoped, but the knowledge he now had was potentially dangerous for the night visitor – and for himself.

※※※※※※※※※※※※※

Inspector Mankad's careful investigation into the Patel killing was finally starting to produce some results. 'Slowly, slowly, catchee monkey' was his catchphrase, picked up from some gangland Hindi movie. He didn't waste time and energy, or arouse suspicion and envy, in hyperactive investigations. He waited for the information to come to him. And he remained detached in case the political wind was blowing too much in the wrong direction and necessitated a tactful retreat. His intelligence came from his network of carefully cultivated informers. He looked after them: never compromised his sources; ensured that, if they found themselves behind bars, there would be special privileges, segregation from their gang enemies and early release. And, in this case, a friendly journalist had also done his bit, not least in signalling to the underworld that the ever approachable Inspector was on the case.

He had established already that two of the Sheikh's more unsavoury and violent foot soldiers had been responsible for Patel's killing. They had abducted him after work at knifepoint and taken him to a van. At

135

some point he had been killed and mutilated, before or after death wasn't clear, and his body deposited into a large open drain whence it had been washed some way downstream to little Ravi's harbour by a night-time downpour. Mankad discouraged his energetic assistant, Sergeant Ghokale, from arresting these small fry, and instead awaited developments. Informers reported that one of the two, Afzal, had been flashing around unusual amounts of money, buying an expensive gold necklace and watch, gambling and drinking bootleg liquor. And he had been shouting his mouth off, trashing the Sheikh as a 'has been' and a 'nobody' and making it clear that he was moving in more elevated circles now. His body was found on a rubbish tip shortly afterwards. And the other, Taheem, had disappeared.

Then, this morning, at the police station, another breakthrough of a kind. His division had launched a sweep-up operation in one of the baastis, netting a few petty criminals and many others who were merely bystanders or in the wrong place at the wrong time. Such raids kept the politicians off their backs – demanding 'action on crime' – and occasionally, but rarely, produced a serious villain. One wretched piece of humanity, his face covered in blood and snot, was dragged into Mankad's office. Mankad disapproved of his colleagues' methods as inefficient and unprofessional but had been careful to keep his views from more senior officers and, occasionally he acknowledged, there was a tiny nugget of gold among the spillage. This man, Jadhav, he was told, had some information if he could talk to the Inspector.

Jadhav was not forthcoming and clearly terrified. Mankad gave him time to settle, allowed him to go under escort to the lavatory to clean himself up and offered him sweet tea. Eventually a few words started to dribble out.

Jadhav was at the bottom of the criminal food chain. Not clever or brave or confident enough to belong fully to a gang, let alone be trusted with a weapon, he was called in to do menial tasks and paid a few rupees for his efforts. The few rupees helped his family to survive. A few nights ago he had been called to one of the better, pukka, buildings in his baasti. There was a body on the floor, blood and bits of flesh and bone lying around. He was told to help carry the body to a van in jute sacking and then to clear up the mess. He had received five hundred rupees, much more than usual, and told to maintain his silence. This hadn't, however, withstood the police interrogation.

The description of the body and clothes fitted that of Afzal, one of Patel's killers. But Jadhav couldn't or wouldn't say anything about the people who had employed him. All he would say, over and over, was 'Trishul', meaning 'trident'. Mankad knew the names of every gang in Mumbai and every serious gangster. This was a new one: a Hindu symbol, a common sight in religious pageantry, the three-pronged trident carried by the god Shiva and used to kill every Mumbaikar's favourite deity, Ganesh. What on earth was this about?

Then he recalled when he had seen tridents in action. It was a televised recording of events a quarter of a century earlier, when a mob led by militant Hindus, some of them holy men, sadhus or sanyasis, brandished tridents, as they set about destroying the ancient building disputed between the two religions. To a modern-minded citizen of the new India, like Mankad, these displays of religious fanaticism and hatred were an embarrassing relic of the past. But he was uncomfortably aware that many Indians did not share his relaxed view of these matters. Some of them were now in powerful positions. There was surely a link between the Hindu militants of the hut and criminals who adopted the iconography of that religion. It was not a link a humble policeman wanted to explore too far. These worries almost spoilt his lunch.

※※※※※※※※※※※※

Before setting off for London, Deepak Parrikar had dinner with his father. Parrikar Senior was unusually agitated; more than Deepak could remember. Their earlier heart-to-heart, exposing the Sheikh's visit and the attempted blackmail, hadn't exhausted his soul searching.

'Your mother: a lot of health problems. She is very unhappy. Talks a lot about when she is gone, what will become of the family. She asks how I will cope on my own. Funeral preparations. I try to tell her: you have years of good life. But she doesn't listen.'

Deepak had heard the tale often enough to know that it was a preliminary to other matters.

'Then there is the business. I don't want to trouble you with small things but we have many problems in Mumbai. Construction, development, very difficult. Workers all the time threaten strikes. Greedy politicians demand more money. Tenants stop paying rent. Police are no use. Also those Hindu fanatics are strengthening their hold on the city. They don't respect me. Always problems but never so bad.'

He paused, to give himself time to eat and gather his strength for the most difficult part of the conversation.

'Now this Patel thing. We have done favours for the Sheikh but I know him; he will want more to leave us in peace. Now we are in the papers. Maybe more to come. People say I keep bad company, I'm too close to gangs. I am trying to stay clean. To keep a good reputation for you, your brother and sister. To protect the family name.'

His first real conversation with his son had released a torrent of emotions. For the first time he reflected seriously on his life and his legacy, on his own powerlessness, his inability to protect his employees, his openness to blackmail.

He tried to explain to his son his complicated feelings towards the man who had almost certainly ordered the killing of Patel and was now seeking to inveigle him into some dangerous operation. In times past he would have taken on the challenge, met muscle with muscle. He was not a squeamish man and in his younger days he had had a fearsome reputation, holding his own in an underworld where might was right and the weak were trampled underfoot. Now he no longer felt able to fight.

The Patel episode was a turning point. Parrikar told Deepak that he had come to a decision. He would quit the Mumbai property market. He would sell the land and property freeholds that he had accumulated. The tax-wallahs would take a big share – but he knew how to minimise the hit. A sizeable sum would be invested in the businesses his family would inherit. But much of the money would fund the Parrikar Foundation. This would be to India what Ford or Rockefeller was to the US. It would be bigger and grander than the Tatas' charitable arm. His head was reeling with ideas for schools and hospitals for the poor. All the details would be ready when Deepak returned from London.

'Daddy-ji, stop worrying,' his son comforted him. 'The family understand that you want to get out of this dirty business and become a respectable company. It will happen. Look, I now have to tie up this big deal. I go tonight. If it succeeds, we will have a strong business for years. It gives us good links to US and UK companies. And with the big chiefs in Delhi. Then I want to launch a capital raising issue in London and New York. You will be there: the founding father, the man who turned a small-time Mumbai company into a global business empire.'

Deepak's next meeting was in London and its purpose was far removed from the family business. Kate had come to see him at the earliest opportunity. It only needed a few seconds to establish that neither was in the mood for polite, exploratory, conversation. A dam broke sweeping away their pent-up emotional and physical restraints. It was late in the night before, exhausted, they slept a little and then talked until the morning, sharing their past and beginning to map out a possible future together.

When she caught a taxi back to the office in Victoria Street the following morning she tried to rationalise her emotions. There was no sense of guilt. No regret. But a deeper feeling, tinged with worry that she was falling in love with Deepak.

The sense of detachment and calculation she had maintained with her previous lovers, and her husband, had largely gone. She found her emotions difficult to explain and that was the point. There was something new that went beyond attraction and physical compatibility. She needed to see him again but without any clear sense of where it would lead and conscious of the risks. He had said something very similar about his own feelings.

Kate forced herself, nonetheless, to focus on the dangers. She inhabited a world where risk taking was a way of life, but also where there was little room for error. There were many politicians with lovers or mistresses, of the same or opposite sex. In an increasingly secular and liberal culture such behaviour shouldn't matter. But there was also an insatiable appetite for scandal: for exposing the hypocrisy of politicians who preached family values and practised the opposite; for 'love rats' whose 'betrayals' proved that they couldn't be trusted with the nation's secrets. Or, simply, the all too understandable pleasure of powerless, anonymous people, seeing the powerful and celebrated caught with their pants down. She remembered the chief whip's warning about envious colleagues. So far she had covered her tracks well, she thought.

When she arrived at the front door of her department, her team had assembled to set off for her next visit – to the Pulsar factory. She hoped that her face would not betray too much evidence of her wonderful night.

CHAPTER 9

THE RIOT

Russia Today, 9 July 2019:

Sources in the Indian Ministry of Defence report that a Pakistani F-15 fighter was, several days ago, shot down by Indian ground to air missiles after encroaching into Indian air space. Both Indian and Pakistani official spokesmen have denied knowledge of the incident. But there are reports of a heavy Indian military presence in the desert area in Rajasthan where the fighter has allegedly been downed.

BBC World Service, 9 July 2019:

Reports by the Indian Defence Ministry state that its forces are on 'heightened alert' and there has been some movement of troops to disputed areas in Kashmir. The Pakistan military authorities and an unusually high number of reported military flights close to the border are believed to be responsible.

Kate's magic carpet sped up the M1 on the way to her factory visit. The quiet hum of the official car; the aromatic smell of the polished upholstery; the space to stretch her legs; the simple luxury of being chauffeured around by the ever obliging Denis: these were part of the ministerial lifestyle she could definitely get used to. She was tempted to daydream and there were pleasant memories of last night to daydream about.

But she also felt a nagging discomfort when she had time to reflect on where her magic carpet was heading. The breezy salesmanship of the Secretary of State and the Prime Minister had obscured, initially, what her job entailed: that and her instincts to get behind British business. Over the last few days, however, Susan's drip-feeding of confidential files had left her in no doubt. She was a salesman in an arms bazaar for technologically advanced weapons that were being sold into a dangerous and tense conflict zone.

She looked in vain in the morning papers for any evidence that the British press took the matter seriously. Her office had, however, equipped her with clippings from news agencies that showed precisely how serious the matter was. But it was too late now to have a fit of conscience. The factory was fast approaching.

At the factory, final preparations were under way for the visit: business as usual; no fuss; no one to get excited. But, naturally, everyone wanted to create a good impression. Long-serving, loyal employees like Mr Khan would have a chance to shake the ministerial hand. Steve's message to the union – forget that the Minister is a Tory; jobs are at stake – was received without dissent. He had also had a quiet word with council officials to ensure that there were no disruptive traffic works planned and that refuse lorries didn't trundle past the front door at the wrong time. As agreed, there was a low-key media presence: one TV camera for regional television and to take a pooled clip for other channels should the Minister choose to say anything significant; and a couple of journalists, school leavers sent along by the local free newspaper. There was to be a plaque unveiled by Calum and the Minister and Calum had prepared a short speech purged of any controversial references to Scottish nationalism or irresponsible capitalism.

Then, about ten minutes before the scheduled arrival, down the road came a group of demonstrators waving banners – 'Stop the Arms Trade', 'Aid Not Arms' – chanting and singing hymns. They were orderly, polite and respectful towards the two police officers deployed at the entrance to the factory. A radio message was sent to the ministerial car, alerting the Minister and suggesting a brief, courteous greeting to the protesters.

Then down the road came a much larger group, not earnest and white but angry and brown. Their placards were less polite – 'Tory Murderers', 'Stop Killing Muslims'. The Socialist Worker and Respect banners vied with green flags with Arabic script and, at the back, the black flag of ISIL. As the crowd of around two hundred reached the entrance, the ministerial Jaguar arrived. The driver, acting on the earlier intelligence, pulled up and, before he could reconsider, the car was surrounded. Kate decided to face what would be a critical but polite crowd and demonstrate character for whatever media was observing. As she left the car, it was clear that the crowd was anything but polite. 'Tory scum' was one of the kinder barbs. Eggs and tomatoes were among the objects thrown and her blue business suit and elegantly groomed blonde hair were soon streaked with red, yellow and brown. One man, his face contorted with rage, spat in her face. The police presence had been swept aside and she was largely on her own.

Nothing in her previous experience had exposed her to angry crowds and personal abuse. She was well aware that her government and party weren't universally liked but to meet hatred face to face was new. She realised with hindsight that a streetwise and courageous politician would have seized the moment, demanded to address the crowd and bravely defended free speech in the hope that posterity – and the evening news – would witness her courage under fire. But she was shaking like a leaf and thought only of reaching the safety of the entrance, which, with the help of the outnumbered policemen and a few other helping hands, she eventually managed.

By the time she had calmed down and cleaned up there was no time and little appetite for the formal business. A hastily convened meeting with Calum did not advance far beyond acrimonious exchanges about the security failure. The Minister's aides were beginning to panic over the media impact. The first images were appearing on YouTube. Twitter was trending at vertiginous rates. The TV camera intended for a tame pooled clip had captured enough to be running on the news channels. Something needed to be done.

Frantic calls back to the No. 10 press room produced confused reactions: yes, the Minister needs to be out there calming the storm and being the voice of authority; but, no, we don't want to advertise a security screw-up; we don't want speculation about what Pulsar is doing; and we don't want to advertise the fact that the black flag of ISIL has spread from Raqqa and Mosul to the streets of an English town (the holding line was that these were British anarchists). After some bad-tempered exchanges, Kate was pushed in front of the camera to address one question with a bland answer.

'A new and challenging experience for me. But we live in a free country. Critics of government have to have their say. There are some people who believe in unilateral disarmament, who don't seem to care about the British jobs that go with having a defence industry. They are entitled to their point of view but the government won't change its policy. Thank you. No more questions.'

By then the police riot teams had arrived. But too late. The crowd had already dispersed. The Minister was able to leave with more dignity than when she arrived.

The post-mortems began immediately. Calum sat with his head in his hands in the boardroom. 'Shit; shit; shit. I never wanted this fucking visit. Fucking politicians. Trouble. Now we shall be like those animal experiment people: hounded from pillar to post by single issue fanatics.'

'I don't think it's that bad,' interjected Justin Starling, the head of security. 'A one-off. Nobody mentioned the Indian contract, thank God. We can get on with business as usual.'

'I am not so sure. What troubles me is that the protesters knew exactly what was happening and when. They got under the radar. They must have an inside source.'

Back at the department, Kate was rushed into a meeting with the Secretary of State and a number of officials responsible for the visit planning, security and media who looked as if they were preparing themselves for a public execution.

When the group had assembled, Jim Chambers paused for effect, watching the officials visibly shrink into their chairs. 'So, what the fuck was that all about? Which idiot told the local police that this was just a nice, informal, low-key visit that didn't merit any extra security? Who was the clown who managed the media operation that made our Minister a laughing stock – through no fault of her own? Absolute bloody mess. We've got the PM lined up to sign an important arms contract of which this is a key part. His people are on the phone to me asking what the hell is going on. *Grip*. The PM's favourite word. He wants to know that we are *gripping* the situation. What do we know about this company? Security?'

There was a bit more bluster from the Secretary of State and a few pointed references to the Overheads. But he had achieved his objective: to reassure Kate; to shake up the officials from their culture of buck-passing and complacency; and to be able to report back to the PM that he was, indeed, *gripping* the situation.

The main post-mortem took place shortly afterwards in the COBRA meeting room below the Cabinet Office. The PM had pulled in the heads of SIS and MI5, the Metropolitan Police Commissioner to speak for the Counter Terrorism Command, the National Security Adviser and the Secretaries of State for Defence and Business, with the High Commissioner participating via Skype from Delhi. The PM was at his best in these emergencies and opened the discussion with quiet authority.

'I want to be reassured that we are still on track for this defence contract. Pulsar is a part of a much bigger picture. Until this demo at the Pulsar plant everything seemed to be under control. I can't overestimate how important it is. Potentially billions in new work. Thousands of jobs across the UK. And crucial for us and the Americans in our efforts to get closer to the Indians.

'We don't talk much about it, but we all know that the biggest threat of nuclear war comes from the subcontinent. We have done the war games. You will have seen some of the reports on the wires in the last few days. Sabre rattling, almost certainly, but these are nuclear powers with a history of real conflict. President Trump and I are agreed that we must help India acquire the capacity to intercept a first strike. Israel is kitted out. So is NATO. India has to be.

'Yet the key technology is in a small British company run by a maverick Scottish socialist: a technological genius and a successful hustler in the funding markets, granted, but a shambolic manager who runs an operation that leaks like a rusting ship. Am I right? What do we do about it? Chief?'

The head of MI5 spoke for the domestic security services. 'We have been giving the place a thorough going over. Perhaps we should have done so sooner. The position is this. There have been the usual attempted cyber-attacks from China and Russia that all our defence subcontractors get. But the firm has the know-how to deal with them. And the bad guys don't seem to have twigged how important the company is.

'So far so good. But there are these reported break-ins. And we have established that someone has successfully hacked into some of the technical material. We suspect it is an inside job by someone who knows their way around.

We don't yet know who or why, nor what they found—'

'But tell me,' the PM interrupted, 'how did the protesters know about Kate's visit? They seemed to have access to details of the visit planning.'

'Several possibilities including loose talk by someone in the know – a departmental official, a journo, one of Pulsar's management team. We did discover that a key figure in the firm – the top union official, trusted by the CEO – is a local Labour councillor who has recently been meeting Muslim militants.'

'You must be joking!'

'No, Prime Minister. This man – Steve Grant – has met a group a couple of times that includes one of the extremists we have been keeping an eye on. That may be how the Muslim, anti-Indian, activists found out. There are also quite a number of Muslims of Pakistani origin in the factory, mostly Kashmiri, though all those in sensitive jobs have been carefully vetted, and none are known to be radical. And we still have to explain how the anti-arms trade people got their information.'

At this point the National Security Adviser, who had remained silent hitherto, interjected. 'There is another, delicate, matter that I need to mention within the strict confines of this room. We discovered that the Minister, Mrs Thompson, is having an affair with the CEO of Pulsar's Indian collaborator. When he was in London, shortly before the Minister's factory visit, she was tailed to his hotel and left the following morning. There appears to be an ongoing relationship. They try to be discreet but there is clearly an element of risk.'

'I have already been briefed on this of course,' the PM replied. 'And I am the last person to want to lecture my colleagues on personal morality. I just hope she knows what she is doing. I had hoped this issue wouldn't come up, but everyone here should know that this is another complication we don't need.'

The High Commissioner rushed in with reassurance. 'I wouldn't worry about Deepak Parrikar. Got to know him quite well. Good man. Totally straight and on side.'

The National Security Adviser agreed. 'Frankly, I am more confident about the Indian side of this operation than our own.'

In his summary the PM was able to be reassuring. 'The good news is that our media haven't cottoned on to the strategic issues. They just loved the idea of a Tory minister being pelted with eggs and tomatoes and haven't got beyond that. Our American friends haven't picked up that we have a problem. The Indian operation seems to be under control. But, obviously, we need tighter surveillance and careful management at this end. So, we proceed? Any objection? No? Thank you.'

Steve was shaken to the core when, next day, he saw the front of the *Herald*, a friendly local paper that he had slavishly provided with press releases ever since his election to the council. His full-on mugshot, making him look like a convict preparing for life in prison, appeared alongside that of a bearded militant waving a black flag. The front page had another picture – the selfie – showing him grinning among his Muslim friends. The headline, 'Local Labour Man Link to Bombers', was followed up by the 'sensational' revelation that he had held 'clandestine' meetings with local 'extremists' and is believed ('according to well-informed sources') to have 'played a key role' in managing the demonstration.

He knew he had to get to Calum quickly. His position at the factory, years of close working and trust, would be destroyed if it were believed he had put his firm's future, and workers' jobs, at risk by an act of disloyalty. When he arrived at the factory he could feel the chill. Eyes were averted. There were no greetings. He could see Shaida in her glass office huddled over her PC, while her support staff were uncharacteristically silent. Calum had the newspaper in front of him. There was also a stranger in the corner of the room who didn't introduce himself. Calum broke the ice.

'You will be pleased to hear that I don't believe what I read in newspapers. Muckrakers. But I want to know what this is all about, as does our friend here from the Spooks,' he said, pointing to the silent man.

Steve had already prepared his defence. 'I did meet a few local Muslim students. But that doesn't make them terrorists or me a sympathiser. I try to talk to all sections of the community. But the leak – absolutely not me. Nor have I said a word to them or anyone else about the confidential stuff we do here.'

Calum was easily reassured. 'I have never had any reason to doubt your loyalty to the company. I must believe what you tell me.'

The man from the security services was less easily reassured. 'If the leak wasn't from you, who do you think it was?' he asked.

'No idea.'

'Well, I do have some ideas. One possible lead is that one of the local militants, who has been on our radar for some time, was at your meeting. He happens to be the son of one of your union colleagues, a Mr Ashgar Khan, and brother of a young woman who is the chief finance officer whom I believe you also know. Could it have been them?'

'No, I don't believe it,' Steve retorted. 'They are totally loyal, honest people who would never have got embroiled in an extremist movement. I know about the son and they worry about him. But anyway, none of them had the inside knowledge to set up that demonstration.'

'So, we come back to you. You did have the knowledge. You met some of the troublemakers. All we lack is a motive. What I need from you is a detailed account of your meetings. Who was there? Who chose the participants? Who organised the events?'

So far Steve had managed to avoid mentioning Shaida and, as he saw the net closing fast, he judged silence to be the safest recourse.

'I note your silence. As it happens you don't need to implicate your – friend – Ms Khan as she came to us first thing this morning when she heard about the press story. She admitted that she set up the meetings. Like you, she denied any wrongdoing. I am inclined to believe both of you. The story of Islamic fanatics causing trouble and being abetted by soft-headed politicians is just a little too convenient. But I am recommending to the company' – he glanced at Calum whose expression betrayed total confusion and powerlessness – 'and I am sure the chief executive will agree, that you and she should be suspended pending a fuller investigation – though of course this is not my company. It may well be in your interests not to see your workmates for a while; I imagine the mood on the shop floor won't be too friendly. And if someone else is at the heart of this, it may be helpful to give him or her the impression that you are in the frame. Let's leave it there. Here is my card if you have anything else useful to tell me.'

Calum shrugged his shoulders. 'Sorry, laddie. I am sure we will be able to sort this out.'

As the conversation drew to a close Steve realised this was an opportunity to get off his chest the uncomfortably heavy weight of confidences shared. He turned to the man from MI5 – Liam, according to his card – who hadn't volunteered any information on his precise role, and said:

'I don't know if this is of any relevance to your enquiries or who exactly I should speak to. But I was told various things in confidence several days ago about some of the Muslim activists in the town.'

'Go on, I am interested.'

Steve then passed on what he had been told about Mo and the group and described the episode with the preacher at the mosque entrance. He was desperate to avoid having to admit that Shaida and her father had any knowledge of the matter, which made it appear that he had acquired the information through divine revelation.

Calum interjected: 'Stop messing about, laddie. He's got a soft spot for this young woman who heads up our accounts department. That's how he knows about this stuff,' he added in case Liam hadn't already worked this out.

'Why didn't you tell us sooner?' Liam responded. 'I would have thought someone in your position would have gone straight to a senior police officer and asked for help and advice. No matter, you were trying to protect the young woman who, I have to say, appears totally professional and uncompromised. As it happens this is not new information. I obviously can't tell you all that much. But we now know quite a lot about the local radicals. When whole families went off to Syria we knew we had a serious problem here and have been keeping tabs on worrying individuals. Ms Khan's brother Mo is just a confused and angry young man. In our view he isn't – yet – committed enough to do anything really dangerous.

Such people become a genuine concern if they fall under the sway of a powerful personality. A potential terrorist? Not really. Strapping on a suicide vest or planting a bomb requires a higher degree of motivation and organisation than he or his close friends currently have. Sounding off about the "jihad" or watching nasty videos is a real cause for alarm, and makes them potential recruits. But they are a step away from actually doing something evil.'

'Well, that's a relief. I realise I should have talked to you earlier. Sorry. But it appears no harm has been done.'

'Actually, you may have helped us – unintentionally. We have been studying the pictures taken by your friends, particularly the group photos after your mosque visit.' Liam removed a set of enlarged photographs from his briefcase.

'Look carefully at this face here. It is blurred and indistinct. He was turning away and seemingly didn't want to be caught on camera.'

Steve picked up the image and studied it. 'He looks familiar. But he didn't say anything at the meeting. I didn't really register his presence.'

'That's the point. He operates in the background. But, if it is who we think it is, we are very concerned. The name is Tariq, Tariq Ahmed. Born in Birmingham, various aliases. Became committed to the cause and terrorist methods in his late teens. We believe he has been in Iraq and Syria. He recruits. He's an organiser. Careful not to blow himself up. There are "useful fools" who can be persuaded to do that. In fact, we believe he leads a breakaway group, a mutation of ISIL, which doesn't support indiscriminate killing – for tactical rather than humanitarian reasons. Rather, he believes in targeted assassination – we think he organised the killing of that Egyptian general in London recently – and attacks on symbolically important sites, like the raid last year on the drone manufacturing plant in Lancashire that set back production for months. We think he's planning a political spectacular. He is very persuasive. Your friend Mo is the kind of impressionable young man who may be sucked into joining him.

'We want Tariq Ahmed badly. But he is elusive and doesn't leave incriminating traces. Where you can help us is trying to get your friends to talk about him: where he is, what he is doing. If at all possible, get him to one of your meetings and we can put a tail on him. No heroics needed.

'As for the preacher man – he is just a nuisance, absorbing a lot of police time and resources. But always very careful to stay inside the law. Like a fast downhill skier, he knows how to stay upright. And if he falls, there are expensive lawyers in the background who will help him to his feet. Frankly, we believe the community should take responsibility for policing people like that.'

Steve started to take stock of what he was getting into. He had been in a room with a dangerous jihadist and was now being asked to help track him down. He reflected wryly on the elusive Shaida whom he had followed into this quagmire: the reward, so far, one peck on the cheek.

'Obviously I will do what I can to help,' he told Liam, 'though I doubt it's much. Quite honestly, this is a very different world from the one I'm used to.'

For the first time Liam showed a flash of anger and Steve focused properly on this figure in the corner. Unexceptional in appearance and informally dressed, he could have been a secondary school teacher with tie askew and a well-worn jumper under his jacket. His voice rose several decibels, opening up his Brummie intonation.

'You are bloody right that you are going to help us. I would say you have an obligation to help. This is as much your responsibility as mine. You chose to get involved in the politics in this town and – as you are discovering – you can't just float above it. Actions have consequences. When we see and hear evil we have to act.'

Steve was too pulverised by the events of the last few days to think of any riposte beyond mute acknowledgement.

※※※※※※※※※※※※

In Mumbai, the *Bharat Bombay* investigative team received warm praise and hints of promotion from the editor for their latest splash: 'Revenge', an exclusive story based around the discovery of the body of one of the Patel killers, accompanied by a gruesome photograph of the bullet-ridden corpse that didn't leave anything to the reader's imagination. *Bharat Bombay* had now followed up the story with a weightier piece: 'Business Empire in Trouble', linking the killing – at one remove – to the Parrikar family company.

The editor swallowed hard before relegating a salacious story about Miss India to accommodate a business scandal. Although his instinct was always to avoid trouble and to give pretty girls priority over price/earnings ratios, the editor had had the Parrikars in his sights for some time. His cynical, knowing mind was irritated by the new, fashionable image of the Parrikar companies and the debonair Deepak. The editor had been around long enough to have heard most of the gossip about Parrikar Senior's exploits and knew that The Caring Corporation rested on the foundations of the less-than-caring Mumbai property business. He also knew that the best time to kick a man was when he was down and the stream of stories about the weakening grip of the Parrikars provided a safe base from which to attack. Now, thanks to his impressive young team and his squad of sleuths, there was a story and two suggestive, but usable, photos of an infamous mafia don arriving at Parrikar Senior's office and Parrikar Junior embracing an attractive female British VIP at the company's guest house. There would be no comeback. The Parrikars didn't advertise with his newspaper. And any recourse to Indian libel laws would now run into hard fact. Anyway, the courts system was bogged down in cases decades old and held few real terrors.

The editor was not the only person to see the potential

of the story. Jimmy Anderson had eked out a living as a foreign correspondent in India for many years ferreting out titbits from the Indian popular press. His translation skills and eye for a good story ensured that he was able to finance a comfortable lifestyle, at the bottom of the journalistic food chain, looking for morsels passed over by loftier members of his profession. As he made his way through the day's collection of newspapers in half a dozen vernacular languages, he spotted the *Bharat Bombay* story. It didn't take long to register that the picture of the British Minister might be of some interest in London. Within an hour he had a translation of the story and a scanned picture on their way to the political editor of the *Mail on Sunday*.

CHAPTER 10

THE SCANDAL

The Pakistani government officially welcomed a visit from Prince Abdullah Al-Saud, a close associate of the Crown Prince, to discuss closer cooperation between their intelligence agencies and training for Pakistan volunteers who were fighting against anti-Islamic forces in the Middle East. He visited a battalion that had acquitted itself with distinction in the fighting against 'atheists and apostates' in the Syrian civil war. He denied claims in India that the volunteers were also being infiltrated into Kashmir in preparation for a new guerrilla offensive and terrorist attacks on Indian cities. Commenting on reports of military incidents along the Indo-Pakistan border the spokesman quoted the Defence Minister as saying: 'Pakistan is not afraid. We are not looking for a fight but Pakistan should not be underestimated. We have battle ready warheads. God forbid there is to be conflict but, if it happens, it will be, for us, a jihad.'

After the drama of the factory visit, Kate opted for a quiet weekend at home – reacquainting herself with her daughters and husband.

'Mum, are you OK?' enquired Tilly, the youngest, over breakfast before pony club demanded her attention. 'We saw that demo on YouTube. It was awful. That horrible man who threw things at you. Those men with beards shouting and screaming. Have they been arrested? We thought you were really brave.'

'It's the job. We can't be liked by everyone. I wasn't brave actually. I was quite frightened but I'm OK now.' She turned to Penny, her middle daughter. 'Your dad tells me that there has been some bullying at school. Penny?'

The girl burst into tears. 'You're never here. I wanted to talk to you about it. A really horrid girl was talking about you – said the government was full of bad, greedy people and you were one of them. That you had taken money from her family. And now they couldn't afford a holiday. She screamed at me. When I argued back the teacher told us both off.'

'I'm so sorry, darling. But you stood up for me. I am proud of you.' She gave Penny a big hug but a spasm of fear jolted through her that these girls, passing through adolescence, unsure of themselves and needing her, were becoming strangers. Being a minister of the crown was all absorbing. And now there was Deepak.

Jonathan had left early for a Saturday morning round of golf with some clients from Singapore who were placing a lot of money in the central London property market and particularly liked Jonathan's tasteful conversions. She was inwardly relieved not to have to try to act normal in his presence. She could take refuge in her ministerial box for the rest of the day and in the evening there was a dinner party: his friends rather than hers. She looked forward to it, as she would be able to hide her feelings in the hubbub of polite conversation. She was, however, dreading the return home as Jonathan was usually amorous after a few drinks and a night out. Excuses would be needed.

In the event the excuses weren't required. At 10pm, as the dinner party was starting to warm up, a light flashed on her mobile – a text: 'Emergency, ring immediately. Susan.' Kate's private secretary knew not to disturb her unless there was a real emergency, so she slipped quietly outside to return the call, full of trepidation.

'A crisis, Kate, brace yourself. I have just seen tomorrow's headlines. You are on the front page of the *Mail on Sunday* with that dishy man you went out with in Mumbai.' Hearing no reply, Susan pressed on. 'Actually, the story is pretty thin and the picture is blurred. But you won't like the headline – "Bonking for Britain". Someone, goodness knows who, has said that you were out for the night. Then, inside, there is a big feature with pictures of the family and your "betrayed" husband with an unnamed "friend" expressing incredulity that you have double-crossed such an amazing hunk of manhood. The editorial is ghastly: "Minister travelling the world at tax-payers' expense… jobs at stake… PM to blame for packing the government with under-qualified women in the interests of political correctness".'

Kate was too numb to reply. Eventually she asked, plaintively: 'What do I do now?'

'Turn off your mobile. Talk to your family before they hear about tomorrow's papers. I imagine the Secretary of State, possibly the PM, will want to speak to you in the morning. I will talk to the press office about a statement… "Minister has no comment to make on press gossip. The PM has complete confidence in her", that sort of thing. We will brief out that you are fully focused on your job, building on the success of the Mumbai visit.

'One more thing. A little bird told me that you saw Deepak, privately, when he was in London. The press don't have that. Let's hope they won't find out. Hopefully this is a one-off. Next week's chip paper.'

Kate regarded this last sally as scant consolation. She thought she had covered her tracks carefully, but she was beginning, belatedly, to understand the meaning of the phrase 'being in the public eye'. Paranoia competed with shock, embarrassment, fear and confusion. She feared above all for the impact on the girls. But the hopes she had built up for the new man in her life could also now be dashed. She thought of herself as a confident and competent person, but this was something new, and outside of her comfort zone in every way.

She somehow stumbled through the rest of the evening and there was some calming, easy-listening music on the car radio so that she didn't have to make conversation with Jonathan on the way home. When they arrived back, she sat down in the living room and said: 'Can we talk for a few minutes?' She told the story as coherently as she could. She reminded him how close they had been to disaster over a decade ago when she had learnt of his string of affairs and had retaliated. But now she had broken the golden rule: don't get caught. 'Sorry... what else can I say?'

He normally managed to sustain his urbane charm even in the most awkward situations. But he responded with a long, angry silence. He didn't do shouting, let alone domestic violence. His weapon of choice was non-communication. Eventually she could bear it no longer, and said: 'So what do you want me to do? Leave? Pack my bags?'

After another long silence he replied, very quietly: 'If you want to run, that is up to you. I wouldn't advise it. I assume you value your relationship with the girls, if not with me. I am not a saint, as you have just reminded me. But we seemed to have a marriage that worked. The problem this time is that, through your carelessness, we have become public property. I will have to run the gauntlet of supercilious bastards at the office, the golf club, the gym. I guess you have the bigger problem. I hope you have good media advisers. Tell me one thing: I take it you don't actually love this Indian guy?'

'That's the problem, I think I do.'

'You think! *I* think you need to make up your bloody mind.'

There was nothing more to add. He went up to one of the spare bedrooms. No backward glance. No banged door. She knew he would settle into an Ice Man routine for days, even weeks. There would be polite greetings: 'Yes, darling; no, darling.' Forced conversations. The ball would be entirely in her court. To stay or leave. Anxious children: 'Ask your mother.' Queries from friends, relatives: 'Everything is fine. Speak to Kate.'

She felt terribly alone. She would have to tell the girls in the morning. They would need reassuring that Mummy and Daddy weren't going to break up and abandon them. Yet that seemed a likely destination.

She couldn't sleep. When she finally dozed off as dawn was breaking, she was roused by noises outside: a car door slamming, voices, scraping, the crunching of the gravel drive. Opening the curtains to investigate she saw a young peroxide blonde woman in her drive setting up a camera tripod. One van was parked at the drive entrance and another, with a satellite receiver on top, was pulling up. Then she saw a head appearing above the garden hedge followed by a long-range camera, aimed at her. She hastily withdrew and returned to bed, shaking with a mixture of anger and fear.

Half an hour later, there was a loud knock on the door. It was just after 6.30am. She waited. The knocking continued. Soon her daughters would go down to see what was going on. So she hastily dressed and went down and opened the door. There was the young woman with a man carrying a portable TV camera just behind her: 'Good morning, Mrs Thompson. I am from Sky. Do you have any comments on the *Mail* story? Do you plan to resign?'

She felt a surge of rage, a need to release the bottled-up emotions of the last few hours; indeed the last week. 'How dare you!' she shot back. 'Get out of my garden or I will call the police.' She slammed the door. The journalists stayed put and when they knocked again, very loudly, Kate opened up to avoid waking the house.

The female reporter looked about sixteen but she had the condescending manner of a matriarch offering to help a confused adolescent in distress. 'I appreciate that we are disturbing your domestic life, Mrs Thompson. But you are a big story – coming after the factory demonstration. Either we hang around and make a nuisance of ourselves, and wake the neighbours, or you cooperate by giving me a clip that we can use during the day and we go away. I suggest that you cooperate. Why don't you put on something smarter and we will rendezvous with you on your lawn in a few minutes?'

Kate did as she was told. And she returned to the camera team prepared for the interview. She looked back at the house. She saw three puzzled young faces glued to a bedroom window. 'Minister, would you like to comment on the press story this morning?' the journalist began.

'No, I have nothing to say. I am getting on with my job in government.'

'Can you tell me something about the man in the photo?'

'He is the CEO of Parrikar Avionics – he will, I am sure, be making a statement in Mumbai.'

'Are you in touch with him?'

'No.'

'Do you plan to resign?'

'No. As long as I have the confidence of the PM I shall remain in government. That's all. Thank you.'

As good as their word, the camera crews left. But she saw that the paparazzi were still there waiting to capture anyone moving inside and outside the house. She would have to go back and explain things to her daughters.

At 8am the Secretary of State rang. 'Sorry to hear your news, old girl. Bloody reptiles. Pity we can't shoot them. I've been there myself, more than once. Just spoken to the PM. He agrees with me that, while this is a bloody mess, you haven't done anything illegal or broken the ministerial code. Saw your clip. Well done. Didn't drop any balls. Continue to stand your ground. No nonsense about resignation. We will come in behind you and the PM will be very robust on Marr at 9.30.'

As the morning wore on she felt more and more like a trapped animal: fearful about what was to come next. The girls had brought her a cup of tea and given her a hug but she didn't know what to say to them nor they to her. Then her friends called, reassuring her but furious that she hadn't shared her secret. 'Seems a very handsome man but you might have told us!' 'I bet Jonathan hit the roof. But how are the girls taking it?' 'Darling, you are a star! Top item in the news, two weeks in succession.'

She realised that she should ring India. Deepak's mobile was off, so she tried the home number he'd given her for an emergency. A woman answered, in English, with an educated Indian accent, so Kate mumbled: 'Sorry, wrong number.' Half an hour later Deepak rang back.

'I've heard about the media storm in the UK,' he told her. 'It's on the BBC website. No one here has really picked up on the picture. My wife made some comment about "your British crumpet" and I asked, in a friendly way, about her Bengali novelist. We both laughed. Seemingly, no harm done.

'The problem is my father. A really scurrilous hatchet job by one of the local papers. A lot of lies and innuendo. But they have made the connection between Dad and a serious mafioso: killer, kidnapper, general hoodlum, a Muslim with family links to Pakistani-backed terrorists – though the police have never laid a finger on him. Dad knew him years back. Did some business together. One of our good people, a project manager in Mumbai, was murdered recently and the press are suggesting that there is some gangland feud and implicating my father. He has never been under public attack like this before. He is in a really bad way. Look, when will we see each other again?'

'Soon I hope,' she replied.

'But let the storm die down first,' Deepak suggested.

Kate realised as she ended the call that she had developed a strong emotional bond with this man five thousand miles away, in marked contrast to the stranger in the next room who was making his late breakfast, humming with affected unconcern.

※※※※※※※※※※※※

To avoid stares on the train the following morning, her private office had organised a ministerial car. When she entered the department there was the usual 'Good morning, Minister'. But no one engaged her eyes. And when she reached the ministerial office there was a big bunch of flowers from her private office staff. She threw her arms around Susan and then her deputy and felt a deep pang of gratitude to the team she had appointed.

The respite didn't last long. A message came through from the whip's office that the Speaker had allowed an Urgent Question from the opposition on Anglo-Indian relations.

The question was clearly designed to make mischief. The fact that the Speaker had allowed it owed more to the deep animosity between the Speaker and the Prime Minister than to any real urgency. The Secretary of State would field the question and her job was to sit next to him looking calm, dignified, and deeply interested in the bilateral trade balance.

The opposition spokesman was a boring man with little sense of occasion who specialised in reading out, verbatim, notes written for him by a researcher. His impersonation of a man reading a telephone directory in a dull, humourless monotone, however, merely highlighted a series of unintended double-entendres referring to the 'penetration of our market', the 'climax of our recent exchanges' and 'growing intercourse between our two countries'. The schoolboy tittering on the back benches gradually swelled to a crescendo of hysterical laughter while the spokesman ploughed on oblivious and Kate, who had always blushed, turned deeper crimson as her humiliation grew. She was no longer listening when the Secretary of State rose to his feet, easily dealt with the opposition's feeble question and calmly swatted aside others from the back benches.

Towards the end of the session, however, the Speaker called an Asian MP who had earned the nickname the Member for Islamabad East and rarely ventured into unfamiliar territory, like British politics. He read out a question, which he stumbled over and which had clearly been written for him.

'Can the Secretary of State tell the House if he has issued an export licence for missile related technology to India, for the company Pulsar?'

Jim Chambers hesitated for an agonisingly long time and then replied: 'I will have to look into the matter and reply in writing to the Honourable Gentleman.'

At the end of the session the MP stood up again on a Point of Order and said: 'The Secretary of State has refused to answer my question about the way the government is recklessly fuelling the arms race on the subcontinent. We have all heard the news stories that relations on the subcontinent are very tense. I demand a debate on the issue.'

'The Honourable Member,' replied the Speaker, 'is not making a Point of Order, as he well knows. But he has made his point, which will, I am sure, be noted.'

As indeed it was, by several listening journalists who had already made the connection with the recent demonstration. Near panic descended on the department's officials and the Secretary of State who could see their project unravelling. Kate's love life was forgotten, for the moment.

In Islamabad General Rashid, head of Inter-Services Intelligence, was summoned to a meeting with the Prime Minister, the Defence Minister and the military High Command. The Prime Minister sought advice on how he could respond to growing public unrest over the government's lack of response to 'Indian provocation' and, more generally, to show that, as the world's militarily strongest Islamic country, Pakistan would not let its co-religionists be 'systematically humiliated'. A decision was taken in principle to carry out an underground test of the most powerful weapon yet developed by Pakistan – with Chinese assistance. It would have the capacity to obliterate Mumbai or Delhi. The decision would be reviewed after a month in the light of international developments. General Rashid was also asked to prepare an urgent note on 'robust' options involving covert special operations.

***

Ganesh Parrikar had aged a decade in twenty-four hours. He had spent his business life mostly in the shadows and was close to completing his life's work: transferring a profitable but ethically dubious business empire to his family who would build a recognised, respected brand in mainstream business across India and overseas. He had, of course, worried in the past that the rumours around his business activity might be given oxygen by the press, but whenever a scandal threatened, he had had warning, and a few telephone calls, from lawyers to editors and advertisers, sufficed to close it down. This time, he had had no warning. His enemies, and the press, no longer feared him. His vulnerability was painfully apparent.

When he saw Deepak he broke down and sobbed. Deepak had never seen his father in this self-pitying state.

And, as in most Indian father–son relationships, there was a reserve, a deference of the young to the old. He didn't know what to say or how to help; he could only try to reassure him.

'Daddy-ji, that picture was nothing. It just showed that man entering your office, nothing more.'

'No, son. My reputation is now ruined. Respect has gone. What I am now is some tin-pot hoodlum.'

'Daddy-ji, I have a suggestion. You told me about your plans for a charitable trust. Apart from the Tatas, and Azim Premji at Wipro, our big business tycoons have splashed their money on lavish weddings, jewellery, gold statues and mansions. You have a vision for helping the poor. Get the press people together. Tell them what you are doing and plan to do.'

'A press conference? No idea what to do. Can you do it for me?' Deepak saw that his talent for PR and the reputation management of modern business was now needed to rescue his father. A pity the Parrikar clan hadn't gone down this road sooner.

After a few days, the storm in London was starting to die down. Press coverage petered out. Kate remembered the phrase about next week's chip paper. But her relationships were not so easily disposed of. She escaped tension at home by staying at her London flat, with regular calls to the girls who were confused and distressed. She sought reassurance from Deepak and, while it was clear that her feelings were reciprocated, her lover was increasingly preoccupied by his father's psychological fragility.

Then she was called in by the Prime Minister. He was in his small study next to the Cabinet Room: a cosy billet with thick carpets and settees, and a desk covered with family photos. In this misleadingly informal setting many of the key decisions affecting the country were made. When Kate entered, the grim faces of the PM, the Secretary of State and the Cabinet Secretary told her that this was likely to be a difficult meeting. The PM spoke first.

'We have a problem, Kate. Our American friends, who were going to supply the Indians with a lot of expensive kit alongside ours, are getting very nervous about this Indian deal. The President doesn't major on subtlety as you know, but he is concerned that premature disclosure could jeopardise the big plans he and his business friends have for building up an alliance with India. To cut a long story short, they are thinking of pulling out, or at least putting it on the back burner. They are very worried about the UK end of things. This company, Pulsar, seems to leak like a sieve; erratic management; an ethnically diverse – that is, Muslim – labour force; demonstrations. You know the story. Then this question in parliament that suggests that the Pakistanis grasp the significance of what is going on. Problems at the other end too. The Indian partner has had a bad press – the old man who controls the family business has been involved in some unsavoury, gangland nonsense.

'The big picture is that we and the Americans want to work with India but we don't want to burn our bridges with the Pakistani military who are important in stabilising Afghanistan, holding down the Taliban and helping with counter-terrorism. And you will have seen that there has been an escalation of military tension on the Indo-Pak border. Our assessment is that a lot of this is just rhetoric, but these countries have fought three wars already and almost fought a nuclear war not too long ago. So the advice is: kick the ball into the long grass.'

The PM was orating from his armchair, his gaze directed at the ceiling. But when it came to the difficult part of the conversation he twitched nervously, paused for an uncomfortable period and forced himself to look vaguely in Kate's direction.

'This brings us to you. You have been unlucky. But if we get into a story of cancelled contracts and lost jobs, the *Mail* and the *Sun* will have you in their sights. My suggestion is that you leave the government quietly, now, before you are chased out. You can sort out your family issues. I will pay warm tributes. The chief whip will find you something important-sounding to do on the back benches; or perhaps in the whip's office. Then, the summer recess is coming up; you can disappear for a month or so. Sorry, Kate. Politics is a cruel business.'

She left the room mumbling 'thank you'. No one else spoke a word.

✖✖✖✖✖✖✖✖✖✖✖

Kate walked back to her department through the rear entrance of Downing Street onto Horse Guards Parade. As the military personnel relaxed their grip on their submachine guns to let her through the iron gate, she attracted a friendlier grin and more rapid attention than, she suspected, her male colleagues would have done. She savoured the moment since there wouldn't be many more. She recalled the phrase about 'fifteen minutes of fame'; her fifteen minutes was up and in political equivalents it had been shorter than that. It hadn't quite been the shortest ministerial career on record but she was definitely in contention.

Up past the Treasury, down Storey's Gate and along to her department to say goodbye. Susan had been told – and when they met a few tears were shed. They hadn't worked together long but strong feelings of mutual respect and affection had developed. They sat down to exchange contact details and promises of lunch to catch up on gossip and go over the messy formalities of her departure (she smiled at the fact that, while she was there, staff from the government's art collection were moving in her choice of paintings to replace the ghastly Victorian horror).

As she was about to leave, Susan hesitated but then said: 'There are a few things I haven't troubled you with but I want you to know. I am not sure I should be telling you, but, technically, until the official announcement this afternoon, you are still our Minister.'

Kate managed to raise a smile. 'Go ahead. I'm all ears.'

'A few days ago Caroline, the Secretary of State's principal private secretary, called me in for a chat. Caroline is pure gold, a brilliant civil servant and utterly loyal to her boss. But she is a stickler for process. Would never allow anything to pass that isn't absolutely kosher. She was quite upset.

'Long story. I won't give you all the details but it concerns the export licences that are needed for Pulsar's equipment, as part of this big deal. Licensing is a separate, semi-legal process distinct from the stuff you have been doing and the licences would normally be cleared by the dedicated team of officials and, if necessary, one of the other ministers. Questions were raised both here and in the Foreign Office about what the Pulsar equipment might be used for. At first sight, it is exactly what it seems to be: part of a defence system.'

Susan paused, looking around to check that no one was listening in before continuing.

'But our technical people point out that there are other potential applications of a less wholesome nature. Powerful electromagnetic pulses that can knock out electric controls over a wide area could be misused by the wrong people. Our people think that we may be at risk of contravening the Anti-Proliferation Treaty we are signed up to. The officials are, of course, very cautious. Remember Saddam Hussein's supergun? More recently the department was given a rollicking by a select committee for approving the sale of a consignment of window cleaning fluid for Syria. Turns out that the fluid contained chemicals that have nastier uses and there was enough of it to clean the windows of Damascus for several centuries. So they recommended refusal for Pulsar.'

Kate nodded. 'All this is consistent with those secret papers you showed me, so what is the issue?'

'The issue is the so-called Red Admiral. Apparently he stormed down to where the officials sit and started haranguing them. "Obstructive jobs-worths" was among the more repeatable epithets. Claimed to be speaking on behalf of the Secretary of State and for the PM at one remove. Completely out of order. A lot of us wonder what the Admiral is doing in the department anyway. He is a "consultant", not an official or even a "special adviser". He's attached to the MOD. But the Secretary of State gave him a room over the objections of Parsons, the permanent secretary. Parsons raised the whole issue of the Admiral with the Secretary of State but he brushed it aside. He got a lecture on "Overheads" not understanding the need for an entrepreneurial culture.'

'Maybe he is just an overenthusiastic trade ambassador for UK plc?' Kate suggested.

'That's what we all want to think. But what upsets Caroline is that this isn't the first episode of this kind. A few months ago there was a controversy over licences for some advanced communications equipment from a firm in Northern Ireland. For Russia. Had all kinds of applications, including strategic military uses. Post-sanctions an absolute no-no. But the Red Admiral waded in, going on about how an American company called Global had rescued the plant from closure, turned it round, saving hundreds of jobs in an unemployment black-spot. The equipment was totally harmless, he claimed, designed to improve the safety of civil aviation. Made a big fuss. The Irish peace process would be seriously damaged, etc. I don't know exactly what happened but somehow the licence was approved.'

'What am I to do with this information?'

'I don't really know,' Susan replied, 'but Caroline and I thought you had a right to know. We'll keep in touch.'

CHAPTER 11

THE INFORMER

Financial Times, London, 12 July 2019:

City analysts at Goldman Sachs have published an analysis of trends in the defence sector. They have highlighted the growing importance of a private US group called Global Analysis and Research which has entered the global top 10 by turnover for the first time. It has recently acquired several British SMEs in the sector and there have been rumours of takeover interest in others, including the Midlands-based company Pulsar.

News that the contract was being 'put on hold' came at a bad time for Calum. His mainly American investors, who normally made a virtue out of not interfering, were becoming restless. They had taken him on trust that he could manage a complex project outside the comfort zone of NATO contracts. India, like other emerging markets, was relatively high risk with unpredictable politics they didn't understand and a reputation for corruption that would test the patience of their lawyers, worrying about US and UK legislation on overseas bribery. But, so far, assurances about a 'clean' Indian partner and political backing from the relevant governments had kept doubts at bay. Now they were being told by their contacts in the State Department and the Pentagon that the high-ups were getting cold feet. Perhaps this contract, on the basis of which they had agreed to stump up substantial amounts of capital, wouldn't materialise.

During an urgently convened telephone conference of leading investors, the man from BlackRock confronted Calum directly: 'Your Plan B? We assume you have one.'

'My Plan B is making Plan A work. The contract is a win-win: jobs, strategic fit, good news all round.'

The riposte was strong: 'Unfortunately the politicos don't see it that way. They are running scared. Wishful thinking isn't good enough.'

'Well, if the project is put on hold I will have to lay off some of our people and just keep those I need to fulfil the existing contracts. We may have to lose five hundred or so. It may cause a strike, which is why the politicians over here will do what they can to keep the project afloat.'

One of the big institutional investors chipped in: 'To be frank, we would be more comfortable if you went ahead with restructuring plans. You have shown before that you can manage the workforce and sell them necessary downsizing. We try to keep out of your way but we have been scrutinising your cash flow and it doesn't look good without this contract. I have to think about the moms and pops whose money I look after. Sorry, but you know the score.'

There was a grunt of approval around the group, though no reaction from the newest investor, a group called Global Analysis and Research, which had acquired a significant stake in the last few weeks, buying out smaller holdings. Calum worried about them: a somewhat mysterious US-based group that had built up, rapidly, a portfolio of high tech supply chain companies, not unlike his own.

A few minutes later he called Steve into his office. Steve was still at the company, albeit in a state of limbo as his suspension hadn't been formalised. Calum had shelved the issue, as was his habit with difficult personnel decisions.

He explained that he had just come off the phone from his leading investors, and that there was a problem. 'I have no choice but to lay off staff who aren't needed for ongoing work. There are some short-term contract workers but there will be redundancies. I need you to explain this, and sell it, to the workforce. You haven't covered yourself with glory over the demo, laddie, but now I need you. Stop the hot heads doing anything silly. Give them hope that we may be able to turn this round, if the workforce play ball. We did this together all those years ago.' Steve was unable to do more than mumble agreement.

✕✕✕✕✕✕✕✕✕✕✕✕✕✕✕✕✕✕✕✕

Steve wandered down to the canteen. Usually he was surrounded by friendly faces: his loyal committee of shop stewards; admirers who looked to him for political leadership or personal advice. Today there was a frosty silence. One exception was a man he knew to be a troublemaker, Brian Castle, who he suspected of having links to far-right groups. Today he was brandishing a tabloid that specialised in horror stories about asylum seekers and illegal immigrants, especially Muslims. 'See this, mate. Big story about our town. Teenage terrorists. Clerics trying to impose sharia law on the rest of us. Big families ripping off benefits. Maltreatment of women.'

So that Steve wouldn't miss the point Castle thrust the paper on the table in front of him jabbing his finger at the more inflammatory accusations, which were helpfully circled in biro. 'Your bloody fault,' he said. 'Your lot let 'em in. And this isn't Bradford; it's just down the road. You should be bloody ashamed of yourself.'

In normal circumstances Steve would have seized the opportunity to stamp his authority on the canteen; put Castle firmly in his place; reunite the workforce. Today he had nothing to say but just looked blankly in front of him.

Shaida, like Steve, was thoroughly disoriented by the events of the last few days. The walls of the carefully segregated compartments into which she divided her life were giving way. Her brother's troubles had invaded her professional life. And she'd let that happen because of a weakness for a man at work. She realised that she could have sent Steve packing but had, instead, found what seemed like a good way of developing their, so far platonic, relationship by involving her family. She acknowledged to herself that she wanted the friendship to deepen but had no idea how to make this happen in a way that wouldn't compound the disaster she had helped to create.

There was one consolation. Calum had made it clear that she was essential to preventing the company capsizing. With restive investors, he badly needed someone beside him who understood the numbers and could present them in the best possible light. Her job was safe.

Then she had a visitor to her office, Liam: 'just a routine security matter'. But it was more than that.

'Your brother. We have uncovered some uncomfortable information about him. Some compromising messages he sent that could lead to his facing anti-terrorism charges.'

'But you told me when I contacted you about that article that he wasn't a threat.'

'This is new material. I still think he is a bit player. But it isn't good. And the publicity will not be good for you and your family.'

'Are you threatening me?'

'No. This is a worst case scenario.'

'So. What is a better case scenario?'

'You help me.'

'I have already helped you.'

'I think I can help to get your brother off the hook. If you are willing to work with me.'

'Meaning?'

'You help me with information. In particular material from his computer. I know you are quite a whizz in that area. Something we have in common. You should be able to get access without being traced.'

'Blackmail in other words.'

'Call it what you like. I prefer to think you will help because it is right.'

'I detest these Islamic militants as much as you do. I know the way they treat women. But spying on my own people… and my brother… I can't do that.'

Liam could sense in her slight hesitation an opening.

'I don't normally talk about myself. The Service doesn't encourage it. But let me explain. My parents were Northern Ireland Republicans who settled in England. Armchair Provos who brought me up to hate the British state: Easter Rising; Bloody Sunday; Bobby Sands. All that stuff. As a student I was on the hard end of the hard left. Drifted into anarchist groups. Violent anti-globalisation protests. I got myself arrested throwing bricks at the police. Some of my group wanted to go further. Bombs. Not to kill people but to frighten the capitalist class. Unfortunately the class warriors were inept. A young woman, a passer-by, had her legs blown off by mistake. I was already rethinking my values and that tipped me over the edge. I went to the police. Grassed on them. Put my comrades behind bars. The Service saw potential in me. Poacher turned gamekeeper. Anyway, too much about me: the moral is that when we see and hear evil we have to act. I believe you understand that.'

Shaida said nothing and he took her silence as acquiescence. 'If you are with me there is a small task that you can help me with immediately. It involves your colleague Mr Grant who definitely owes us a bit of cooperation. I want you to ask Mo to pass on the message that Steve is very keen to meet the same group again at the mosque, and others, especially those of a more jihadist bent. It is just possible that we may get a lead to one of our targets who we know to be active in the town. He has been in touch with your brother and attended one of the meetings. Can you help set that up?'

<hr />

Ganesh Parrikar received a message brought by hand to the servants' quarters at his home late in the evening before he retired. It was a request from the Sheikh, dictated to a trusted intermediary, for an urgent visit to an exclusive private hospital where he lay seriously ill following a heart attack. The Sheikh might not have long to live. He needed to talk. If Parrikar followed the enclosed instructions his visit would be strictly private except for the Sheikh's immediate family, currently gathered at the hospital.

He hesitated. His old associate had betrayed and blackmailed him, organised the killing of one of his employees. Now he wanted some comfort before he met his maker. But the tone of the message contained a hint of desperation. Perhaps there was something Parrikar did not know. He summoned his driver and headed to the hospital, entering as instructed by a back entrance and reaching a floor at the top of the building by a service lift. He discreetly entered an ante-room to where the Sheikh lay. His wife and daughter were weeping silently and when Parrikar entered they rose to greet him, mumbling their thanks. The shrunken old woman with the grief-stricken face was barely recognisable from her beautiful and self-confident self of a generation ago when the Parrikars had given the family refuge. Her daughter had been a child then.

When Parrikar was ushered in to the Sheikh he saw first the panoramic view of Mumbai by night and then the inert figure on the bed fed by tubes and attached to wires, with the rhythmic clicking of the machines the only sound apart from weak, uneven breathing from the patient. Parrikar sat beside the bed and the Sheikh opened his eyes with a flicker of recognition. A clammy, trembling hand sought out his visitor's. They sat together in silence for a while until the

Sheikh tried to speak in short, rasping gasps.

'My good friend… thank you… thank you… want you to understand… They tricked me… made me… afraid… my son.'

'Who is "they"?'

The Sheikh moved his head.

'You don't know?'

'No… afraid… my son.'

'Your son Ali? Someone threatened to kill him?'

He nodded slightly but definitely.

'You had Patel killed?'

He nodded again. '… or kill Ali.'

'Who is "they"?'

'Gang?'

There was a long pause. Exhaustion? Fear?

'Trish… Trish…'

'Trishul? Is that what you are trying to say?'

There was a faint nod. The Sheikh turned away and closed his eyes.

Parrikar held his hand for a while then left him to sleep. He doubted he would see the Sheikh again. He left choked with emotion.

On the way out he gently embraced the Sheikh's wife and daughter and they thanked him through their tears. He would go over the conversation in the morning with Deepak and try to make sense of it. What he had learnt was that the Sheikh had been merely part – perhaps an unwitting part – of something bigger and more threatening.

Deepak was unable to add anything when they spoke the next day. He had never heard the term Trishul used outside of Hindu iconography. 'A gang? How would I know?' He realised that his contacts in Delhi wouldn't be able to help with this one. He had the idea of consulting Inspector Mankad. 'I don't rate him or the Mumbai police but it is his job. We can at least try him.'

Deepak arrived, feeling out of place and awkward, having been dropped off by his chauffeur at Dharavi police station where Inspector Mankad held court. To add to his embarrassment there were press photographers at the entrance who were waiting for a well-known figure from Bollywood to arrive in handcuffs and who snapped Deepak instead on the basis that he was probably a minor celebrity. Then there was a long wait as his briefcase and the contents of his pockets were examined at great length by an X-ray machine and its numerous operatives. Not satisfied, the operatives insisted on a detailed hand search of the briefcase, extracting a packet of condoms for prolonged public examination. The humourlessness and officiousness of the operation added to the hilarity of the proceedings, though Deepak was in no mood to laugh. Then he had to run the gauntlet of the dozens of shouting, jostling visitors, relatives, job seekers and hangers-on who seemed to populate the entrance to every Indian public building in contrast to the quiet, orderly, air conditioned oasis that was Parrikar House.

That, and status, was why Deepak had initially summoned Inspector Mankad to his office. But the Inspector made it clear that he was not to be summoned but might find time for a meeting at the police station. He was a different man from the diffident, and deferential, officer who had been present at the official inquest into Patel's death. Deepak had quickly pigeonholed him, without much thought, as a typical Mumbai police officer: not very bright; obsequious to his superiors and the rich and powerful; bullying to his juniors and the poor and powerless; and probably on the make.

This case and the publicity around it had, however, energised and transformed Mankad. For the first time in his career he had appeared on the front page of newspapers and he was getting closer to his dream of the day when 'Mankad catches his man' led the news. He and his journalist contact had inflated each other's reputations with a steady flow of leaks from the police enquiry. Mankad realised that the 'political' element in the case was dangerous but he had also grasped that with danger went a certain power. Everyone assumed that he would not be going public unless there was a Mr Big somewhere guarding his back. His superiors, who would normally grab any glory or forbid him from going near controversial cases, gave him a free run while wondering who Mr Big was. And as the enquiry gathered momentum, more and more little birds came bringing titbits of information to his office.

The real test had come when his sources identified the group who had been present when Patel's killer had been executed as punishment for his undisciplined loquaciousness. Two accessories to the murder had been members of the state assembly. This was in itself no great surprise. In some of the more lawless states like Uttar Pradesh or Bihar over half the assembly members had been charged with murder, rape, kidnapping and other serious offences (though only a few had been convicted and imprisoned). Those two were arrested and charged on Mankad's orders and were now sitting downstairs in what some humorist had called the 'custody suite'. They resembled caricature villains whose heavily oiled hair, long moustaches, record breaking stomachs and betel stained teeth suggested that they had styled themselves on a popular movie gangster. Their initial sense of outrage had turned to sardonic humour and threats to invoke the help of friends who, they claimed, reached to the top of government. Mankad did not allow himself to be fazed and kept them behind bars. Before long the villains had greased palms sufficiently to ensure a steady supply of luxury food and journalists who could regale the world with stories of their suffering in prison because of an over-zealous, misguided obsessive in the Mumbai police. Nonetheless, Inspector Mankad had them where he wanted them and another flock of little birds felt confident enough to bring information to his office and to his rapidly expanding team who were combing the baastis with unusual care.

Now this Deepak Parrikar wanted to see him. Mankad admired Deepak's role as a global – and seemingly honest – businessman, as well as a glamorous figure. But in their brief previous acquaintance he had come across as aloof and condescending: a Westerner patronising the natives. So he could wait. And he was required to wait for half an hour outside Mankad's office on an uncomfortable bench with a number of unsavoury characters and with no respite from the heat. When he was finally shown into Mankad's small office there was a blast of cold air from an old, rattling air conditioner turned to maximum volume and lowest temperature. The room stank of paper and cloth rotted by condensation. It felt and smelt as if fresh air had never been near the place. But the Inspector looked suitably impervious; and the walls were decorated with – now mildewed – pictures commemorating his progress through the ranks and, pride of place, his gallantry medal.

Parrikar sought to settle himself and to open the conversation but he was interrupted several times by streams of messengers and tea boys and, then, heavily laden clerks bringing in more files to add to the collection on the desk. Parrikar noticed that, despite the heaps of paper, there was also a computer on the desk but it was ancient, seemed to have no power source and was probably the result of some, brief, failed attempt by a 'new broom' to modernise. At last he secured the Inspector's attention.

'I have come to discuss the progress of the investigation into the death of Mr Patel.'

'We are making good progress. Arrests made. You will have seen in the newspapers.'

'Yes, I have. I see that the alleged killers are dead or have disappeared.'

'Yes, unfortunately. But we have arrested some people who were behind it.'

'Perhaps I have some useful information.' Deepak proceeded to pass on the account of his father's visit to the Sheikh.

'Your father is not here. Why?'

'He is not well. And badly affected by recent events.'

'Sorry to hear that. Your father made a bad mistake in dealing with this Sheikh. He is responsible for much trouble.'

'But you have never arrested him... Anyway, what about this "Trishul"?'

'I have heard of it. It's a new gang.'

'Is that all? Why would a serious mafioso like the Sheikh be frightened of them?'

'That is what my current enquiries are about.'

'Let me put a theory to you.'

'I prefer facts if you have any.'

'Please hear me out,' Deepak said patiently. 'My father and I believe that the Sheikh is just a pawn in a much bigger game. Ever since the Pakistani-inspired terrorist raid a decade ago and the Dawood gang involvement with the Sheikh's brothers, he has been something of a pariah. Other criminals are reluctant to work with his people. Although he stayed here rather than flee to the Gulf, he is weakened and struggles to hold on to his territory. Perhaps this new group – Trishul – exploited his weakness. Used threats to make him do what they wanted including the pressure on my father.'

'Theory. Short of facts. But it makes sense. It fits with the facts I have. Anything else?'

'No. Well, perhaps I should tell you what I have already told the country's security services.' He described the request to place a 'nephew' in his factory. 'As long as the Sheikh was running his own operation it made sense to imagine that he might have had some pressure through his family and its connections with Pakistan to facilitate some infiltration into the country. But how does that fit into this Trishul organisation running the show?'

'I have no idea and it is the role of our very able security services to investigate. You have told them. Not a police matter.'

Deepak struggled to extract a little more from this one-way conversation with the taciturn policeman. Perhaps he wanted money? But Mankad hadn't hinted at it and if he proved to be one of the puritanical minority of honest police officers, Deepak would be most unwise to proposition him. And, anyway, Deepak had scruples of his own about corruption. Perhaps he needed encouragement from further up the police hierarchy, but pulling rank was also a risky business and Deepak didn't know who to go to in any event.

'Thank you, Inspector. You have been very helpful. I hope you can use my information.'

'No problem. It's useful.'

'Before I go, can you give me some advice? What do I do to protect my family, my business?'

Mankad thought for some time. He was used to being patronised by people like Parrikar, but humility threw him. 'This is more than usual goonda trouble. The Trishul gang has big political friends. Maybe very big. You don't. So they squeeze your family, your company. They will keep squeezing until you join them. Or you get your own friends. It's up to you. Politics is not my business.'

<hr />

Deepak did not have long to wait before the next move. As dusk settled over Mumbai harbour and with the cicadas in full voice, a group of men slipped along the lane to the Parrikar Chemicals complex. The workforce had gone for the day and the only human presence on the site was a small security detail and the skeletal staff required to keep some of the machinery in twenty-four-hour operation. The men knew their way around – they had worked in the factory until the recent cutbacks – and they headed for a shed close to the water's edge. There was a storage tank with a sign warning of the dangers of extremely hazardous substances within. But the men knew how to avoid hazards to themselves and carefully loosened a series of valves that released the contents of the tank into the sea. The liquids mixed silently and invisibly, creating a lethal cocktail that would kill any living object that imbibed it over a wide area. The men then tightened the valves, cleaned them of fingerprints and quietly disappeared into the Indian night.

⬛⬛⬛⬛⬛⬛⬛⬛⬛⬛⬛

Several miles away in another part of the Mumbai suburbs, Iqbal Aziz waited until the evening activity in the local bazaar had started to die down. He slipped quietly along the lanes behind the main shopping street until he came to the yard marked on a map that was now being slowly digested inside him. The gate, as he had been told, was unlocked and he picked his way through piles of building materials until he reached the door of a shed, which opened, with some difficulty, as he pushed. There was a dim light inside from a low-powered naked bulb and just beyond the sparse illumination he saw, half hidden, the outline of the man he had come to meet.

His short stay at Parrikar Avionics had been almost too straightforward. Security had been lax to the point of negligence. No one had taken any particular interest in him. The Indian staff where he was carrying out induction training were friendly and welcoming without being too inquisitive. His mission was to find out what he could about the factory's activities and to report back via coded messages left under a loose brick in a wall at the Muslim cemetery. He had so far managed to construct a detailed map of the layout of the plant, an organogram of the management hierarchy and description supported by photographs of new machine tools that were being installed. He had blended into the local scene very easily.

His Indian collaborators, part of the Sheikh's network, had organised for him a nondescript flat in a township a short bus ride from the plant. He aroused little interest as he commuted back and forth and, at night, surfed the dozens of channels on Indian TV. He felt comfortable and there was enough familiarity in language, food smells and sounds to remind him of life in the spreading suburbs of big cities back home, like Lahore. There was even a mosque nearby whose calls to prayer reassured him and which he occasionally answered. The one cultural divide he struggled to deal with was the presence of Indian women: much more visible, colourful and confident than back home. In the smarter shops and restaurants, they dressed in Western clothes, some disporting themselves in what he regarded as semi-nudity. He had been to Western cities and wasn't a stranger to the adult channels on hotel TVs. But this outward sign of secular values and female independence in an Asian society very like his own he found simultaneously repulsive and exciting.

Tonight, the routine was interrupted by the message at his drop: to meet the contact who, he had been advised, would meet him in an emergency or if there were a change of plan. There was a change of plan. No need for further intelligence gathering. He was to disable a key piece of equipment and then make a quick exit. He would be helped to escape and the network would organise his safe transport back to Pakistan.

The man who passed on these instructions remained well out of sight. He was not there, in any event, to hold a conversation but to transmit orders. Iqbal Aziz had many questions but couldn't ask them. Why abort a successful intelligence gathering operation that was just getting into its stride? Why was he to be involved in explosives, an area where he had minimal expertise? Were his activities being seen, back home, as a 'success' or 'failure' (since he was banking on this final piece of field work giving him a crucial promotion to the upper echelons of Inter-Services Intelligence)?

At the conclusion of the briefing the man handed him the 'kit' with some minimal instructions. The following night he was to carry out the operation. A bicycle would be waiting for him afterwards to bring him back to this place after which he would be sent on to a safe house before returning to Pakistan. He left the way he had come and returned, unseen, to his flat.

CHAPTER 12

ESCALATION

Reuters, 14 July 2019:

Following a massive explosion on the Delhi metro unofficial estimates of casualties are as many as 200 dead and many more injured. Leading Indian ministers have blamed the terrorist attack on Islamic militants infiltrated from Pakistan with the connivance of the Pakistani authorities. The Home Minister, normally regarded as a 'moderate' in the BJP government, has spoken of a Muslim 'fifth column' aiding and abetting terrorists. As news of the explosion spread through social media, mosques were attacked in Ahmedabad and Indore and there are unconfirmed reports of mobs attacking predominantly Muslim districts with retaliation in Hindu minority areas. The Pakistani Prime Minister, Imran Khan, has put out a statement condemning the terrorist attack, disclaiming any responsibility and expressing sorrow for the victims - noting that similar attacks have also recently occurred in Pakistan, allegedly with Indian government connivance.

It was after dark, next evening, in the factory on the outskirts of Mumbai. Iqbal Aziz (aka Hussein Malik) had stayed behind after work, hiding in the men's lavatories. His mission tonight represented a dramatic escalation of activities. He was equipped with plastic explosives and had been given instructions about where to put the packages through the perimeter fence for collection, unobtrusively, later – thereby avoiding the risk of a routine check on his bag when coming into the factory for the day. He had now retrieved them. He had also memorised the exact spot where he was required to place the explosive before detonation. This was his first mission involving violence but he was told by his Indian contact that what was being asked of him was easy and his controllers back in Islamabad considered it an essential part of his task.

He secured the explosive, as instructed, in a vent from the factory power unit and prepared the timing device. There was silence in the pitch black night. Then he heard a click behind him and turned towards a gun a few inches away from his face. Floodlights were switched on around the factory and he was suddenly illuminated like an actor on a stage. He could see that he was very far from alone. The audience was a small army of black-jacketed Indian anti-terrorist troops who had been waiting for him.

In the minutes that followed as he was spread-eagled on the ground, then strip searched, he realised that he should have seen the signs of a sting operation. Now he had to brace himself for an uncomfortable interrogation and to discipline himself to follow the instructions he had been given, even when in great pain.

General Rashid wasn't totally surprised when he saw, on the CNN newsfeed in his office, his bright young protégé Aziz being paraded across the screen by his Indian captors. He felt for Aziz, who could anticipate some very rough questioning from interrogators who may well have learnt their trade from the Russians, just as his own had benefited from US expertise. He noted that the Indians had been smart enough to equip Aziz with explosives – even though he had no clue how to use them – qualifying him to be a 'terrorist' rather than a mere agent. This enhanced status carried the prospect of hanging or, more likely, a higher price if he was exchanged.

But the risks had been explained to Aziz. And since General Rashid suspected that his networks were compromised, he had prepared Aziz for what would follow. Not to be too courageous. Hold out for a while and then talk. Give the Indians lots of information. Ninety per cent of it correct, which the Indians already had; the other ten per cent new, plausible and wrong. That ten per cent could prove very useful if the current skirmishing and sabre-rattling got out of control and a fourth war broke out between the two neighbours.

Aziz hadn't picked up anything useful in his brief snooping expedition. But something more valuable perhaps? The group on the TV screen clustered around the hapless, bound Aziz contained some interesting faces. One he recognised. Sanjay? Sanjivi? Desai. What was he doing there? Some research for the boys.

With this, and the bomb in Delhi, there would be a busy day ahead.

Steve had a very difficult two days as the redundancies were trailed and he urged moderation. The company needed time to work out the various options. Nothing was gained by rushing into industrial action. Even those who bought the arguments for a measured approach were surly and resentful, since his indiscreet behaviour was generally believed to have contributed to the company's problems and the (apparently) lost order. At a time when unemployment was rising to levels last seen a decade earlier in the wake of the banking crisis, there was little tolerance for carelessness with people's jobs.

His reputation in the local party, and the council, had also taken a nosedive: no longer the unblemished hero and hope for the future. In any event, the leftist move of the party's national leadership and the influence of new members meant that the brand of politics that Steve represented was no longer fashionable.

He received an abruptly phrased summons to the office of the council leader, Councillor John Gray. John was a retired lecturer from the town's further education college: liked, if not respected, by his colleagues as a decent, safe, uncontroversial man who kept the peace between the endlessly feuding factions and over-sized egos. The borough council had several longstanding Lib Dem wards. Another, which had once been represented by the BNP, now had a trio of community independents, who maintained the tradition of white, working class hostility to the town's Asian population. But, these apart, the council was overwhelmingly Labour.

Maintaining discipline required keeping two of the big beasts of the council tolerably happy. One was Les Harking, the regional organiser of Steve's union, Unite, who had a hard left background on Merseyside and whose permanent sense of grievance was only partly appeased by being put in charge of the town's planning, as well as a seat on the union national executive. Councillor Mirza made sure that the three wards with a large Asian vote delivered the right result, without too many questions being asked about the size of the postal vote. He had responsibility for social services and there were growing mutterings in the town about the abysmal standards in several residential care homes owned by various members of the Mirza extended family. Steve's political career had flourished thanks to the patronage of John Gray and the grudging acquiescence of the others he had managed, so far, not to alienate.

The final member of the panel worried Steve the most. Bill Daniels was the Labour group's oldest and longest serving councillor. He had been first elected in the dawn of political pre-history when Harold Wilson was Prime Minister and sometime before Steve was even born. His political contribution was negligible. He never spoke in the council or council committees and he performed no obviously useful function. But his very antiquity gave him status. Like a long surviving veteran of the Battle of Britain he regaled his colleagues with accounts of his dog-fights in the class struggle over Bedfordshire. Until recently his reputation had been sustained by the belief that 'old Bill' knew everyone in his ward and solved all their problems through assiduous casework.

This reputation had taken a severe beating in the last municipal elections. The Lib Dems had decided to fight the ward seriously – the first real contest for decades. Their simple weapon was a voters' questionnaire. The answers told them that hardly anyone in the ward knew who 'old Bill' actually was and no one could recall anything he had done. The Lib Dems buried the ward in campaigning Comments and came within two votes of unseating Bill when there was a swing from Lib Dems to Labour elsewhere in the town. Since his near humiliation, Bill had launched his own personal crusade against the Lib Dems, generating a degree of tribal passion never previously seen in his almost forty-five years on the council. One of Steve's biggest political mistakes had been to let slip in a group meeting that he felt there was quite a lot of common ground with the Lib Dems and that the party's interests might be served by letting the Lib Dems have a clear run in the leafier suburbs and rural areas where Labour stood no chance. For this terrible heresy, in the eyes of Bill Daniels, mere burning at the stake would be compassionate.

As a senior figure in the Labour group, Steve would normally be at the top table, setting the agenda. On this occasion he was placed at the end of a long table, which required him to look deferentially at his interrogators: his four senior colleagues. He saw that on the wall behind them were photographs of party leaders going back to Kier Hardie but, he noticed, excluding the traitor Blair.

Gray clearly had little appetite for the proceedings and looked, embarrassed, into the middle distance. Les Harking, however, was keen to get down to business. He had spent a lifetime intimidating college-educated managers and making an example of union 'scabs'. Cutting down tall poppies in the party was another speciality and here was one in front of him. 'Comrade,' he began, 'the party's regional executive has asked us to investigate your conduct. We have been informed that there are to be substantial redundancies at your company. We want to know about your role in this disastrous state of affairs. Some of our Brothers are not sure whether you are acting in their interest, the bosses', those of a group of pacifists or religious fundamentalists. They say you were a good rep but have fallen into bad company. They say you encouraged a demonstration against your own industry. And now you are telling our members that they have to accept redundancies imposed by the people who control your firm: private equity barons and hedge funds in America. The suggestion is being made that you are bringing the Labour Movement into disrepute.' Bill Daniels grunted his agreement.

Before Steve could answer, Councillor Mirza wanted to have his say. 'Steve, my people are angry. They are good, loyal people. They work. They pray. They give no trouble. They support our party. Now they say you are making friends with some dangerous people; troublemakers, militants. I speak for the community. They say to me: "Why does this councillor interfere and not respect you?"'

By this time Steve had woken up to the fact that he was on trial in a kangaroo court. He realised that he was sweating uncomfortably, and his heart started to race. His union experience told him, however, not to get into a brawl when he was outnumbered but to insist on due process. His prosecutors clearly didn't like him and had their own agendas. They almost certainly resented his reputation as a moderniser in the workplace and in the party. No point arguing the toss with them.

'Colleagues, I have very good answers to these charges. They are ridiculous. But I want to know what is the constitutional basis for this meeting; that it is properly constituted.' Harking and Daniels protested vehemently and Steve stood up, preparing to walk out.

This intervention gave John Gray the opportunity to pour oil on troubled waters.

He intercepted Steve on his way to the door and put his hand on his shoulder. 'Steve, calm down. We are not accusing you of anything. We all value your political and union work. We just want you to know that some of our colleagues are concerned. This town has enough problems without divisions in our own ranks. You are a good colleague, Steve. You have done excellent work for the Movement. Let us forget this meeting happened. Just take on board the worries of your colleagues.'

Despite the reprieve, Steve felt angry at the pettiness and spitefulness of colleagues with whom he had worked together to run the town for the last few years. He reflected that his effortless rise had so far shielded him from some of the uglier realities of Labour politics.

Preoccupied by these thoughts, he failed to notice a half-familiar figure loitering at the entrance as he left the town hall. But the man was determined to see him and followed. Steve initially panicked as he thought he was being tailed but then was able to put a name to the face: Mehmet, the night watchman. He paused and Mehmet asked if they could go somewhere private for a conversation. Steve was reluctant; life was already complicated enough. But there was a hint of desperation in the man's eyes. They found a coffee bar nearby.

'It is union business,' Mehmet started.

'I haven't anything to add to what I said about redundancies at the branch meeting. Sorry. Nothing I can do about that.'

'It isn't about that. I have been dismissed. I am not entitled to anything. I am an asylum seeker. I was sacked for misconduct. They said I was asleep on duty. Lies. The reason is that I know bad things are happening at the factory.'

'You know about "unfair dismissal"?'

'Yes, but I don't qualify. Not working here long enough. I came to you because you are a fair man. And you fight for the workers. Maybe you can't help me, but you must know about the bad people there.' The man was patently sincere and in distress.

Steve was now sufficiently engaged to let Mehmet tell his story, from the university classrooms of Asmara, to the battlefields on the border of Eritrea, the nightmare journey across Sudan and Libya, the terrifying experience under a lorry crossing the Channel, months in crowded bedsits around London, scraps of jobs, mostly illegal, and now –

after his papers came through – permission to work and this job on an industrial estate. He was not stupid, he insisted. He knew when things were not right. His reports on night-time visitors in the factory: ignored. And then early one morning observing the head of security clearly up to no good. Shortly afterwards he was dismissed and told that he would be well advised to disappear quietly. Any stories he told would not be believed and the company had influential contacts in the government who would ensure that he was returned to Eritrea. But rather than disappear, he wanted someone to know.

Steve wasn't sure how all this fitted into the bigger picture but there was enough to demand a proper investigation. So he rang Calum with the intelligence he had gleaned. And he remembered that he was still carrying the card of the man from MI5 – Liam – and called him too.

<hr />

The following day Steve had a call from his boss. Calum and Liam had confronted the company's head of security, Justin Starling, that morning. Calum had already started to have doubts about Starling's competence and had remembered the holes in his CV, which he had overlooked on the basis of the Red Admiral's character reference. The intelligence from Mehmet confirmed existing suspicions that not only was he not doing his job very well, he was actively working against the company and, perhaps, the country. A threat of criminal sanctions and the Official Secrets Act persuaded him to come clean about his activities on the basis that charges would not be pressed.

Sometime ago Starling had been approached by a US company called Global Analysis and Research that was stalking Pulsar and wanted, in due course, to make a takeover bid. In the meantime, he was to pass whatever confidential information he could gather about Pulsar's intellectual property. And to help soften up the company for a cheap takeover, he was to help destabilise it. For that reason, he had passed on in advance all the details of the Minister's visit to the anti-arms trade group and the Islamic militants. He had the run of the place at night with access to a full set of security codes, and a large, if unquantifiable, amount of Pulsar's proprietary anti-missile technology was now in the hands of a rival company in Louisiana. That company happened to be the same large minority shareholder that Calum had, belatedly, realised had Pulsar in its sights for an aggressive takeover.

It had been difficult to establish Starling's motives beyond a generous enhancement of his package if the takeover materialised. Eventually, cross-questioning established that Starling had a guilty secret. Some years ago he had been suspected of, and charged with, indecent behaviour with children. But the evidence had been inconclusive and the case had been dropped. He had no criminal record but Global had obtained information that had eluded Calum's checks. They could control him.

All it had required was a glowing reference from the Red Admiral to get him installed at Pulsar.

British intelligence had no great interest in pursuing the matter further. The damage was primarily in the form of intellectual property theft from Pulsar, a private enterprise. And an American company with apparently close links to the Pentagon could hardly be treated as if it were Chinese or Russian. If Calum wanted to take action it was up to him. He did want to take action but the lawyers would move slowly, at best, and, in the meantime his company faced an existential threat from Global's expanding shareholding. He needed political support, soon.

Steve was the first call he made, lifting the suspension with immediate effect. Calum had a guilty conscience, in any event, that Steve had taken the rap for the demonstration and had a reputation to rebuild. When the problem was explained, Steve immediately saw both the threat and the opportunity and started making calls to his high-placed Labour and union contacts and journalists to whom he had fed good material in the past. Shaida was involved in the discussions and given the job of trawling the internet for references to Global and its finances. This was a covert operation she was altogether more comfortable with than snooping for Liam.

What she found was not reassuring. The company was founded and chaired by a somewhat reclusive American called Aaron Le Fevre. He had been a very senior if somewhat murky figure in the Pentagon with Donald Rumsfeld and then on the staff of Vice-President Cheney. Shortly after 9/11 he left government to establish Global, which had expanded rapidly on the back of Defense Department orders. As Shaida dug through the press references she picked up a couple of articles based on blogs from a – now deceased – investigative journalist in Seattle, Lee Wright. Wright worried about Global's rapid expansion, taken in conjunction with Le Fevre's political history. He spoke to the CEOs of a couple of companies Global had taken over and, while the two businessmen were reluctant to talk, they said enough to leave the strong impression that dirty tricks were involved. Global seemed less interested in the health of the companies it was taking over than in getting its hands on their proprietary technology. In each case, the companies specialised in anti-missile defence, or missile technology more generally. Wright died shortly after in an unexplained shooting incident. Then Shaida found the link to the company in Northern Ireland making advanced communications equipment, and which Global took over and turned around.

She was also able to piece together a consistent pattern from an analysis of share prices and company valuations. All of the companies taken over had experienced a major crisis leading to a sharp drop in their share price. At that point Global stepped in to 'rescue' them: a white knight for companies in distress. Data on Global itself was patchy but it showed prodigious growth and profits. Global was not yet in the Premier League with the likes of Lockheed

Martin but it soon would be. More detail, however, proved hard to find. The full company accounts could not be traced any further as they were lodged in various offshore holding companies based in the Cayman Islands.

The name Aaron Le Fevre also cropped up in a different context, as a member of a group of US businessmen, security insiders and Republican congressmen called the Crusader Knights who were preoccupied with confronting the threat of militant Islam in all its forms. In a speech reported in a newspaper in Le Fevre's native Louisiana, he had advocated an 'alliance of civilisations': the Christian West and Russia, Israel and Hindu India, with Islam the common enemy. This kind of talk had gone down well with the Trump people, and press cuttings showed him at various Trump Tower events.

Islamic radicals were also the subject of conversation at the finance department's coffee machine where Steve was waiting to discuss his next rendezvous at the mosque. When Shaida arrived she anticipated the question.

'Your heroics won't be needed after all,' she explained. 'Apparently there was a police raid last night in the town. Some jihadists were caught. And lots of incriminating stuff: an arsenal, in fact. Guns. Explosives. It appears, however, that the main target, Tariq Ahmed, got away. Some of this was on local radio – you must have missed it – and Mo had picked up the news on social media. His reaction worried me – he was overjoyed that Tariq Ahmed had escaped.'

Shaida hesitated, not sure how much of what she had already shared with Liam as informant she could now share with her friend.

'I haven't discussed these things much with you recently, Steve. But Mo has become incredibly difficult to talk to. Secretive. He's started locking himself in his bedroom and goodness knows what he's doing and looking at on his computer. On the odd occasions he communicates at meal times he starts ranting about how the British are to blame for all the violence in the subcontinent: the history of divide-and-rule, Partition, all that. Now the British are to blame for supporting India and not understanding the suffering of our people in Kashmir. My mum and dad and I are "deluded". Coconuts he calls us: brown on the outside, white on the inside.'

※※※※※※※※※※※※※※※

Back in Mumbai, the Parrikars were also anxious, waiting for the next blow to land. They experienced several days of bad publicity after the pollution spillage from their chemicals plant came to light. Another example of the company's 'irresponsible capitalism'. There would be one official enquiry by the Environment Agency and another by the state government. Villagers were being mobilised by people who claimed to be environmental NGOs to demand compensation. There would be big fines. A speech Deepak had made recently on the 'Greening of the Planet' had become the subject of newspaper cartoons and a source of ridicule among the English-speaking intellectuals.

And then one of Parrikar Senior's most loyal project managers had received threats similar to those made to Patel. He was speedily given leave of absence to head off a similar fate. Disruption of the defence contract was, for the moment, forgotten.

The telephone rang in Parrikar Senior's downtown office. His PA came through to tell him that there was an urgent call from the Prime Minister's office in Delhi: Santosh Joshi, the PM's private secretary. 'Highly, highly confidential, Sahib, I will connect you.'

'Joshi here. The Prime Minister has asked me to speak to you on a serious matter.'

'Of course. It is an honour.'

'Let me get to the point. The PM is concerned about the defence contract. There are serious problems in London, and America – they are saying the contract may be delayed, even stopped. It would be a disaster if that happens.'

'But you stopped this plot. Clever operation.'

'No thanks to sloppy security in your son's plant. And your family is a big part of the problem. Your dirty business has alarmed the Americans and your son isn't satisfied with our local prostitutes; he has to show off this English woman in front of the cameras. It's created a scandal in the UK.'

'Sahib, we only want to do good for India. We will do what is needed.'

'You will need to put in more cash. The Avionics plant must be fully tooled up and ready to start work once the contract is sorted out.'

'That is difficult. There's no other work for the factory at present. Banks will not lend without the contract being agreed.'

'That is your problem, Mr Parrikar. Your Mumbai businesses have plenty of cash. The Revenue Department tells me that they are thinking about investigating your tax affairs. If you don't want them on your back, you had better cooperate.

'We also want to sort out your son's amateurish operation. We could nationalise Parrikar Avionics but we don't operate that way. We are pro-business, not like Congress and their Communist friends. So, we will work with you to strengthen the executive team. We have someone in mind. You may know of Sanjivi Desai, a highly talented engineer who now advises the PM on national security issues. He is also well connected and respected in the US, so he ticks a lot of boxes. He will be parachuted in to give your son advice.'

'We will discuss this.'

'No, you will do it. The Prime Minister wants it. He also thanks you for your help with the last election – your donation was well received. He doesn't want to lose the respect he has for you.'

'Yes, Sahib.'

Desai soon started making himself at home. With perfunctory notice he arrived at the Parrikar Avionics site with a coterie of 'experts' and 'advisers', mostly Americans of Indian origin whom Global had recruited from Californian high tech businesses and had been rapidly given visas to operate in India. A PhD from MIT or Caltech seemed to be the minimum qualification.

When Deepak arrived at the factory, the visiting team had already thoroughly intimidated security and his personal staff, and had taken up residence in his office. Before Deepak could protest, a distinguished-looking man in a beautifully tailored Nehru suit leapt up from an armchair, a hand outstretched in greeting.

'Good morning, Mr Parrikar, you won't be surprised to see us. Forgive the invasion but we came early to get down to business. The Indian government has suggested that my team can help upgrade your operation so that it can meet the tough specifications required by our Defence Ministry and by the US and UK partners. The current security situation with Pakistan is a reminder of why this project is important. To be frank, our political masters have been none too impressed by the lax security and some of the unprofessional operations here. This is too important to be just a vanity project for your family. I am here to help. Global Research and Analysis is at your service. Let me introduce the team.'

None of this surprised Deepak. In the last few days, since he first heard of Desai's proactive role, he did the rounds of his friends in business, politics and the media who broadly shared his world view: essentially patriotic Indians, but outward looking, cosmopolitan and secular. Several of them gave him anecdotes and titbits of information. Desai was a senior, if rather obscure, figure in the first BJP – Vajpayee – government operating in the interstices of politics and administration, part of the national security apparatus that was built up after India's drubbing in the border war with China, and he was now a major force. His origins were obscure but he was identified in leftist magazines as one of the more fanatical products of the RSS, the ideological and paramilitary arm of the ruling party in Delhi that included the Prime Minister among its alumni.

When Congress came back to power, with its secular allies, Desai disappeared to the US, building up his already impressive qualifications in electronic engineering. US citizenship followed. Then he worked with right-wing Republican think tanks and published several pieces disseminated on Alt-Right websites about a Muslim 'fifth column' in both India and the USA. He met Le Fevre at a fundraiser for the – successful – Republican gubernatorial candidate in Louisiana, 'Bobby' Jindal, one of the new breed of Indians making it big in America. Desai and Le Fevre wove together their respective conspiracy theories, an ideological marriage made in heaven, and before long Desai was on the board of Global. Now, through his business, he straddled the two worlds of US and Indian politics.

One of the advantages of Deepak's Western education and US experience was that he was not easily intimidated by the likes of Desai. He decided that attack was the best form of defence.

'Thank you for the offer of help,' he replied. 'But I didn't ask for it and I don't believe I need it. We have never had complaints before in all our years of supplying the Indian armed forces. And let me be clear; this is our family business. It will remain so whether I or one of my siblings runs it.'

Desai smiled his killer-shark smile. 'We'll soon see who calls the shots here!'

Deepak tried to understand how Desai fitted into the recent tribulations of his family company. He went over in his mind the pieces of the puzzle. A gang called Trishul appeared to be targeting the business. And if the police were right, it was linked to politicians from one of the extreme nationalist parties that were powerful at state level. The Sheikh had been involved in the Patel murder and also in helping place the Pakistani agent in Parrikar Avionics. At first sight these seemed totally disconnected events. But perhaps they were connected after all.

It was odd that a man with the Sheikh's pedigree was allowed to function unobstructed by the authorities and had surfaced at such a convenient time. Perhaps he had been turned, blackmailed, by the people who now controlled the secret parts of India's increasingly sectarian state in which Desai was an important player. A Muslim gangster would be a good foil, and easily deniable.

But this was surely paranoia: conspiracy theory run riot. The theory had a coherent logic, but conspiracy theories often did. Like the internet fantasy stories peddled by dangerous cranks about 9/11 being orchestrated from Tel Aviv. But, then again, Mr Le Fevre was one of those people on the American extreme right who were reported as believing and promoting the story that, although Hitler was a bad man, the Holocaust was really the creation of the grand Mufti of Jerusalem and the Islamists.

What persuaded Deepak to believe the worst of the people threatening his family firm was the reaction of his father, who had sunk into self-pitying despair after his public humiliation in *Bharat Bombay*. But when Deepak had hesitantly set out his theory, his father sprung to life, finding it totally believable and exactly the kind of stunt that could have been pulled in the smaller universe of Mumbai slumland. He knew from experience that the frenzied religious massacres that occurred every generation or so owed far more to political manipulation than to any real difference or division. He had seen the religious militant nationalists increasing their power in Mumbai and believed them capable of anything. Fortified by this insight, his father's street fighting instincts resurfaced. They decided to stand and resist rather than capitulate to the people trying to control their company. And that involved following the advice of the policeman. They needed political friends.

Kate had returned to her constituency routine. She declined the very junior ministerial role she had been offered, a sop to her pride, but such a minor sop that leaving the government seemed more dignified. She was welcomed with open arms into the club of the dismissed, overlooked, angry, mischievous, disloyal and congenitally rebellious who occupied a corner of the tea room. She enjoyed her first experience of defying the whips.

Her constituency surgeries swelled in size, she suspected, because her brief notoriety had attracted the curious as well as the needy. Coming to the end of a long and tiring session a man came into her office with a pretty Asian woman, who looked vaguely familiar, to discuss what he had described when making the appointment as a planning problem. When they sat down he said, looking at Stella: 'We would like to see the MP alone. We have something highly confidential and political to discuss.'

'Planning?' Kate asked.

'No, when you have heard what we have to say you will understand the need for privacy.'

'This is very irregular. I am not sure I wish to have such a conversation.'

But Stella, her sense of affront getting the better of her curiosity, was already on her way to the door. When it was closed the man began. 'Let me come clean. I gave a false name and I am not a constituent. In fact, I am a Labour councillor. My colleague here is chief finance officer of Pulsar, the company you visited recently.'

'I could hardly forget,' Kate replied. 'But, look, I really think you should leave. You are completely out of order.'

'Please hear me out. What I have to say has a direct bearing on your departure from the government and, also, on your friend in India – if the newspapers are right about that. I am the union man at Pulsar.'

'So I can thank you for the eggs and tomatoes, can I?' Kate said, still bristling with annoyance at the invasion of her advice surgery on false pretences.

At this point Shaida endeavoured to steer the conversation towards the reason for the visit. 'We briefly met after you were manhandled by that mob. We have come to show you these.' She took out her bundle of documents and talked Kate through the Global story as quickly and clearly as she could.

Kate listened with mounting incredulity, and then anger. 'If all this is true, we have been well and truly done over. But it is history; water under the bridge. I don't know about you but I am trying to move on.'

Steve insisted: 'No, it isn't history. This American operation is closing in on Pulsar; probably on your Indian friend's company too for all we know.'

'Well, in that case, why come to me? Why not take it to the press? Your Labour people can publicise it; raise it in parliament.'

'Yes, I could do that. I could take it to the *Guardian*.

They would have a lot of fun with the story: right-wing extremist American destabilising and taking over British high tech company. I could also take it to our front bench people who would no doubt make hay with it and demand that the government use its powers to block takeovers where national security is involved. But, as you know, our politics is tribal. Grandstanding is satisfying but it is less likely to get results than working on the inside.

'We have come together because we are not just concerned for ourselves – but with the people I have represented in the factory. We genuinely believe that this Global outfit is sinister and needs to be stopped. You have contacts in government that I don't have and they, in turn, have contacts in the US. You also have direct access to people at the Indian end.'

'I think you overestimate my influence,' responded Kate. 'I am not exactly flavour of the month at the moment. As you know I am now on the back benches and persona non grata with the people you wish me to influence.'

Steve felt they had done enough to press her. 'All we can ask is that you do your best. I suggest the following. I understand that there is an important debate in parliament on Monday. You will get a chance to corner your former boss, Jim Chambers, at the division, even if he won't see you before. Tell him what is going on. I will try to line up some press publicity for the Wednesday that might prompt a question in PMQs or could be the basis of an Urgent Question. Ideally, you could raise it. But that is for you – I am not an MP and not sure how these things operate. The key point is that all of this will come out. Let's work together to make sure it comes out in a good way.'

Kate drove home trembling with fear, excitement and nervous exhaustion and had to pull in to a layby to compose herself. She had been through the most difficult and traumatic few weeks in her entire, admittedly rather cosseted, existence and, just as she was coming to terms with her stalled career, she was being thrown back into the maelstrom.

She was, as the Prime Minister had suggested with heavy sarcasm, spending more time with her family. It was proving an ordeal. She had come to loathe her husband's twin-track campaign of angry silence and icy politeness. She had been called 'darling' more frequently than ever before in the sixteen years of their marriage but he somehow imbued the word with accusation and malice. He had made it clear that he wasn't going anywhere and he was waiting for her to produce the white flag of unconditional surrender and an abject, grovelling, apology. The girls weren't much help. After an initial display of solidarity with Mum, they had all retreated into adolescent sulks, making clear their embarrassment with their parents and their refusal to try to understand the world of adult emotions, let alone politics.

The house was quiet so she rang Deepak, who tried to be supportive and as sympathetic as the intermittent mobile reception would allow.

'I would like to be there with you. And I miss you,' he said tenderly. 'Things aren't as bad for me but my father's mental state is brittle and my mother's health has taken a turn for the worse. How are you feeling?'

'I am coping. Jonathan is insufferable. The girls are tricky. But, otherwise, I think the crisis is bottoming out. For the British media I am already ancient history. And this evening I learnt a lot more about the political background. About this company and what it is up to here and in India.'

'Their man Desai is much in evidence here. I am beginning to see a way forward.'

'Me too. Talking to you gives me more confidence. With luck, we'll be together again soon.'

She decided to act quickly rather than wait until Monday. She had kept the Secretary of State's home number and, to her surprise, he was both in and willing to take her call. The bonhomie was almost overwhelming.

'My dear Kate, how are you coping? I am so sorry things turned out badly. It must be awful. How is your lovely family? I am sure it will all work out for the best and we will have you back in government before long.' Even if she applied a high discount factor for his natural bombast and insincerity it was clear that, up to a point, Jim cared. Perhaps a guilty conscience that she had come to grief on his watch, on his project. And it was part of his character to enjoy being the saviour of damsels in distress.

What she thought was a dispassionate account ran, however, into a wall of scepticism: 'A Labour councillor…? That hopeless Scottish socialist trying to run the business… Eritrean asylum seeker…' As she went on she realised that her list of witnesses for the prosecution making accusations against a well-connected US company was far from convincing. She hadn't even got as far as the young British Pakistani woman. While he didn't say so explicitly, she could imagine him formulating the obvious questions: 'Are you on the brink of a nervous breakdown?' and 'Have you been reading too many spy thrillers?'

She was able to keep his attention by referring to the documents about Global and Le Fevre that the two had given her and which she undertook to scan immediately. When he rang off, he gave little indication that he was persuaded of the need to take the matter further. But she knew him well enough to know that the one thing that would have got through to him was the threat of an ambush in parliament, and bad press, and that she had done the right thing by warning him.

The Secretary of State never rang back, but then, she hadn't asked him to.

Other telephones were, however, ringing furiously. In his Sloane Square flat the Red Admiral was busy trying to retrieve a situation that was in danger of slipping out of control. All thanks to the carelessness of Starling, interfering politicians and some wretched African asylum seeker who would soon be back on his way to the jungle if he, the Admiral, had anything to do with it. So: favours called in across the Pond, in the Pentagon; Whitehall contacts alerted and suitably briefed; his friends among defence correspondents given the correct spin for when the story got out; and then, reassurance to his old friend, Jim Chambers, and his associates in Louisiana that everything was under control.

Meanwhile, Kate waited on tenterhooks for several days until the story appeared in the *Guardian* as Steve had planned and predicted. It was backed up by an editorial that had the flavour of an anti-American rant and was, she judged, unhelpful. The piece was placed low down on page seven, having been bumped off the front page by a Labour 'split' story. There was no traction. The rolling news channels and social media took little interest.

What did gain traction, however, was a powerful front page lead in the *Telegraph* under the headline 'Asylum Seeker Betrayal'. Readers were told that 'sources close to No. 10' had given the paper exclusive background on 'an act of treachery' at one of the country's important, high tech defence companies. 'An African asylum seeker with a mathematics background' had managed to hack through the security codes of the company where he was employed and was passing valuable information, for money, to commercial rivals. He had also stirred up trouble at the plant by informing Muslim militants and Marxist groups about an impending ministerial visit, leading to a violent demonstration. The article noted that the plant had a history of union militancy and Muslim extremism among the labour force.

Fortunately, the *Telegraph* reassured its readers that 'quick action by the company's head of security and by the country's intelligence services had contained the damage'. The Home Secretary was investigating how such breaches of security could be prevented in future, by ensuring that those foreign nationals who were allowed to work were excluded from sensitive sites.

Talks were taking place, encouraged by the UK and US governments, to develop a 'partnership' with a leading US company, Global Analysis and Research, to 'secure the long term future of the plant and ensure that Britain's leadership in a key area of military technology is fully protected'.

No one noticed that the *Guardian* story related to the same set of events, so different was the account.

Kate had, as recommended, put down an Urgent Question but it wasn't called. Instead, the Labour MP in whose constituency Pulsar was based raised the matter with the Prime Minister, who replied with a carefully drafted statement:

'I am aware of these accusations and the government is studying them carefully. There is a suggestion that criminal activity may have been involved concerning an asylum seeker and it will be dealt with firmly and quickly by the appropriate authorities. I also want to reassure the House that the government has been in contact with the US administration and with the Indian government and the contract is proceeding as planned. Furthermore, we are in contact with the Pakistani government and have reassured them that the contract is purely for defensive equipment.

'I wish to reassure the House that the US company that is acquiring a controlling interest in the company has given the government a set of written undertakings to protect jobs at the factory. Demonstrating confidence in Britain's future outside the EU, it has committed itself to establish a major new development facility close to the existing site, potentially employing several hundred scientific personnel. Britain is, truly, open for business. This is good news for jobs in the Honourable Member's constituency and underlines this government's commitment to jobs and to the defence industry. We are, after all, the Workers' Party.' (Jeers, hoots.)

Calum called in Steve to brief him on the latest developments. Steve saw the empty tumbler on Calum's desk and caught a whiff of the products of a Highland distillery. Calum normally never drank in the office, but today his face was flushed and looked seriously agitated.

'Well, laddie, you came out of this OK. The *Guardian* story. Now there is the local paper: "Zero to hero". The journalist who stitched you up a few weeks ago now has you as "the man who saved the plant". Your lads have secure jobs, for now, that's for sure. And, if you did half of what you are said to have done, I guess you deserve a medal. But this whole thing stinks. I have been completely fucking shafted. We have been taken over by a dodgy American company run by some right-wing ideologue, and this is supposed to be a great victory for our brilliant fucking government – and you for that matter. These people now have access to all our IP, or the bits they hadn't already nicked. That fucking Admiral, who I trusted and who brought in that pervert to spy on us, now – believe this – has us under his fucking chairmanship.

'They want me to stay and manage a handover delivering this contract. But – after my golden goodbye – I have to work out how to spend my early retirement. Can't spend more time with my family: I don't have one. Any ideas, Steve?'

Steve had never encountered Calum in this morose, self-pitying, semi-alcoholic state. Their relationship had worked because it was not a friendship. Calum was the boss; Steve the worker who wore overalls and collected his pay cheque like the other workers. There was mutual respect but distance. Now, it was clear, Calum wanted to unburden himself. He unearthed a bottle of whisky from a cupboard, poured himself a full glass, neat; then remembered that Steve was in the room and offered him a drink, which he declined.

'I realise now just what a bunch of fucking wankers we have running this country. Useless. PR men. Snake oil salesmen. Never done a proper day's work in their lives. Probably never been inside a factory; certainly never worked in one.'

He paced around the room gesticulating, spilling half the contents of his drink on the floor. But he was in full flow, absorbed in his own, drunken, eloquence. 'What have those idiots done for our manufacturing? I go to my engineering dinners. Poor sods from Rolls-Royce and BAE. They've got bean counters at their elbows. Cut this. Cut that. Shareholders on their back the whole time. No interest in making anything any more: design, development – the things we used to be good at. Before long Rolls will be bought out by Ning Ping fucking Inc if the Yanks don't get there first. Post-Brexit export drive? What a fucking joke.'

Steve would normally agree with all of that. But he was desperate to leave as he saw Calum downing two more large glasses of whisky. 'I know you want to go,' Calum said as he put down his empty glass. 'Just one word of advice. I've seen you eyeing up the Khan lassie. Her people don't like us messing with their women. They'll have your balls off if you're not careful. Fighters. Once wiped out a British army.'

'That was the Afghans.'

'Same difference. Stick to your politics.'

At the factory, Steve's reputation was largely rehabilitated. He had been puzzled by the differing interpretation of events in the *Telegraph* and the *Guardian*. But these were not papers read by his workmates. Their jobs were safe. Expansion was on the way. The local paper and the local MP claimed it was a great outcome. Calum and Steve didn't want to pour cold water on a good news story, just yet.

The conversation with Calum had worried Steve more than he let on at the time. He was unlikely in future to have the intimate, trusted role he currently enjoyed. The new owners would presumably know of the part he had played in trying to expose their dirty tricks. Jump or be pushed?

He would not be short of things to do. He had recently been voted onto the national executive of his union. And the ancient and anonymous local Labour MP had recently decided to stand down, creating a vacancy. He would start as favourite for the succession.

As for the prospect of emasculation to protect the honour of a woman from the North West Frontier, that all seemed rather academic. Shaida had given little encouragement. Even on the trip to visit that MP in Surrey Heights, which she had managed to sell to her parents as essential for the benefit of Pulsar, she had remained aloof and rebuffed any sign of familiarity.

So he was unprepared for their next encounter at the coffee machine. Shaida smiled as she walked up to him. 'Good news,' she said. 'I plucked up the courage to tell my dad I was planning to go on a date with you. Told, not asked. There was no response. No fatwa.'

He was, as always, several steps behind her, and he struggled to find a suitable reply. 'Maybe you can come and help me deliver some Labour leaflets,' he said tentatively.

She laughed – she wasn't sure if he was being serious or had a nice line in humour. 'That sounds really exciting. Maybe my brother can come along as chaperone.' Then her long, deep chuckle told him what he needed to know. She really did care for him.

━━━━━━━━━━━━

In another part of town, where the more sordid bedsits were interspersed with gap sites for housing parking lots and illegal businesses operating unlicensed taxis and distributing qat and hashish, a police van sat waiting for orders. There had been a tip-off about someone described as an illegal asylum seeker. The Home Office wanted him removed, and quickly. The police were on hand in case Border Agency staff encountered serious resistance. There was no reply at the door so the police were summoned to break it down.

The flat was empty. Signs of a hurried exit were evident. The only sign left of the former occupant was a photo found under the bed of an African-looking woman and young children photographed in happier times.

The occupant was, in fact, watching the raid from behind the curtains of a nearby flat belonging to a friend. Unlike his former workmates at the factory he actually read the British broadsheets. And, when he read that article in the *Telegraph*, he realised that he had been betrayed, though by whom and why wasn't clear. Anticipating that the authorities would come after him he had quickly moved in with his friend, stayed off the streets and awaited developments.

Being a refugee was not a new experience. He had survived before and would survive again. But he felt a bitter anger at a country that had taken him in and given him hope and then spat him out again. It was a long time since he had prayed to Allah. But Allah would guide him to do what was right.

CHAPTER 13

THE ABDUCTION

Associated Press, 25 July 2019:

The official Chinese news agency Xinhua has reported that a flotilla of Chinese warships has made a 'goodwill' visit to friendly countries in the Indian Ocean. The vessels passed close to the Indian Andaman Islands en route to Dacca; sailed around the Indian coast to Karachi as part of a visit hosted by the Pakistan navy, before 'rediscovering the maritime silk route'. Indian sources are said to be investigating claims that the Chinese vessels had strayed into Indian territorial waters and have insisted that India would meet the 'maritime threat'. President Trump tweeted that China was 'again demonstrating aggressive and expansionist tendencies and aggravating the risks of nuclear confrontation in the subcontinent'.

The events in the subcontinent rippled through the respective communities in Britain. The governments in Delhi and Islamabad, prompted by their allies overseas into a belated disavowal of collective suicide, were seeking to maintain a sufficiently belligerent position to satisfy their hot-blooded militants in politics, and the military, while simultaneously trying to turn down the temperature dial. But it took a while for their acolytes to get the message. There were continuing reports of sectarian mobs running amok. Funerals for the first round of casualties fuelled demands for revenge, feeding another round of attacks. Politicians on both sides reflected on the fact that it had been easier to inflame bigotry than to put out the fires. Hate-filled speeches continued to resonate with the faithful and were amplified in the retelling and in the diaspora.

Muslim communities in Britain were mobilised for a protest demonstration denouncing the Indian government. Cooler heads at the local mosque cautioned against it: the militant cleric would demand to be heard; the black flag wavers might appear and dominate the media coverage; the factory where hundreds of local Muslims worked would again be at the centre of unwanted attention; the English Revival – a virulent, post-Brexit, nationalist group – might organise a counter-demonstration that could produce violence. The police also expressed concern and strongly advised cancellation.

The police advice was not heeded. A lot of people felt the need to let off steam and exercise their democratic rights. About a thousand of them gathered near the town hall. Their numbers included many of the same characters who had marched on the factory but, mercifully, not the black flag wavers. About a hundred English Revival protesters turned up, too, separated from the Muslims by a thick blue line. These activists – almost all young men with shaven heads, bulging muscles, bare torsos and tattoos – were clearly not here for a political seminar. The political descendants of Mosley's blackshirts, the NF, the BNP and EDL, were enjoying an upsurge in their fortunes and here was a perfect platform to demonstrate their contempt for foreigners in general and brown-skinned Muslims in particular. Tucked away around the corner were a substantial number of police riot vehicles in the event of trouble.

Steve observed all of this from the window of his office in the town hall and saw that he was not the only watcher. Plain clothes officers with cameras were filming the event, capturing faces for posterity, a fact that had registered with a significant number of demonstrators whose faces were masked. Steve did, however, notice a few familiar faces from his meetings, one of which was Mo.

The organisers lined up a series of speakers including a well-known MP and a Muslim peer who were politely received, and, then, less celebrated but more animated, there was a man in traditional Kashmiri dress who had honed his oratorical skills on the street rather than in the Palace of Westminster. The political heat rose perceptibly and it was approaching boiling point when the preacher whom Steve had seen at the mosque clambered onto the rostrum. He started slowly, switching between heavily accented English and an Asian language familiar to his audience. As he picked up speed he held up a picture of the Indian Prime Minister leading to outraged shouts and chants of 'Pakistan Zindabad. Pakistan Zindabad. Allahu Akbar. Allahu Akbar.' As he concluded his peroration and prepared to leave the stage, his supporters at the front grabbed the picture and set fire to it, waving the blazing poster in front of a conveniently placed TV camera. A choreographed outburst of spontaneous anger.

The controlled nature of the demonstration was not understood by the police officer commanding the line who saw arson as a prelude to anarchy and instructed his men to intervene. By advancing into the crowd they inadvertently created a bridge-head for the English Revival to charge into. Before long, fists were swinging and heavy boots were finding tender flesh. Although small in number relative to the size of the crowd, the Revival had a vast superiority in street fighting skills. They cut through the crowd flailing fists as they went, before orchestrating a well-planned tactical retreat by which time the police had re-established their line. As the troops from English Revival marched off in triumph down the nearest street, chanting slogans and waving captured banners, the Muslims counted their wounded. Steve could see from his vantage point that his group of friends had borne the brunt of the attack. Mo was clutching his face and his white tunic was covered in blood, the badge of martyrdom.

‖‖‖‖‖‖‖‖‖‖‖‖‖

The demonstration was captured, too, on network television and YouTube. Scenes of Muslims in Britain being beaten by white racist thugs, while (mostly) white police officers milled ineffectually in the background, provided further evidence for millions in the Middle East, Africa and Asia, already inclined to believe that Western countries were involved in a crusade against Islam. Taken in isolation, the British news was bad enough. But the bulletins also had dramatic coverage of gruesome massacres carried out by Assad's forces, accompanied by Russian advisers, 'mopping up' the last centres of radical Islamic resistance at the end of the Syrian civil war; a revival of hostilities in Gaza; and reports of brutality in the 'concentration camps' established in several European countries to hold suspected Muslim militants. Le Fevre's dystopian and self-fulfilling narrative found a perfect echo in the Muslim world. And that world included many millions in India and Pakistan following the news on Al Jazeera or social media.

‖‖‖‖‖‖‖‖‖‖‖‖‖

In Pakistan, a Cabinet meeting was reconvened to which the military High Command, including General Rashid, were invited. It was decided that the military would press ahead with preparations for a 'worst case' scenario, including an underground nuclear test to demonstrate Pakistan's preparedness.

In Mumbai, the atmosphere was tense. From the top of Parrikar House Deepak could see several columns of smoke from some of the densely populated slums where sectarian violence had broken out. He received strong advice from his management team to work from his apartment. But he was determined to have a presence at the factory to face down Desai's uninvited 'advisers'.

He set off as usual from his apartment block with the added precaution of an armed security guard alongside the driver. The roads were eerily quiet but not in any way threatening.

But as the Bentley approached the main highway to join the stream of traffic to the north, a transit van pulled out in front of it from a concealed drive. Deepak's car screeched to a halt. And then another van pulled up behind, blocking it in. Armed men in hoods jumped from the two vans and converged on the car. Deepak was pulled out of the back; as he resisted he heard several shots in the background as the guard fired at the assailants and they fired back.

Within seconds he had been bundled into the back of the van, his legs tied with cord, his arms bound behind him and tape stuck across his mouth. The van drove off at speed onto the main road. It had all happened in less than a minute.

Lying in extreme discomfort on the rattling metal floor of the transit van, with two hooded men pointing guns at him, Deepak struggled to make sense of what had happened. His bodyguard presumably dead? Driver? Probably also dead. He was still alive; and had his captors wanted him dead, they had had ample opportunity already. Kidnap was the obvious explanation; there had been several cases in the past of Bollywood stars and rich individuals, or their children, being abducted in this way. He was certainly worth a lot more alive than dead. Or, conceivably, they had something seriously unpleasant in store for him, like the late Mr Patel.

After a journey of fifteen minutes or so – still well within the city limits, he reckoned – they turned onto a rougher track. Judging by the hubbub of human noise and the smells, savoury and unsavoury, penetrating the vehicle, they were trundling slowly into the heart of a crowded slum. Eventually the vehicle came to a halt. Deepak was blindfolded, then dragged out of the back and brought into what he judged by the echo to be a substantial building with a concrete floor, set aside from the main part of the community. His blindfold was removed and he was thrown into a side room, on the floor, still bound.

His captors – he guessed half a dozen – slammed the door and left him, bruised and terrified, in the dark.

<hr />

Kate's mind was in turmoil. She hadn't slept on the overnight flight to India and she filled the time watching films, not really concentrating. She had received a call from Deepak's sister Veena very early in the morning, explaining that a few hours earlier Deepak had been abducted. The police knew where he was and had a building surrounded. Negotiations were taking place. But his captors were violent and irrational. No one could say when the crisis would come to an end. Veena knew how Deepak felt about Kate and wanted her to be properly informed. Kate decided on the spot to go out to India and booked the evening flight. She then had a tense conversation with Jonathan, explaining that there was an 'emergency', unspecified, and she would be gone for several days; he would be in charge of the girls. An indignant Stella was told that she would have to cope with the weekly advice surgery on her own. Polly, the researcher, was entrusted with the job of tactfully fielding other queries and manufacturing excuses.

As she tried to compose her thoughts, she was prepared for the fact that Deepak might be dead when she arrived in Mumbai. Another part of her toyed with the idea of a successful rescue and a future in India: the life behind her was a mess, both her marriage and her short political career. In front of her was the possibility at least of real love allied to useful work with her business associates. But she had her daughters and the umbilical cord was long and strong. Nor did she really want to run away from failure. Now, altogether more alarming outcomes seemed more plausible than a romantic ending.

On arrival she went to the airport information desk where Mr Parrikar's driver would collect her. When she arrived at the desk she was approached by an attractive but tearful young woman who introduced herself as 'Bunty' Bomani, Deepak's PA. She spoke very quickly, full of emotion, and tried to explain the sequence of events of Deepak's abduction. Kate was to come to the family residence where the rest of the Parrikars were assembled.

The driver, whom she had last met on her late night tryst, was uninjured and had recovered sufficiently to drive her there. The morning traffic was no worse than normal and they made reasonable time. But Kate was not remotely interested in the passing scenery. This was the latest big emotional shock in a few weeks – the riot, the discovery of her affair, her departure from government, now this – the worst of all.

Her first four decades of life had been largely free of trauma. She had lost her father in her twenties but he had been a rather distant figure and when he, metaphorically, disappeared beneath the waves, the waters had closed over him remarkably quickly. There was childbirth, yes, but compared to some of her friends, it had been smooth and uncomplicated. No major illnesses. Healthy, normal, children. A love life, until very recently, satisfactory if nothing much more, or less. She realised that she would need to pull herself together when she met Deepak's family. But in the car she let herself go. Bunty took her hand and they wept together. It seemed obvious that Bunty also had an attachment beyond the professional but Kate did not need or want to probe.

When they arrived at the Parrikar home on Malabar Hill, the drive was full of cars and there were a couple of police vans and uniformed and armed men standing around or communicating through walkie-talkies. A crowd of onlookers was gathering at the gate: people who sensed, from the activity, that something untoward was taking place. She saw in the gardens the incongruous but remarkable sight of a peacock in full display: a timeless courting ritual rather wasted on the preoccupied human audience.

Kate was ushered into the house, a luxurious bungalow overlooking the city and bay below. She had remembered enough of her visit preparation to offer a Namaste to the elderly couple in front of her whom she took to be the parents: a shrunken, crumpled, unshaven, toothless man in pyjamas and an equally diminutive elderly lady in a cotton sari who insisted on trying to stand to greet her despite obvious pain and frailty.

Kate had discussed at some length with Deepak, in happier times, how she should be introduced to the family; but of course he wasn't here. There was an awkward silence and, then, a pretty woman in a sharp Western business suit stepped forward. Veena, the sister. She took command of the situation switching effortlessly between cut-glass English, which would only have come from an expensive private school education in the UK, and the language understood by her parents. She introduced Kate to the other people in the room including a rather silent brother and took her to a side room – 'operational HQ' – where a policeman was simultaneously fielding several mobile phone calls while his two assistants waited for instructions.

'This is Inspector Mankad,' Veena explained. 'He is helping us and understands the background to Deepak's abduction. There is a SWAT team surrounding his place of captivity but the Inspector is liaising with us on a ransom demand.'

Veena steered Kate by the elbow to a quiet corner of the big room where the parents and others were gathered. Kate had time to notice the beautiful, thick, handwoven carpets and the stunning artefacts of brass and wood that would have cost a fortune in a London gallery. No one was in a mood for conversation but Veena offered to explain what she could of the background.

'I don't know how much Deepak has told you?'

'A bit,' Kate responded. 'The murder of this Patel. Exposure of the family's business secrets. Then the trouble at the factory. An American company called Global and a man… Desai? There is a link with Global in the UK where it has been trying to take over the company that was to be Deepak's business partner. I had a rather exciting visit there, which you may know about. But, to be frank, I have only a hazy understanding of what is going on here and Deepak seemed too preoccupied to give me the full story.'

Veena began her explanation. 'You have the bare bones. There is a shadowy organisation, basically a criminal gang, in Mumbai called Trishul. Has its roots in the murky world where the militant, more fanatical nationalists and religious fundamentalists, who are now a big force in politics, and growing, overlap with the criminal underworld. Politicians and criminals have always fed off each other in this city, as they often do in other countries, but the sectarian element is particularly poisonous now. Goondas – as we call them – think that, if they wave a saffron flag, they will get immunity. Perhaps they are right.

'Our friend the Inspector – who is actually a lot smarter than he looks – has a handle on how the Trishul gang or gangs work. They have been muscling in on several well-established companies like Daddy-ji's making demands for protection money. Control over land and property gives them leverage and the construction industry is notoriously corrupt. This, in turn, attracts the politicians who need money for elections. The Trishul gang has been building up its network of political friends from an extreme Hindu nationalist party in this part of India, and related groups:

some of them religious extremists. One clever ploy, however, was to work through the Sheikh, a Muslim who was vulnerable to pressure because of his family connections in Pakistan and was also close to Daddy-ji.

'But there is another level to the Trishul operation that lifts it beyond the mafia-type outfits we are used to. There is some kind of link up with like-minded people at a national level, in politics, the armed forces and the intelligence services. The extremists have been hard at work in the last few weeks fanning the flames of Indo-Pak conflict – you have seen the news, and read the papers. One of the key figures is the man called Desai who is at the centre of a web of these political, intelligence and military people in Delhi. He is also involved in that US company, Global. This group dreamed up the idea of using the Sheikh's connections to bring in and set up a Pakistani agent leading to the exposure of a "sabotage plot", raising tension between our countries another notch. Deepak was in their way and – anyway – these people despise his secular, liberal, Western values.

'Deepak alerted his friends in Delhi – there are a lot of them already alarmed by the drift in Indian politics. They made the mistake of placing too much faith in the leading family. "Madam", like your Mrs Thatcher, was tough as old boots but her grandchildren and their hangers-on are absolutely clueless. Some of them are deeply corrupt. Deepak was one of a group of businessmen financing a secular "front"' to mobilise opposition. His own experiences in Mumbai were featured in a big exposé in the weekly *India Today*. He said too much; mentioned Desai; implied that the Pakistani spy was set up. There are some things you don't say even in a democracy like ours. Now this… which we think is connected but aren't sure.'

Veena hadn't paused for breath. But, for the first time Kate could see how the pieces of the jigsaw fitted together including her own small corner. Veena turned away but Kate could sense that she was trying to compose herself to maintain the front of business-like conversation. But it was clear, from the way Veena clenched her fists and dug her fingernails into the palms of her hands, that the calmness was a façade that might soon crumble. After a deep breath, Veena took up the story again.

'Deepak was seized by an armed gang yesterday on his way to the factory. The gang who took him have been tracked down to a slum area quite near here and are surrounded. Inspector Mankad's working theory is that it is a group related to the gang who killed Mr Patel and also linked to the extreme ultra-nationlist party. He knows where they hang out and, sure enough, the gang were seen there unloading a bound man from a van. It seems to have been a thoroughly clumsy operation or perhaps they didn't expect to have a competent and honest police officer on the case. Anyway, a team of paramilitaries has taken over and we are praying that they get Deepak out alive.'

Kate could see that Veena was now close to breaking point and they lapsed into a long silence, broken only by the shuffle of servants and the clink of glasses as tumblers were refilled with an inexhaustible supply of lime juice. An hour passed. Two. Then as evening approached on the second day of the crisis Inspector Mankad emerged from his room. 'Something is happening soon,' he announced. 'Our men are surrounding a building where he is. I want someone from the family…' Kate realised that he could mean identification of a corpse. She wasn't sure she had the stomach for what was coming. But when Veena stepped forward and announced that she would go with the police, Kate insisted on joining her.

The procession of police vehicles made its way through the city led by motorcycle outriders. The journey was nonetheless infuriatingly slow through streets jammed with pedestrians, cycles, motorbikes, rickshaws, mopeds, buses, cars and animals. The sirens and flashing lights of the police helped a little but they were just part of the urban cacophony and kaleidoscope and the crowds parted only slowly and reluctantly.

After what seemed an eternity they arrived on a road surrounded by a sea of shacks spreading to the horizon in each direction: the townscape of Dharavi and the neighbouring slums. There was a helicopter hovering a hundred yards away with a searchlight penetrating the gathering dusk and the fog of woodsmoke. And people everywhere with police trying and failing to marshal them behind an official-looking tape. Kate could see the excitement on the faces of the adults and the wide-eyed wonder of the children: better than the cinema, and free. And unlike the communal troubles of recent days, this drama could be watched in safety.

Kate and Veena were told to stay with their police car and not to come close to the action. Tension grew with the crowds building up, the noise level rising. Then, suddenly, there was the dull thud of an explosion, a brief crackle of gunfire and a plume of smoke rose from somewhere beneath the probing light of the helicopter. The crowd gaped and then cheered, but whether supporting the police or the putative villains wasn't clear.

After a few minutes a senior police officer beckoned to them to follow him into the settlement. They passed through narrow lanes, trying to step over rather than into the open sewers and avoiding the mangy dogs, chickens, pigs and children. When Kate recalled these events long after, one image stuck in her mind: passing a fetid rivulet, a storm drain, and seeing a little boy, totally indifferent to the chaos and excitement around him, poking with a stick at his imaginary navy and in particular steering a large paper boat, the flagship of his fleet.

Eventually they came to a more open area on raised ground and in the middle was an extensive single storey building – a meeting hall? perhaps a school? – with smoke rising through its roof. They were directed inside where police and paramilitary officers with automatic weapons were examining several corpses splayed on the floor. No Deepak.

Kate saw that there was a side room, with a half-open door guarded by a policeman, and pushed her way inside. There was a body on the floor, inert, facing away from her, with blood covering the ears and the back of the head. She knew immediately who it was, or had been. She turned the corpse towards her to look at the familiar face and gazed at it. Then, an eyelid started to quiver. She heard the rasp of a breath. She screamed for help and heard the clatter of boots coming up behind her.

<hr>

Deepak Parrikar managed a smile through the bandages covering his head. Several times in the last few days, spent mostly unconscious, with concussion, his doctors had feared for the worst. But he came through. His injuries were still severe but no longer life threatening.

He was gradually coming to understand what had happened. In the chaotic shoot-out, a bullet had entered his body causing severe blood loss and damage to bone and muscle but missing his vital organs. The greatest damage had been done not by the bullet but by a metal rod when one of his captors had seen him try to wriggle to safety. The surgeons had nonetheless been able to heal the skull fracture and contain the swelling of the brain.

It would take some time yet for him to comprehend his new celebrity status. The raid had a television audience of millions. The narrative was stripped of its complexities: Deepak was a champion of secular values, almost killed by extremists embedded in the world of gangland. The politics of the abduction, the exposure in the national press of the links between the extremists and organised crime provided a catalyst for attempts to bring together the various secular parties and factions in a common front to fight the 2019 general election. Deepak was deified somewhat prematurely by those imagining that his soul had already ascended from its earthly capsule.

The Prime Minister, no less, had seen the value of distancing himself from his party's more violent and extreme elements and their unsavoury allies like the ultra-nationalists. He sent a message of sympathy and support to the family. The abduction and attempted murder of a leading industrialist, supposedly for political ends, outraged opinion formers in a way that casualties of recent riots and the daily suffering of countless Dalits, Muslims and Christians in village India had not. The more pragmatic elements in the ruling party had drawn the conclusion that a show, at least, of inclusive secularism was a necessary requirement to staying in office. The Prime Minister had concluded his handwritten note with a tantalising comment, that he was considering a proposal that he would shortly make to Deepak 'to play a major role in India's political life'.

The drama had affected some of the other actors too. Mr Desai had withdrawn back into the shadows. There would be time again to exploit his particular skills, his links with the Mumbai underworld and his influential American friends, But, for the moment, what was needed was a blander, more emollient face.

Inspector Mankad was lauded for his efforts even though the attempt at negotiation was confused and the wild firing of the police was responsible for several deaths and at least some of Deepak's injuries. Instead of being despatched, as he feared, to some fly-blown police station in the rural depths of Maharashtra he was rapidly promoted to Superintendent within his current command, albeit on the clear understanding that his Trishul enquiry would be limited to some of the more egregiously venal and less elevated politicians involved.

All of this and the other missing details of the last few weeks were explained to Deepak by the two women who had moved to the centre of his life. With his parents no longer able to function effectively and deeply scarred, psychologically, by recent experiences, control of the family company had effectively passed to Veena with the consent of her other, less assertive, brother, Manu. She had prised out of her father's tenacious grip most of the financial secrets of the property empire and had set about restructuring it on more conventional business lines, as well as establishing the charitable trust for her father, albeit less generously endowed than he envisaged.

Parrikar Avionics already had a strong senior management team capable of operating, at least for a while, without their CEO and without Mr Desai's unsolicited advice.

Sitting next to her was Kate who, in a short but intense period of mutual need, had become a close friend and confidante. Both the family and nursing staff insisted that her presence had led to a measurable step forward in Deepak's recovery. The same was not said of the more reluctant, dutiful, visit from Delhi of Rose Parrikar. There were months of gradual rehabilitation ahead but full recovery was now probable rather than merely possible.

※※※※※※※※※※※

Kate's visit to India was an item on the agenda of an emergency meeting of the executive committee of the Surrey Heights Conservative Association. 'I hesitate to raise this difficult issue,' said the Chairman, Sir William Beale, non-executive director of several companies and, once, a powerful figure in the City, a former Lord Mayor of London. 'But several of you have asked me to put it down for discussion. I recognise that there is a lot of feeling in the association about the behaviour of our MP in recent months. We all had such high hopes of her, especially when she became a senior figure in our government. Who would like to speak?'

Most of the members present put up their hands. 'I am absolutely disgusted,' said one, 'we might as well have a

Lib Dem or a socialist as our MP.' 'She campaigned for Remain. Just shows the contempt those people have for decent British values,' interjected another. The discussion centred initially on her wayward, rebellious voting record since she had left the government – 'sacked' insisted one of the members – and a variety of strange causes she had taken up far removed from the interests and prejudices of Surrey Heights. There was the series of parliamentary questions she had asked about a missing asylum seeker from Eritrea: 'I ask you… where the hell is that?' 'It's some rat-hole in Africa, for God's sake.' 'How many people want more asylum seekers anyway?' Then there was the infamous debate on social housing where she admitted she had been wrong to oppose more of it in her constituency: 'I suppose she wants to bring every single mother in Britain to live here.'

But these were merely the hors d'oeuvres. The main course was 'the Indian boyfriend', or 'the coloured gentleman' as one of the elderly members preferred to call him. 'I don't have anything against them myself. But I didn't expect to see our MP chasing one of them to India like some silly school girl.' 'And what about her lovely family? I have been told she now spends her time – when she is in the country – at her flat in London, not at home.'

One brooding figure had not yet spoken. Stella was still simmering with resentment after being relieved of her duties as Kate's casework officer (and the associated remuneration). She had had to make way for a bright young woman called Anne-Marie. She had started to produce letters to constituents for the MP to sign that made some sense, answered the questions asked and were not padded out with party propaganda. For this, Kate had been profoundly grateful, since Stella's letters – which Kate had given up trying to improve – had become a source of ridicule in the correspondence columns of the local press. But Anne-Marie's faultless spoken English was delivered with a French accent, the product of her childhood, and this reinforced the sense that, thanks to the MP, 'bloody foreigners' had penetrated deep into the inner sanctum of the local party at a time when Britishness was being rediscovered and continental miscegenation was being discouraged.

Stella served up her dish of revenge with icy venom. 'I think I can claim to know Mrs Thompson better than any of you. I have worked… tried to work… with her since she was elected, which some of you may remember I masterminded. She has some good points, of course, but I speak for all of us when I say I am deeply, deeply, disappointed. I felt particularly let down – actually, betrayed is what I felt – when for the first time in many, many years the MP did not turn up for our annual fete. She was, I believe, in India.' Gasps of disapproval followed.

'We can sit here and complain. Or we can do something about it. I have taken the liberty of exploring with party HQ the procedure for deselection. You may recall that, a few years ago, one of our Yorkshire MPs was deselected for not carrying out her constituency duties as she should. I have established what the procedure is and,' with a final, triumphant, flourish, 'we should *do* it.'

The nods and grunts of approval were taken by the Chairman as assent. But there was a belated objection from one of the local councillors who remembered how much enthusiasm there had been for Kate when she was first adopted. He could also claim to speak for the under-eighties in the local party and had a job – as an estate agent. 'I think we should be careful. There will be more bad publicity. The other parties will exploit it. Mrs Thompson hasn't done anything illegal or abused her expenses. Her visit was in the summer recess when other MPs were on holiday. And my wife tells me that her friends admire her for being broad-minded and an independent thinker.'

This novel thought threw the Chairman off his stride but Stella moved quickly to close the rebellion down. 'The mood of the executive is clear. I suggest we vote on a motion to convene an extraordinary meeting of members with a resolution of no confidence in our Member of Parliament.' Agreed thirteen to one, with one abstention.

<hr>

A few weeks later parliament reconvened and the National Security Council was summoned to a special meeting in the COBRA room under the Cabinet Office where Cabinet ministers, intelligence and service chiefs consider matters of exceptional sensitivity. There was one item on the agenda: aircraft carriers. The Prime Minister opened proceedings.

'Some of you were here when we last considered the future of our two new aircraft carriers, the *Queen Elizabeth* and the *Prince of Wales*. It was a mess then and it is now a bigger mess. Thanks to our dear friend Gordon Brown, whose legacy this was, we have an unnecessary, unwanted pair of white elephants. The project was designed to create thousands of new jobs not a million miles from his constituency, to keep the Scots loyal to Labour – what a joke! – and keep the Admirals happy – sorry, Chief, not you, you were probably still commanding rowing boats at the time.' Prolonged laughter followed.

'When we last looked at this, during the Coalition, some of us,' he said, looking at the then Chancellor, 'wanted to scrap the programme. We flunked it. The Scottish referendum was in the offing. The *Telegraph* ran a big campaign, prompted, I suspect, by the top brass in the navy, to keep the carriers. How could we save the Falklands again without them? A lot of wishful thinking about how the carriers could be adapted to carry the F-35 (which, of course, we hadn't bought and couldn't afford). And the frigates we would need to protect the carriers could also be built on Clydeside to provide more jobs for the Scots.

'You can guess what has happened since. All the warnings about the difficulties of adapting the F-35 to fly off the carriers proved to be spot on. The costs have escalated out of control. Then, we have had a series of own goals. The bloody Commies in Unite have been working to rule to make the job spin out longer. Then we had to agree to use British steel to avoid a scandal over our using cheap Chinese steel for the navy. Almost doubled the cost. Now, the Chancellor tells us that he can find no more money down the back of the sofa. His borrowing targets are looking worse by the week. There is no more money left.'

The Chancellor nodded in agreement while pulling a face to signal his annoyance at having his failures of financial control given such prominence.

'We will have to make some difficult choices. What I am absolutely clear about is that we cannot compromise Trident. Going ahead with the full replacement was the best decision we made after getting those wretched Lib Dems off our back. Within these four walls Trident is a complete waste of money, isn't independent and isn't a deterrent for our main enemy, the terrorists, and belongs to a bygone age. But the public and our friends in the press love it. It keeps us on the UN Security Council. And it has helped us to stuff the Labour Party.

'But, of course, it is costing us a bomb.' (Nervous laughter.) 'We thought the four subs and missiles would cost twenty billion pounds back in 2010; now we will be lucky to get away with a hundred billion. Unless we decide to abolish the army as a fighting force or put the air force back into World War Two aircraft, we have to choose: Trident or the carriers.'

The PM turned to Jim Chambers. 'Jim, I asked you to help us set out the options. What do we do?' The Business Secretary had little background in defence but enjoyed the Prime Minister's confidence. The Defence Secretary smarted at the snub but he knew he could lose his job if it emerged that he had been sitting on the cost escalation numbers for months and had done nothing about the issue; so he nodded deferentially, while Jim Chambers spoke.

'As you say, Prime Minister, it is a bloody mess. If this had happened in my businesses, heads would have rolled by now.' He looked very pointedly at the Chief of the Naval Staff, Admiral Cooke-Davis. 'But let me give my honest assessment of what we can do. Well, first, we could throw money at the project to finish it as quickly as possible and get the ships into service. We could pay for them by jettisoning not just the planes but also surface ships to defend them. Fill the decks with helicopters or something else to use the space. But, big buts. The naval people say that without planes or protection the carriers will be as much use in a fire-fight as cruise liners. We shall be slated by our own chaps on the back benches and in the press. And we shall have revolting Scots telling us we have stabbed them in the back over the frigates. So, no go.

'Second, we could pull the plug completely. Park the damn things in the Cromarty Firth with all those oil rigs. But we have gone too far for that. Her Majesty has already blessed the *Queen Elizabeth*, and the *Prince of Wales* is half built. Portsmouth is already kitted out to maintain and service them. Revolting Scots are one thing. We can't have south coast marginal seats also put at risk. And the navy and its friends in the media would crucify us. No go.

'So my recommendation is that we press on with the programme as best we can – finish equipping, build the destroyers and the frigates, buy some jets for appearance's sake. But sell the second carrier rather than keep it.'

'Who on earth will buy a carrier that we don't want and can't afford?' piped up the Scottish Secretary who hadn't been kept in the loop.

'Ah! Our people in Delhi have been talking to the Indians about this for several years,' Chambers replied. 'The Indians have a carrier building programme like us – two vessels and also horribly behind schedule and over-budget. One, the *Vaishal*, is in service; the other, *Vasant*, is years away. There is a lot of national pride involved in building their own. But the recent trouble with Pakistan has seriously rattled them. They need money to press on with missile defence. They also have the Chinese in the background with a new naval presence in the Indian Ocean. An extra carrier delivered quickly from us (at a discount!) would be timely – and they can put their converted MiGs on it, I believe.'

'Brilliant, Jim. Spot on,' the Prime Minister crowed. 'And after your recent success with the Indian missile defence project – now up and running again, I am glad to say – I have every confidence we can carry it off.'

'We did have some casualties.'

'Yes, the gorgeous Kate, poor girl. But she will get over it. You might try to use her Indian contacts – you know who I mean...'

The Chief of the Naval Staff set out all the reasons why the export proposal was a terrible idea and why the Treasury should pay for the full programme of naval modernisation. But his service colleagues pointedly declined to endorse spending commitments that would impinge on their own budgets.

It was left to the Foreign Secretary to warn of unintended consequences. 'Sorry, colleagues. Someone has to spoil the party. Even assuming the Indians want the wretched thing and can afford to pay for it – I assume we are not giving it away – we need to think about the wider implications. India and Pakistan have been involved in a confrontation that has been perilously close to war. Things are still very tense.

'Now the Chinese are involved. At Pakistan's request they have a flotilla of vessels including their own aircraft carrier circling India. We hear they may have strayed into Indian territorial waters. The Americans are seriously alarmed; this is the first time the Chinese have ventured militarily west of the Malacca Straits, in strength, since

Admiral Zheng-He went to Africa in the fifteenth century. If we get involved in fuelling an escalating naval arms race in the Indian Ocean, it could be highly destabilising. Please think again.'

'Thank you, Foreign Secretary,' the PM said with a nod. 'But I am going to have to overrule you. The rest of us are agreed – aren't we? No more Boy Scouts. It's "export or die". Post-Brexit, India is our best hope of breaking into big non-European markets. We have to get our priorities right. So, gentlemen, we are agreed. But hush-hush. I don't want to read about this meeting in the press. The Cabinet has been leaking like a paper boat recently. It must not happen again.'

<hr />

It did not take many minutes for the report of the National Security Council to reach the Red Admiral. And as soon as he could organise a secure line, calls were placed to Louisiana, Delhi, Tel Aviv and Moscow.

The Admiral's stock was already high with his business colleagues and his expected commission would go a long way to paying for the ocean-going luxury yacht now on order. The Pulsar contract, if not the bigger aircraft deal, was now agreed and waiting for a formal signature. Now a big naval project offered tantalising opportunities for Global Analysis and Research and its network of associates. The carrier would need protection against attack from aircraft and missiles and the Pulsar/Parrikar Avionics technology would be invaluable. The carrier could also take adapted MiGs, and friends in Moscow could perhaps come up with an offer the Indians would find irresistible. The flourishing, but very secret, cooperation between India and Israel could find new possibilities in upgrading India's rather antiquated naval communications system. The Admiral had learnt from experience not to get too excited or to over-promise. For that reason, he thought it better not to tell his colleagues about the progress he had made in getting Global established as a leading Tier 1 Supplier in the UK's new Trident replacement programme. But the possibilities were mouth-watering.

<hr/>

Steve and Shaida had their first row. The 'date' had proved less fulfilling than Steve, at least, had imagined: a drink after work in the chaste and discreet environment of a local coffee house. She had exaggerated her father's endorsement. She knew he would never countenance a relationship with someone who, however admired, was not merely from a different cultural tradition but was divorced, with young children. She knew that at some point she would face an awful choice, a fork in the road, that would affect her destiny for ever. She also loved her family and dreaded the thought of having to choose.

Not just that: her emotional energy was absorbed in steeling herself to snoop on her brother and his friends for the plausible, but demanding, Liam. And her mind was absorbed in unravelling the algorithms guarding Global's secrets. Even for someone as self-disciplined and capable as Shaida the strain was beginning to show.

Besides, Steve had become more distant. Since his election to the national executive of his union there had been growing numbers of absences on union business: meetings around the country as well as in London. He had explained that he was sinking under the weight of union responsibilities, the council and the local party. The meetings at the mosque had petered out: lack of time. She understood, but part of her resented being in a lengthening queue for his attention.

Then, he had proposed that she accompany him on a visit to Glasgow where he was meeting the Scottish shipyard workers.

'And what is my role? Researcher? Secretary?' Shaida asked pointedly.

'Well, I just wanted your company.'

'So, this is a double room at the Grand Central?'

'If you like.'

'As your date?'

'Well – I suppose… yes, isn't that what we both want?'

'God! Have you thought what this means? How do I explain it at home? Where do I go afterwards? Do you really know what you are asking of me?'

'I understand… sorry… I should have thought.'

'Yes, you should! I do want to come, but this is an impossible thing to ask of me.'

She could see that their relationship was fizzling out thanks to her distractions and his impatience. She decided on a make or break move: total candour.

'The truth is that you don't begin to understand what makes me tick. I think you have this idealised picture of an exotic Asian female, probably a virtuous virgin, just waiting to be set free. You couldn't be further from the truth. I am tempted to shatter your illusions.'

'Try me.'

'OK. But you won't like what you hear.'

'I'll risk it.'

'Where do I start? Well, at school I was gifted and marked out for higher things: a girl who loved maths. The trouble began when I wanted to be a normal British teenager. Fooled around with my girlfriends. Experimented. One night I got totally plastered. Somehow got to bed avoiding my parents. Then boys. Had my first sexual encounter at – what? – fifteen, maybe less. Then one day on my desk at school there was a Pakistani newspaper with a picture of a girl, my age, disfigured by acid burns. Someone had written across it in red ink "SLAG". Someone from my community had been spying on me.

'My parents got to hear about some of this and I was on the next plane to Pakistan to find a husband. One of my uncles tried to marry me off to a disgusting old man with dyed ginger hair who spat all over the place. My dad – bless him – took pity on me and I was allowed to come back on the strict understanding that I stuck to my books. I did. Got a place at Cambridge. But the family thought this was too high a risk so I finished up doing accounting at the local uni.

'Didn't stop me. I had a series of affairs. Very discreet. A group of Asian girls worked together to organise safe rooms and generally help each other. The nearest thing I had to a proper relationship was with a post-grad Israeli, a soldier with a family back home. I got used to living dangerously and enjoyed the thrill of it. Aren't you shocked?' Shaida looked challengingly at Steve, who knew it was now his turn to open up.

'A different world from mine. I left school at sixteen to care for my dying mother. Never went to university. Then married my childhood sweetheart. When you were discovering yourself at college I was helping – or usually not helping – bring up three toddlers. I lost myself in politics and union work, not affairs.'

'It gets worse,' Shaida replied. 'When I left uni and came here I wanted – needed – to continue my double life. A friend told me about internet dating. Sex without strings. So whenever I feel like it, I ask for permission to go to a "seminar" or "training course" in London and meet a man. Some bad experiences; mostly OK. I enjoy the control. At home I am a meek, submissive female lacking only a husband. I realise this can't go on; deep down I am not a

cold person. But I must have turned you off completely?'
Shaida studied Steve's face closely for his reaction.

'No. I suspected there was a lot more to you than meets
the eye. And since my marriage broke down I haven't
exactly been celibate either.'

'That's a relief.' They smiled at each other, glad that they
had shared their personal stories at last.

That night Shaida did not sleep: not just because of her
own conflicts of loyalty and identity, which had led to this
crisis point in her personal life, but because of growing
worries about her brother's slide back into the clutches
of his militant friends.

⬚⬚⬚⬚⬚⬚⬚⬚⬚⬚⬚⬚⬚

Steve's mind was also in turmoil after this exchange. He
adored her still, but her coquettish playfulness, alternating
between Miss Brisk and her affectionate teasing, so that
she was always just out of range, had become deeply
frustrating. And while he thought he could live with
the newly revealed Shaida it would require a degree of
emotional maturity he had never achieved before. He
could see that, short of a dramatic break with her family,
nothing would ever happen and the love affair would
gradually burn itself out, unconsummated.

There was frustration on other fronts too. The union
election was initially very satisfying: a recognition of his
talents on a national stage. But the sudden switch from

being a big fish in a small pond to swimming in the sea of national union politics was proving exceptionally difficult.

His brushes with Brother Harking should have warned him that his youth, moderate Labour politics, south of England accent and manufacturing background put him in a small minority. The General Secretary was a hardened militant who had built up a fearsome reputation for skilful organisation and bloody-minded negotiating techniques. This 'young lad', closer to Mandelson than Marx, was not exactly welcome.

And the talk around the table about the problems of nurses, council officers, bus drivers and Whitehall civil servants meant very little. He had one soulmate and he was dying of cancer: the gaunt figure of Kevin Dubbins, the legendary negotiator for the car industry whose guile and pragmatism was a key factor in attracting and keeping investment in Britain. All this, his tiff with Shaida, his ex-wife's demands, and, now, another decision that was looming: whether to pursue the vacancy for a parliamentary candidate to replace the retiring local MP, a window of opportunity that might not be open in future.

To clear his head, he decided to walk downtown after supper. He instinctively headed to the part of town where Shaida lived, one of the middle class, increasingly Asian, districts with well-tended, detached and semi-detached houses and expensive cars. Perhaps in his subconscious he hoped he would see Shaida and be able to signal his continuing commitment to her. He saw the house ahead and stopped, realising that his presence, if seen, would be difficult to explain to her parents. As he waited a familiar figure left the house, head covered by a shawl, and made off in the opposite direction.

Curiosity as well as animal magnetism drew him after her. After ten minutes of fast walking she headed towards an unlit piece of open ground and sat on one of the benches. A figure emerged from the shadows and sat down beside her. A man who looked, from a distance, vaguely familiar. He saw them in close conversation until they stood up to go. She handed over a small package and then they walked off in opposite directions. Sexual jealousy was in danger of dominating his emotional response especially after what he now knew of her private life. But the couple showed no signs of affection and his attempt to fit the shape of the man into his database of physical profiles came up with a name that suggested something quite different from romance: Liam, the MI5 officer. This was something that hadn't formed part of her full and frank disclosure.

CHAPTER 14

REHABILITATION

Reuters, 3 September 2019:

There are uncorroborated reports of a major explosion having taken place several weeks ago in the naval shipyards in Kerala. Commentators speculate that, if there has been disruption to the aircraft carrier building programme, it would help to explain the rumours that the Indian navy is looking at overseas options for a new carrier, regarded as essential to counter the build-up of Chinese as well as Pakistani forces in the Indian Ocean theatre. Commentators have also linked the reported explosion to the Iqbal Aziz trial, warning that Pakistani terrorist cells are still active in India.

The Prime Minister summoned the National Security Council to hear a report back from the High Commissioner, via Skype, on his round of discussions in Delhi about the aircraft carrier.

'We are here to brainstorm,' said the PM. 'Unless we crack this we are left with some pretty gory alternatives. Secretary of State? You came up with this idea in the first place.'

'Well,' Jim Chambers replied, 'we can obviously cut the price or throw in some sweeteners, give them an offer they can't refuse. In effect, give the carrier away.'

The Chancellor and the Defence Secretary both grimaced. The former spoke first. 'We can't be too cavalier. The Public Accounts Committee will be all over us like a rash. I can see the terrible headlines at this distance. And I have to balance the books – there will be a serious hit on the MOD budget.' The Chiefs of Staff also grimaced.

'Jim, back to you.'

'I have had one idea for trying to shift the debate in India. That man Parrikar who was the conduit for the last deal is now a big player. I don't know if you have been following events there but Parrikar has become some kind of hero. Shot up by a gang with connections to the extreme nationalist politicians. Now in hospital recovering from his injuries. If he were to endorse the deal, appeal to his secular friends not to embarrass the government, it might help. High Commissioner? I believe you have market-tested this idea in Delhi and it plays well.'

'Yes, Secretary of State. But the man is in a bad way. Out of danger but still in intensive care. Not sure if the family will welcome dragging him back into controversy.'

'There we have an ace card,' Chambers responded. 'Our Mrs Thompson. Currently giving our whips hell and threatened with deselection. She can reach the parts that others can't.' Jokes were not common currency in the National Security Council but he had made his point. 'We can give her a political lifeline. Back to her former glory, serving the country. Back to being Minister of State? Special envoy? Trade ambassador? Foreign policy Tsar? Whatever.'

The Prime Minister didn't look convinced. 'It's a bit weak. Clutching at straws. But I guess we don't have too many other options. Can I leave this to you, Jim? You know the girl better than I do.'

<hr />

Steve had agonised for several days about how to raise with Shaida her link to the British intelligence services. He didn't want to acknowledge that he had been following her, late at night, around the town. That would appear distrustful and he found it impossible to explain to himself, let alone her, what had taken hold of him that night. He thought back to the violent clashes he had seen from his office window in the town hall, which could give him a reason to talk to her at their next lunch break.

'Has Mo fully recovered now? He looked a bit of a mess after that demo.'

'Looked worse than it was. But the experience has radicalised him further. "Why didn't the police protect us?" he asks. He genuinely didn't go to make trouble and he could see that the agitators were deliberately winding up the crowd. But being kicked in the head by British "patriots" in a peaceful demonstration has brought him closer to his radical friends. It is a pity you're no longer taking an interest in him,' Shaida said, looking Steve straight in the eye.

'Yes, I am sorry. I could and should have done more. And I promise I will. But can he not see that he is heading for disaster? His card has already been marked by the authorities – who, incidentally, were filming the demo. After the recent wave of arrests, he is only one or two moves from joining them. I haven't told you this, but a man from the security services, Liam, approached me for information about Mo and his group. I believe you contacted him after that article, to clear Mo's name. I was wondering whether he has been on to you or your family since then.'

She hesitated before answering. 'Since we confide in each other and – hopefully – still trust each other, I can tell you what I am not supposed to divulge even to my nearest and dearest. That man Liam told me that if I wanted to keep the family out of trouble, especially Mo, I should keep in regular touch and inform him of anything I pick up. I don't enjoy being a sneak but it is something I have to do.'

Her words understated the pain she felt. Until now, she had successfully juggled her different identities without ever having to really choose. Now she was being forced to, and it hurt.

'Is there anything happening I should know about?' Steve asked.

'Nothing much you don't know already. But please understand: I can't say any more. I have probably said too much already.'

He held her hand for a few minutes before heading back to his work station, but before he left she added: 'Sometimes I think he is right.'

'You mean Liam?'

'No, not Liam. Never mind. Let's leave it.'

<hr />

Kate received a handwritten letter from her former Secretary of State – 'My dearest Kate… Yours affectionately, Jim' – asking if she would drop by his parliamentary office for a 'catch up'. Having settled into the mind-set of a fully paid-up and thoroughly alienated rebel she was naturally suspicious. And their last serious encounter bore all the hallmarks of his political cynicism: the scapegoating of the innocent night watchman, now disappeared; the backdoor takeover of Pulsar by an American company with some very questionable connections; the side-lining of the talented if idiosyncratic Scottish CEO; the cheerful disregard for the wider consequences of throwing more fuel onto a smouldering Asian fire. Still, the tone of the letter suggested that he wanted something from her: much the safest position to start from. And she was curious.

She went to his office after the last vote of the evening, along the gloomy ministerial corridor where Cabinet ministers held court when not at their departmental desks. Away from the prying eyes and twitching ears of civil servants, this was where the serious, political business of government got done.

'Oh my dear! I am so sorry. How have you been?' Chambers rushed up to plant a kiss on both cheeks, which she accepted before retreating to a safer distance.

'Actually, I am quite enjoying being myself and getting to know something about the interesting characters in this place,' she answered truthfully.

'But I know you have been through hell, Kate. Problems at home. Your Indian friend shot and badly injured. I hear your local association has been making your life difficult too. The awful press.'

'I am coping. But I'm sure you didn't invite me here to offer a shoulder to cry on. I get a sense that you want something.'

'Well, just let's say I think we can help each other.'

She grimaced rather than smiled, and hoped he was taking in her cynical detachment.

'My last experience of helping each other ended with you smelling of roses and me face down in the dung heap.'

'Not quite. But I realise I do owe you. Let me tell you what I can do to help you and then I will tell you what you can do for me.'

'Sounds suspicious. But I'm all ears.'

'For a start, I can get the local Tories off your back. I know Beale, your chair. Not the sharpest knife in the drawer. And a bit past it. But a decent cove. We can help him steer any motion against you into a procedural cul-de-sac.'

'Not sure I care any more.'

'That's silly. You have real talent. People instinctively like and trust you; not many politicians have that. You speak well. Look good. I don't want you to go to waste. And the PM agrees; if we try to rehabilitate you, he will do whatever is needed. And there is something else, more personal.'

Curiosity was beginning to overcome her defensiveness. She waited a few seconds to suppress any sign of eagerness and then encouraged him to go on. 'Such as…?'

'Look, I don't know what the situation at home is. None of my business. Whether you go back to your husband, John, isn't it?'

'Jonathan.'

'Yes, of course, Jonathan. Or ditch him for your Indian friend. It's for you to decide. I am not a marriage guidance counsellor. But I can sense that he is an angry man. Humiliated. Any bloke would be. Maybe we can make him less angry. It would help in any settlement you reach. Money. Access to the children, that kind of thing.'

'I know you have great political skills, Jim. But how on earth do you propose to perform a miracle of anger management on my estranged husband?'

'The Honours System.'

Kate laughed. 'Jonathan is quite vain and status conscious but I can't see an OBE or MBE meaning much to him.'

'I was thinking more of something else. The Lords. I understand that he has been a party donor – not premier league, but generous. And we need people to restore political balance. All those Lib Dems after the Coalition. Then we hoped that when the hard left took over the Labour Party they would stop demanding more. Not so. Every time there is a threatened strike on the tube or the trains we are told that some Fred Bloggs has to be given a peerage. They see it as a rest home for the Labour aristocracy. So, we need more credible Tories. Jonathan, as far as I know, isn't gaga, isn't a certified crook and isn't a foaming-at-the-mouth nutter. We should be able to line this up. Would it help you if it was made clear, privately, that this was all your doing, fighting his corner?'

'I suppose I shouldn't be shocked any more,' Kate answered. 'And I suppose I should be grateful that you have taken the trouble to research what is needed to get me on board. What exactly is it you want me to do?'

'India again. Continuation of what you were doing. This time an aircraft carrier. You are our emissary – we can call you whatever you like including your old role, or some posh new title. Make it clear that you are thoroughly rehabilitated.'

'That's a bit sick, isn't it? Palming off our unwanted weapons like that. I take it you read the newspapers – about how close the subcontinent has been to a new war.'

'Now, don't go all moral on me. We have to earn our living like any other country. The Indians are grown up. Not a colony any more. A big power these days.'

'I know all that. I am not a sentimental pacifist and I know everyone else does it. But—'

'Look, Kate,' Jim interrupted, 'this country became great on the back of trade in slaves and opium. We shouldn't have a fit of conscience about what we are doing.'

'I'm not. But let's get back to what you want of me. Just another visit to make the case for our ships?'

'Not quite. Your friend has a role too.'

'How? He was – if you remember – almost killed. Still on the danger list, if no longer critical. His sister, Veena, is actually running the company.'

'Well, when he is able to communicate, we would like him to signal his support for this contract. His stock, I understand, is very high at the moment. Also, encourage his secular friends in the opposition not to oppose too vigorously. The technical stuff we can handle through the High Commission; we now have answers to most of the tricky questions. It's the politics we have to get right. There will be quite a lot of work coming his way as well.'

'When I last saw Deepak he was a long way from anything taxing. I hope this proposition isn't time specific.'

'There is a decision point in a month. But I am sure we can be flexible.'

Kate thought for a moment. 'And if I come back, even as a trade envoy rather than a minister, do I get my old private office team? I was just getting used to them and I trusted them, until you lot decided to get rid of me.'

'Won't happen again. Promise you. And, of course, your team. We'll find a way round the rules and regulations. Parsons will do the necessary.'

'I am also concerned about what happened last time. The way that Eritrean night watchman was made the scapegoat. The way the dodgy American company finished up running the show.'

'Ah! I knew you would ask me about that. Your contacts, whoever they were, got the wrong end of the stick. I asked the Admiral to look into it. He knew the set-up there. Knew the people.'

'I'm not sure I find that completely reassuring. The Admiral gives me the creeps. Up to no good.'

Jim shook his head. 'My dear girl, you have got him all wrong. A bloody hero. Not just in the navy. His salesmanship – getting the armed forces of the world fitted out with British kit – has created more jobs than all the theories of John-bloody-Maynard Keynes put together. But I know he ruffles feathers. I have already made him apologise to the civil servants. And I'd tell him to keep out of your hair.'

She stood still for a while, taking in how far she had retreated in a few moments from her initial show of cool indifference. Chambers had a special talent, she grudgingly admitted to herself.

'This is a lot to take in. Both what you are offering and what you are asking me to do. Let me sleep on it.'

'That's fine. I half expected you to walk out and slam the door. Can't ask any more, my girl.'

She stiffened but decided not to take the bait.

Even before she left the room Kate knew what her answer would be. Part of her detested the squalid, amoral world she was still part of. If she was a Christian or a socialist she would be indignant, walk away and campaign for a better, nicer world. But she wasn't and couldn't be, either. Or she could quietly disappear back to her family, her friends and her Indian textiles business, perhaps even her lover, a little older, a lot wiser, and put her recent experiences behind her.

But the stronger part of her had no intention of escaping. She had been hurt and humiliated but it was through her own naïvety and clumsiness – and bad luck. 'Don't get mad, get even' was a slogan she approved of. She would get even. Show she wasn't a loser, a weak woman.

To make a success of the second coming she needed a Praetorian Guard that would watch her back and prevent the wrong people getting too close. Susan was crucial. She also needed someone who could deal with the media, do the spinning that high-minded people disapproved of but was what communication was all about.

Then there was the couple from the factory – or perhaps they weren't a couple. The union and Labour man. She would need a line into the opposition and the labour force. And the Asian accountant. As someone usually described as 'handsome' or 'attractive', she had been conscious of being in the presence of a genuinely beautiful woman. And she had been taken with her poise and sharp intelligence: more than the man, she thought, who was given to using five words where one would do, like many politicians. Kate wasn't going to be blind-sided again by not knowing enough about Deepak's British business partners. She would set up meetings with them before the formalities kicked in.

When Steve arrived at Calum's office for a debrief, his way was barred by a formidable woman, large and loud, with a mid-Atlantic accent.

'May I ask you what you are doing here?'

'I have come to see the CEO.'

'Do you have an appointment?'

'We agreed that I would call in first thing this morning.'

'Not in the diary. Your name?'

'Steve Grant. And may I ask who you are?'

'Gill Travers. I am part of the new Global executive team. And you are?'

'Gill. My union represents the workforce here and I still have regular access to Calum.'

'The company is considering whether and how consultation with employee organisations will take place in future. The new owners may wish to change things. We have generally managed without unions in our other operations. Can I also point out, Mr Grant, that you are not wearing a name badge? As from the beginning of this week company policy is that name badges should be worn at all times; by employees as well as visitors.'

'And Mr Mackie? Is he free?'

'No, he is busy. But I can text you with a meeting time. You should in the meantime go to the HR department to collect your name badge and complete a security questionnaire.'

'Security questionnaire? I have been here for over a decade.'

'I understand that there were some serious security issues here. You will know that better than me. We have now introduced the same rigorous procedures we employ in the rest of the group.'

Steve could see that his role as union representative might be in jeopardy with a company unsympathetic to unions. He reminded himself that the reason why he had progressed so rapidly and enjoyed such esteem was the patronage of his boss – now outgoing, it seemed. Pulsar was an enclave of unionism in a private sector increasingly characterised by short-term employment contracts and tokenistic employee participation schemes. He would have to tread carefully.

And in his short absence, he had also found himself in the middle of an impending national storm. He had gone to meet union representatives and organisers in the defence industry in Scotland. As one of only two delegates on the national executive with an engineering background – the other being the ailing Kevin Dubbins – he had been given a rapid immersion in a potentially toxic issue. Rumours were flying about that the aircraft carrier programme reaching its end in Rosyth and the linked frigate programme on the Clyde were in trouble: that the government was thinking of pulling the plug on some or all of it. When he had arrived to meet his union colleagues in Edinburgh and Glasgow there had been an acrid atmosphere, full of suspicion and accusation with cross-cutting themes of Scottish nationalism and socialist militancy. He realised that he badly needed advice. And Calum Mackie, now on his way out and surrounded by gatekeepers provided by his successors, was the obvious source of good advice. But those gatekeepers stood in the way.

He completed the checks he needed to qualify for his name badge – conducted by an earnest young woman who stuck religiously to her script and treated him as if he had just walked in off the street. Then, he took the familiar route through the finance department. Shaida was in her office, clearly not concentrating and in some distress. He invited himself inside the, now familiar, glass office.

'What is it?' he asked with concern, discreetly taking her hand.

'Mo. He has gone. Didn't come back home last night. He took a knapsack and a few personal things. Vanished. No message. Nothing.'

'Who knows about it?'

'I notified Liam on an emergency number he gave me. No one else. Oh my God! He has gone off to fight. Do something mad. I know it.'

Steve wanted to embrace her, but with the Three Witches in the background itching with curiosity and Gill Travers waiting in the wings, he could do nothing to comfort her.

<hr />

The latest domestic crisis had distracted Shaida from what had become a difficult and complex but satisfying task: integrating the accounting systems of Pulsar and Global. The old saw that Britain and America were divided by a common language applied, in spades, to accounting. Superficial similarities masked a wide variety of different conventions and standards. She realised also that the Americans were much less casual about data security. The endless checking of passwords was tiresome but the opening up of blocked passages started to give her a bigger picture of how the group operated. She had been playing with computers and solving mathematical puzzles pretty much since she had left her cot, and it wasn't long before she was able to walk round the secret gardens that the top US management had designed for their own private convenience. Liam, who really understood these things, would be very impressed.

CHAPTER 15

THE TRADE ENVOY

Press Association, 10 September 2019:

At a US State Department press conference, the Secretary of State produced satellite photographs showing what appeared to be movements of troops and carriers of short-range missiles with what could be battlefield nuclear weapons at several points along the Indo-Pak frontier. He appealed to both sides to step back from a 'dangerous confrontation'.

China's President Ji has also offered to mediate. Reaffirming his support for Pakistan's 'historic claims' in relation to Kashmir, he also expressed support, for the first time, for India's 'fully justified stance against terrorism'. He stated that China would 'do everything in its power' to prevent conflict.

Steve was leaving parliament after a lobby of MPs on behalf of his industry, faced with a new round of defence cuts. He felt a pat on his arm. It was that Tory MP – Kate what's-her-name. She gave him a slight, conspiratorial smile and said: 'I think we need to talk.'

'How did you know I was here?'

'Never mind. Not important. Just follow me.'

She signalled to him to follow her up a spiral staircase to the upper floor where she found an empty committee room. Its pervasive sense of gloom, like many rooms on the parliamentary estate, was deepened by a dark Victorian portrait of MPs – all men and seemingly all bearded – engaged in debate.

'Sorry about the cloak and dagger,' Kate began. 'But I am back in government and I need to talk to you, strictly off the record. Our last meeting had mixed results for both of us. I realised then that there is something seriously fishy about the company Global. It has now, as you know, taken over your firm and seems to be spreading its tentacles everywhere. I expect to be dealing with them again in my new role.'

'But how can I help?' Steve asked. 'Global seems to be firmly in charge now and they have the blessing of government. They don't want me. I am on the way out.'

'I don't know how you can help. Maybe you can't. But I need to have one or two people outside government whom I can trust and to whom I can turn for advice and perhaps help. I also want to make contact with your colleague Shaida Khan. Perhaps you can help me set that up.'

'OK. But meeting is difficult. How do I get through your ministerial defences?'

'We can't meet publicly. I have learnt from painful experience that in a high-profile political job I am under more scrutiny than I thought possible. And, however much we have in common, you know that, in both our parties, the greatest crime is fraternisation with the tribal enemy. But there is a way. My private secretary, Susan, has your contact details and these are hers.' She handed over a note. 'Let's keep in touch.'

Steve was left to find his own way out of the parliamentary labyrinth. But if all went to plan he would soon be here in his own right.

Kate landed in Delhi the following morning on the mission agreed with the Secretary of State. It was clear, soon after arrival, that this would be a difficult visit. The High Commissioner was bristling with irritation that he had been misrepresented in London by ministers looking for a way of lessening the pain of defence cuts. Yes, he had said that a carrier sale was 'possible'; but his many qualifications and negatives had been studiously ignored. He was hardened by three years of battering on the Indian door for big arms contracts that had delivered little. Kate Thompson, Indian Trade Envoy, would have to discover for herself that the warm Indian words and friendly reminiscences about life in the UK were usually a prelude to disappointment.

And so it proved. The Prime Minister, the Finance Minister, the Commerce Minister and the Defence Minister were all busy. But, since Mrs Thompson was such an important and valued visitor, a key government adviser, Dr Sanjivi Desai, would be able to see her. She had heard from Deepak about Desai's extreme nationalist and anti-Muslim views, and his seemingly sinister role in Deepak's company. She was intrigued.

His office was Spartan and small by ministerial standards. There was none of the clutter and endless coming and going she was becoming used to. Everything was spotless and meticulously organised: neat and fastidious like its occupant.

'Dear Mrs Thompson – Minister?' Desai began.

'Trade Envoy.'

'Much more important. Delighted to have you back in the country. I am told you cut quite a dash with my colleagues on your last visit.'

'It was certainly a successful visit. Paved the way to an agreement that will hopefully strengthen your anti-missile defences and provide the UK with valuable exports.'

'Absolutely. But tell me more about how things are in the UK. As you will know I was an engineering student at Cambridge before I went to the US. Always go up to the alma mater whenever I can.'

'I was at the other place.'

'Poor you. But no hard feelings. What can I do for you?'

'Aircraft carriers.'

'Ah yes. I was warned that you would raise this issue. The High Commissioner already knows where things stand. Our philosophy is "buyers' navy to builders' navy". But the building of the second of the new class of Indian carriers – the *Vaishal*, a nuclear-powered, state of the art ship – is delayed. Because we feel threatened by the rapid build-up of the Chinese navy, as well as our old friends in Pakistan, we want to plug a gap in our defences, quickly.'

'I think that is where we can help.'

'Help from our British friends is always very welcome. But let me take you through our options. First, the Americans: now that India is an economic, political and military superpower we have developed a close relationship with the superpower that most closely aligns with our national interests: the USA. The Americans understand the Chinese threat in a way that – with respect – you may not; we keep reading about Britain's close friendship with President Ji and his Communist regime. The Americans have a clear-headed view about the threats posed by China and also about the threats posed by militant Islam. I know Western intellectuals make fun of President Trump. We don't. We admire his clear thinking. And the Americans now have a production line of carriers following *Gerald R Ford* and *John F Kennedy*, very much along the lines of our requirements.

'And if that doesn't work, we have our longstanding Russian friends. Never let us down – Soviet or post-Soviet. I don't want to be rude, Mrs Thompson, but your country has a less than stellar record when it comes to supplying us in our hour of need. And we respect Putin. Proud of his country. Good man. Taught those Chechens a lesson. We, of course, are a proper democracy and can't deal with Kashmiri subversives in that way. I should add that the Russians also have surplus carriers that can take MiG-29s, our fighters of choice.'

Kate was wilting under the barrage and the High Commissioner was, conspicuously, leaving it to her to defend her near-impossible brief.

'I think you will find we can more than match whatever the US and Russia can offer,' she began. 'But why don't you come and see for yourself? The *Prince of Wales*, the carrier we are talking about, will be in Portsmouth – where the carriers will be based when in service – in a few weeks' time. There is to be a big ceremony. Perhaps the Royal Family will be there. We would be delighted if you could come as one of our guests of honour. We believe you may well be in London at around that time with your Minister for the big defence sales exhibition?'

'Yes, that is the plan. But *Prince of Wales*? Can't have an Indian ship called the *Prince of Wales*! The Empire is over; though I know some of your countrymen want to bring it back now that you are no longer in Europe. So it would need a proper Indian name. We have *Vikrant* and *Vaishal*. Why not *Trishul* – Trident – a good maritime name?' He laughed loudly at his own joke, perhaps, she thought, too loudly, as if there was more in the joke than was initially apparent.

On the way out she reassured herself by suggesting to the High Commissioner that 'at least the invitation got a good response'.

'I would be careful what you wish for, Mrs Thompson,' the diplomat replied. 'He's a notorious Muslim baiter and will not be universally well received back home.'

※※※※※※※※※※※※※※※

The search for Mo intensified. The police and intelligence services had mugshots, mobile numbers and email access codes to intercept. But there was silence. The distraught Khan family turned to the mosque and community groups for help and in particular to Steve. The worst case scenario had him travelling to Libya, Afghanistan, Yemen or some other ISIL stronghold to train and prepare for battle. A more optimistic view was that he was holed up with friends, perhaps in London, waiting to make the next move. Either way there was no news.

Shaida and Steve decided to convene a meeting at the mosque, bringing together the earlier group to seek their help. The mood was not good. There was still simmering anger over the protest demonstration. Steve's lack of sustained interest was criticised, as was the failure (for which he was blamed) of the council leadership to put out a statement supporting the demonstrators and condemning the police and Indian government provocation. There was angry condemnation of 'traitors' in the community who were 'grassing' to the police, leading to complaints of police harassment of several local Muslim women. They did, however, agree to meet every couple of days to pool information; Mo was, after all, one of their friends and seemed likely to do harm to himself and to others.

At the second meeting there was a modest breakthrough. One of Mo's friends who was monitoring jihadi websites – and was something of an apologist for them – reported a video featuring five masked young men, one of whom had a physique similar to Mo's. The video dealt not just with the usual enemies of Islam but featured in particular the 'atrocities' being committed by anti-Muslim Hindu 'fascists' in India. The video had been shot rather carelessly and showed in one corner a window opening onto a British townscape and what someone claimed was – or perhaps was not – Waltham Forest town hall. But at least they – whoever they were – were in the UK.

Kate arrived in Mumbai at a bad time for the Parrikars. The press stories around the spill of poisonous chemicals still featured prominently in the newspapers: 'Environmental Disaster at Parrikar Chemicals'. The main casualties were fish, not that many were left in the highly polluted waters around Mumbai. But the spillage had also occurred as the tide was rising and carried poisons into a village upstream where the poorer residents washed their clothes and themselves. There were reports of serious inflammation of the skin and damage to eyes. No fatalities, at least yet. But Indian reactions were coloured by the still outstanding damages claims and political toxicity from the Union Carbide Bhopal disaster in 1984 that had killed thousands and injured thousands more. Even a limited chemical disaster was capable of making big political waves.

All of this was explained to Kate when she had barely had time to reacquaint herself with her convalescing lover in his hospital bed. Veena took her into a side room to reveal another major development.

'Kate, I am not a politician like you. But I am learning the hard way that politicians can make or break businesses like ours.'

'That isn't unique to India by any means.'

'No, but we have this link between family businesses, political parties and – to a degree – organised crime that you don't have. It is a bit like Italy, or the US in the Wild West.'

'So what has all this to do with me?'

'A few days ago Deepak had a group of visitors from the ruling party. Seriously big hitters. He hasn't recovered and didn't take it all in. But they were offering him a "ticket" for the next general election in a seat they expect to win.'

'But I thought he couldn't stand these nationalist, religious types. He always describes himself as secular.'

'True. But he did vote for them. Our father gave money last time round. Deepak likes the pro-business bit. And the Prime Minister is – apparently – wanting Deepak to be a champion of his New Industrial Policy. He sees Deepak as part of his efforts to improve his party's image – make it more inclusive: what you call a "big tent".'

'But Deepak isn't in a fit state to embark on a political career or even make decisions about it.'

'That is true. But he understands the importance of protecting his family and the company, which are under siege. He has to have political allies. And he has little time for the opposition: hopelessly divided and still revolving around the leading family, discredited though they now are by corruption and general incompetence. That is why he asked me to advise him; decide what is best for the family. And you are, for me, part of the family.' Veena reached out and took Kate's hand.

'I am, really, very touched by that,' Kate answered, the gesture of solidarity prompting a hint of tears. 'It is the nicest thing anyone has said to me for quite a while. My feelings for Deepak are quite simple. I love him and I think he feels the same. But I am painfully aware that marriage or living together is out of the question. We both have families at opposite ends of the earth. Political career apart, I am not going to abandon my girls to come and live here. So I am reconciled to the idea that there will be occasional, snatched, moments when I visit India or he is in London. Not ideal. But better than nothing.'

Veena nodded. 'That makes it easier to tell you what I plan to tell Deepak. He should take it. Do as they ask. You have a British expression: if you can't beat 'em, join 'em. That is where we are. I really don't know how far all these incidents are connected – the gangland killings in Mumbai, the attack on Deepak, this latest sabotage of our plant; lots of other things you don't know about. I am not a believer in conspiracies but because we are outsiders, because we have no protection, we are vulnerable.

'The family is under terrible strain as a result: my father is broken: my elder brother – next door – has barely survived; my younger brother is becoming an alcoholic; I am really struggling to cope. I have a lovely husband and two small children, and I am failing them, worrying twenty-four hours a day about the company. If Deepak becomes an MP for the ruling party, it won't solve all our problems but it gives us a shield. One thing Deepak will hate is seeing his factory slipping back under the control of that man Desai and his associates – it was made clear that, under the deal with the ruling party, Desai and his cronies will back off. And Deepak can, I am sure, find a way to promote his ideals.'

'Yes, I think I understand,' Kate replied. 'Very few of us are cut out to be great or heroes, taking on the world: a Mahatma Gandhi or a Mandela, or for that matter a Mrs Gandhi or a Mrs Thatcher. I am also a small fish in the big sea of Conservatism in Britain. I detest a lot of the people I have to deal with. Cynical and nasty. I don't even like the party all that much; I drifted into it. But they seem likely to be running the country for the next generation, so I want to stay where I am and do a few small good things. I guess we have both come to the same conclusion in our different countries for much the same reasons.'

The shared intimacy and frankness were infectious. Kate was eager to find out more about the man she loved; his childhood, the things about him that she could only discover second hand. Veena, for her part, was able to shed the fears and responsibilities of recent weeks, and forget, for a while, that she was now the family matriarch. After sharing some of the funnier family secrets, the time came for Kate to leave. She felt that she had found a true friend.

Deepak Parrikar wasn't the only budding politician whose fortune was being mapped out by the women around him. The future Lord Thompson of Surrey Heights was pleasantly surprised to discover that his wayward wife had been scheming to get him a peerage. He was already daydreaming about making a big hit in the Lords and a quick move to a ministerial post, preferably in the Treasury where his well-developed views on freeing up market forces in the property sector could be put to use. Not, he believed, that his appointment was undeserved. Had it not been for the disparity between his salary and bonuses on the one hand and the pathetic pauper's pay enjoyed by MPs on the other, he would now be the local MP. Kate would be doing what he thought she was best at: small talk at social gatherings and charming the old dears at the annual fete. After months of quiet bitterness and recrimination he could see his way to forgiving her, just.

And so, when she returned home, the 'dears' and 'darlings' were not delivered with quite such venom. She discovered that it was possible to have a cordial coexistence: lacking in love or even affection but perfectly pleasant. The girls sensed the change of mood. They had become withdrawn and resentful of their parents: Maggie had taken to teenage rebellion, and to the fury of her father had dyed her hair bright orange. The other two hid behind their iPads in endless typed chatter with their friends. Now, as they picked up the more relaxed atmosphere around the breakfast table, they gradually opened up to talk to their mum again about the things that loomed large in their lives: the preparations for next month's gymkhana, the agonies of GCSE maths, the love affair between the lesbian chemistry teacher and the head girl, the prospect of a skiing holiday. In reality they were enormously proud of their mother and greatly relieved that she was still with them and spending less time at her MP's flat and more time at home.

⬝⬝⬝⬝⬝⬝⬝⬝⬝⬝⬝⬝⬝⬝⬝⬝⬝⬝⬝⬝

Shortly after returning from India Kate was called in to see the Secretary of State, the man responsible for the sudden turnaround in her personal and political life. She was surprised that he had moved so soon to deliver his side of the bargain when she had delivered so little.

'My dear Kate,' Jim said as she entered his office, opening his arms wide in greeting. 'Back from communing with our friends in the subcontinent. How are you? How did they treat you?'

'Thanks, Jim. You will have heard from the High Commissioner that we didn't make any headway on the carrier issue. I tried.'

'To be frank I didn't expect you to get far on that one. Other options are beginning to emerge including a joint Anglo-German project now that Berlin are getting over their hang-ups over Brexit. They want to be involved with us in the Med and the Gulf. Very hush-hush. Please don't talk about it. But the PM and the German Chancellor are enthusiastic and we may no longer need the Indians. What you did – brilliantly as always – was to get the powerful Desai interested in the UK. He is keen to follow up on your invitation for whatever reason.'

'I appreciate that you moved very quickly on the promises you made to me. Even though you've never met my husband, you seem to understand him better than I do: after one of your people dropped a hint about the peerage he has been like a little boy with a new train set.'

Jim gave a snort of laughter. 'Good. And you will also find that there is no more nonsense about deselection. The next step is to have you back in a proper, senior, job in the government.'

Kate saw her opportunity. 'Provided I can do something worthwhile,' she countered. 'I am not interested in simply having a job, I want to do something useful. I thought social housing. As a constituency MP I see some of the havoc in the lives of ordinary people because of sky-high rents and the cost of buying.'

'No, no, no. Far too left-wing. The party hates social housing. We are trying to get rid of it. We want the peasants to own their own huts – sorry! My sense of humour is getting the better of me, again. No, definitely not. Let us stick to our priorities. The PM is clear. Our top priority is the female vote: being on the side of aspirational women. What I had in mind was getting you into one of the departments where we don't normally see many women: Defence perhaps, or the Treasury.'

Kate was inwardly annoyed at his casual dismissal of her ambition to do something she cared about. But she found his brutal cynicism easier to deal with than the mealy-mouthed hypocrisy of most of their colleagues.

She also suspected that he put on something of an act for her benefit. Try as she would, she found it hard to dislike the man.

'Can I think about it?'

'Yes, of course. Perhaps I can help you think about it over a nice dinner at my favourite restaurant.'

'Mmm…'

'OK, agreed. I will set it up.'

Kate's readmission to the fold by the leadership of the party was quickly followed by reaffirmation of her status at local level. The motion to be put before a meeting of association members to proceed with deselection became, at the stroke of a pen, a motion to support reselection. The Chairman's Damascene conversion was quickly followed by the rest of the party executive whose moments of blinding light consisted, variously, of a promise by the Foreign Secretary to speak at the association's annual dinner, an offer by the Prime Minister of the unbeatable prize of 'tea at No. 10' for the fundraising auction and a generous financial contribution from Mr, the future Lord, Thompson: all predicated on the assumption that the current MP remained the party's candidate.

Although the better part of Kate winced inwardly at the party's unerring instinct for the baser qualities of human nature, she also enjoyed the benefits. Being chauffeured around in a political Rolls-Royce undoubtedly had its attractions and she lacked the streak of self-denying Puritanism required to decline the ride. The only bump felt through the suspension was the announcement by Stella that she was resigning from the party to join UKIP because of 'a decline in traditional moral values'. Her resignation was made more significant by the fact that she also took with her twenty years of membership and canvass records and minutes of party meetings including the recent executive no confidence vote in the MP.

<hr/>

The political Trabant that was the modern Labour Party offered a much less comfortable ride, as Steve Grant discovered when he put forward his name for selection as prospective parliamentary candidate for the town's safe Labour seat. It had been assumed for most of the last decade that he was the Dauphin waiting only to be anointed at the coronation. That assumption was soon shown to be dangerously wide of the mark.

Local party membership had more than doubled since the 2015 general election and as rumours spread of an impending selection, numbers surged again in a spasm of socialist zeal. As a former champion recruiter, Steve was no shrinking violet and he signed up many of his union colleagues at Pulsar who, in recent years, had allowed their membership to lapse. To his delight, Ikram, one of Mo's friends he had met at the mosque, had now joined the party. He had emerged as a brilliant organiser, doing prodigious work boosting membership among young

Muslims. And, despite the family's preoccupation with the missing Mo, Shaida had joined in too, enlisting the Three Witches and a dozen of her other girlfriends.

But when Steve sat down with the membership list, once closed, it became clear that he was in trouble. John Gray, the council group leader, had taken on the role of coordinating his campaign and, as they sat together in Gray's council office, analysing the numbers, they found it difficult to identify solid support from more than a third of potential voters. They had conducted a quick telephone canvass of new members and were shocked by the findings: a substantial majority had joined to elect and support the national leadership; few had a party background and many were former Greens or Socialist Workers; their issues reflected the concerns of university staff and students rather than the shop floor; and few had heard of Steve or, if they had, thought favourably of him. Most spontaneously expressed support for Steve's main opponent, Dr Liz Cook, a lecturer in the Social Anthropology Department of a new university in North London where she lived. Ms Cook was head of a university research unit specialising in War, Capitalism and Women and her expertise in this field had led to her becoming one of the architects of the party's new defence policy. She had also been a Paulina and Oxford contemporary of Kate Thompson but these inconvenient facts were kept well away from her CV.

Councillor Gray didn't beat about the bush. 'You've

got a problem, lad. If you want to win, you are going to have to fight. No more Mr Nice Guy.' He raised the possibility of resurrecting the local party's Attack Unit, which was established to fight off a Lib Dem offensive several years earlier. Its task was to destroy opponents using every tactic known to political man, short of those that would lead the candidate to be disqualified, the agent imprisoned and the party bankrupted by libel damages. That still left quite a lot of scope.

Any qualms Steve might have had were swiftly removed when Ms Cook's supporters struck the first blow with a social media blitz attacking the 'Establishment Candidate' for 'lobbying on behalf of multinational companies in the arms trade'. They had also unearthed a grainy but recognisable photo of Steve shaking hands with the then Secretary of State, Peter Mandelson, which told its own grim story of spin and betrayal. Councillor Bill Daniels's complaint about Steve's advocacy of tactical cooperation with the Lib Dems was further proof of unreliable SDP tendencies.

The Attack Unit was soon at work preparing a counter-offensive. One of their young researchers – a student intern – unearthed a copy of the *British Journal of Social Anthropology* with an article summarising Ms Cook's PhD thesis: 'Manifestations of Penile Aggression in the Military Industrial Complex: A Multi-Disciplinary and Multi-Cultural Perspective'. 'Boys toys', in other words, giggled the young woman who had excavated this gem. But after a round of laughter the team agreed that humour was likely to be counter-productive. Some of the membership might be impressed by the long words and a candidate who wrote learned articles about an Ology.

Gray had concluded that a better tack would be to work on two key power brokers: Councillors Les Harking and Mirza. Both had been hostile at the aborted disciplinary hearing but that issue had gone away and both had worked well with Steve in the past. They each had a solid block of support that might, together, get Steve over the finishing line. But they were old pros whose support would come at a price.

Councillor Mirza was the easier nut to crack. He had no real disagreements with Steve, merely a badly wounded ego that required tender massage. Steve was capable of the necessary dissimulation, much as he disliked it. And as he piled on compliments about the Mirza clan's stellar contribution to civic life, he had echoing in the back of his mind the jibes from Brian Castle and others in the works canteen about 'your corrupt Paki friend on the council' whose family was 'ripping off the council with those horrible, squalid, care homes'. The coup de grâce, however, was delivered by the Attack Unit, which sent to Councillor Mirza and his supporters a YouTube recording of a radical feminist rally at which Liz Cook had been a – not very prominent – speaker. Someone in the crowd waved a placard with a cartoon of the Prophet and the words 'male chauvinist pig'. It mattered little that the rally was a long time ago, pre-*Charlie Hebdo*, and that the organisers including Liz Cook issued a cringing apology. The verdict was: guilt by association. Steve pocketed the Muslim vote almost to a man and woman.

Councillor Harking held court in the Red Lion, savouring every second of his political courtship.

Steve sat down at his table with a pint of beer. 'Evening, Les, how are you?'

Les made it clear he was not impressed. He had a copy of the *Morning Star* in front of him and pointedly ignored Steve as he studiously worked his way through it. Steve tried again.

'Sorry, Les, you must know why I want to talk to you. I hope I can count on your support in the selection.'

'Not so fast, young man. Why do you think I would do that?' He was already into his second pint and looking forward to a long evening of drinks 'on the house'.

'We have worked together a long time. Speaking up for the local working class.'

'Sometimes. Anyway you're slow off the mark. This Liz Cook has already been in touch. Impressive. Said I would think about supporting her.'

'You know she isn't your cup of tea. Never been near the town before. A carpet bagger.'

'But I like the politics. For the first time since Michael Foot was leader we are calling ourselves socialists without being ashamed.'

'A fat lot of good that did us at the last election.'

'Maybe different next time. The young people are with us.'

'Some of them. And they don't vote. You know the story.'

'I've been around the block a lot longer than you. I was part of the struggle when you were in nappies. We need our principles back – which your friends in New Labour trashed.'

'You know as well as I do that all this academic waffle from Liz Cook and her ilk isn't taking us anywhere. Working class people are completely turned off. We'll be stuck with the Tories for ever.'

'Don't talk us down, lad. That's all the right-wing media. Can't give in to Murdoch, the *Mail* and the rest of 'em. Stick up for what we believe in.'

They had been round the houses, exhausting these arguments many times before. Les was in no hurry. He was in his element: power broker, career maker and breaker; the grizzled veteran of The Struggle passing on the wisdom of the tribe. He knew, and Steve knew deep down, that as fellow alumni of the University of Life and fully qualified operators of the town's political machine they had far more in common with each other than with the newly ascendant leadership in the party. But before consummating the relationship Les would have to extract serious political concessions. He was willing to be bought but only at a suitably high price. Before the end of the evening, Steve had refused to endorse UK withdrawal from NATO and the restoration of free tuition for students, but had signed up to full nationalisation of the banks and support for a campaign of civil disobedience against the new trade union legislation. His wallet was also lighter after meeting the bar bill.

Steve now had a somewhat incongruous – and fragile – alliance, but an alliance nonetheless, between the party's Muslim supporters and the traditional working class members. And at the public hustings he was at his eloquent best, speaking without notes, and skilfully used his local and working class credentials. But he sensed, from the audience reaction, a bristling anger and rejection of who he was and what he stood for. He was jeered and heckled. By contrast, his opponent read, badly, a tedious script full of clichés and jargon and she was seemingly unaware of which town she was in. But the audience was mostly on her side and whenever she used words like 'neoliberalism', which were not part of Steve's vocabulary, there was fervent applause.

When the votes were counted things looked bleak for Steve, until the postal vote arrived, which he won hands down. There had clearly been some successful exhumation of the dead in Councillor Mirza's kitchen. Steve was home by two votes, in the overall count. It wasn't a glorious victory but he had won. Quite what victory meant in a changed and hostile party only time would tell. For the time being victory was enough. He was still a player.

Shaida introduced herself to Susan in Caffè Nero in the town centre. She was dressed traditionally and modestly and had taken to wearing the hijab when she was on view in public places, demonstrating conformity if not piety. Susan had tried to dress down, in sweater and jeans, but her demeanour was that of the smart, tidy, official that she was.

'Kate has asked me to liaise with you,' Susan explained. 'I do need to stress that I am a civil servant. There are rules. I am not political and here essentially as a messenger. But I know something about the background and my line manager is comfortable with my being a conduit. Kate's message is that any inside information you have on Pulsar, under the new owners, would be very helpful. As you know she believes something seriously irregular is going on there. Any evidence would be better used than when you last approached her.'

'I already got a message indirectly through Steve and my other government contact who I want to help,' Shaida acknowledged. 'I don't like what I've seen of the new owners one little bit. But I need to be careful. They're very security conscious. But in a very mechanical, box-ticking, kind of way. I get to see a lot of email traffic between senior managers that even Calum, the CEO, is excluded from and, to do my job, I see the important money flows. I am also quite good at finding my way around security protocols and passwords. They don't yet seem to have cottoned on to the fact of my brother going missing or my joint activities with Steve and your Minister. But they will, and then doors will close.'

Shaida reached into her bag and brought out a file of documents, which she handed to Susan. 'I've brought along a few copies of interesting-looking financial transactions and I've highlighted a few names – Kate will recognise their significance. There is a lot more. This is just a sample. But, as I said, I am on borrowed time.'

'Kate will be very pleased. Thanks for these. Let me know when you have more.'

'One more thing,' Shaida added. 'There has been some talk of a big exhibition in London in the next month. They want me to be on the company stand. One of the new people – an American – wasn't very subtle: they think a brown female face will help to present the right kind of inclusive image. And the top brass will be coming over and holding a board meeting to coincide with the exhibition.'

'Ah yes. I know all about this event. Every two years Britain hosts the world's biggest arms bazaar. It is theoretically private but the government is heavily involved. We're gearing up for it: lots of VIPs from the defence sales world. A kind of Davos for arms dealers. I imagine Kate will be on parade with the Secretary of State. Useful info about your company; I'll feed it back.'

CHAPTER 16

THE TRAINEE

Dawn (Lahore), 20 September 2019:

It is reported from sources in the Pakistan military that the mooted nuclear test has been postponed and that efforts are being made through intermediaries to de-escalate the 'war of words' between India and Pakistan. Senior figures in the Pakistan army are reported to have expressed alarm at the way civilian 'hotheads' have been allowed to set the agenda.

He had little idea where he was. The van had no windows and his companions didn't wish to talk. When he asked where they were going the answer was 'Better you don't know.' The night journey by motorway – he assumed the M1 – had lasted about an hour. Then ten minutes on a side road and, briefly, a rutted track. Now, a big house surrounded by trees. There was a distinctive smell – pigs, silage? He was too much of a town boy to tell. And there was the occasional distant sound of aircraft far overhead. He could be anywhere.

When they arrived, three bearded men – Asian or Arab, they didn't introduce themselves – provided hot soup and bread and spelled out the rules: no one to leave the house except under supervision; no attempt to communicate with friends or family (mobiles were collected in – 'secure' phones would be issued in due course); and a daily roster of duties, education and prayer. Then into the room came the man who had inspired him, Tariq Ahmed, and who was clearly in charge of this operation. Tariq Ahmed gave him a short nod of acknowledgement.

Mo was allocated a room in the attic and spent the rest of the night awake, wondering whether he had made the right decision when he had said yes to the friend who challenged him to say if he was ready and sufficiently committed to fight for the cause. There was a Holy Quran by the bedside but he didn't open it.

He discovered the following morning that there were six of them: a couple of Asians from Bradford, one from Stoke, a white convert from Birmingham and an African who was from the same town though they had never met. It soon became clear that he and the African had a different motivation from the others who were totally devout; assiduous in the rituals; seemingly entranced by the prayer. Mo's family had pride in their Muslim identity but religion played only a minor and occasional part in their life. As with his Christian school friends, religion surfaced at weddings and funerals and was experienced through feasting rather than fasting.

Mo was more engaged by the political sessions that Tariq Ahmed led and particularly the videos that dramatised the hurt and discrimination suffered by fellow Muslims: the suffering of helpless children during the siege of Aleppo; footage of the Iraq war; the men of Srebrenica being led off to execution; the humiliation of Palestinians at Israeli checkpoints and the bombing of Gaza; the burnt bodies lying beside a rail track after a massacre in Gujarat; torture victims in profusion; Guantanamo. Mo's beating by a group of racist thugs and several experiences of 'stop and search' didn't quite match those horrors but a shared sense of victimhood reminded him why he was there.

Mo felt confident enough to air his doubts: his lack of religious conviction; his disquiet at some of the gruesome practices of ISIL; and his secular views on the role of women. Tariq Ahmed was not fazed. His branch of fighters was comfortable with intelligent doubt; respected ISIL's achievements but not their methods. Mo would be called on to show courage but there was also a role in less demanding work: providing safe houses or storage for weapons; organising protests in support of the cause; disciplining informers; collecting information on potential targets; recruiting in colleges and universities: part of the penumbra of terrorism rather than its core.

But the recruiters had spotted in Mo some spark – created from anger, intelligence, determination – that was the basis of a good fighter. The next big mission did not require suicide from its perpetrators but basic competence and discipline with careful planning and skilful execution using firearms.

Mo was taken to an outbuilding, perhaps once a barn, where a shooting range had been constructed. The structure was well insulated for sound and no one passing nearby would be aware of its purpose. There, Mo was taught to use semi-automatic weapons and small arms as a back-up. He had never handled guns before, but, once he had learnt to suppress the rush of adrenalin and master the action, proved to be the most adept of the group.

Mo also bonded better with the others and joined in the prayers with more conviction. Too much conversation and intimacy was, however, not encouraged. The instructors revealed little about themselves and kept discussion at a general and practical level. If the recruits were interrogated at some point in the future, the information they gave up would be of dubious value.

Then, without warning, the instruction came to pack their small collection of personal possessions and to prepare to leave for a safe house, nearer the planned action, where final detailed instructions would be given.

※※※※※※※※※※※※※※

Steve was concentrating on union work. And this currently involved representing the union on a trip to Portsmouth to celebrate a major milestone in the dockyard's history. The process of transforming the Portsmouth dockyards from a shipbuilding centre to a base for servicing the navy's two new carriers and other warships had been industrially and politically difficult. But his union had been credited with a tough but pragmatic, rather than disruptive, approach that had borne fruit in a minimum of redundancies, and deadlines being met. There would continue to be a role for the skilled craftsmen and engineers who made up his union's membership at the base.

He had never been to this city before and on arrival at the harbour station was struck by the force of the naval presence: Nelson's *Victory*, a symbol of past glories, and the giant Spinnaker Tower, a powerful and optimistic statement of belief in a maritime future. He wandered around the city centre where seamen had drunk, eaten, boasted, brawled and womanised for centuries before looking for his Premier Inn. His allowance permitted something a little more luxurious but he had already discovered that even relatively minor public figures lived under scrutiny. After unpacking he went in search of an evening meal.

By the time he left the restaurant, the city centre was filling up with young people, some of them already quite far gone with alcohol. Despite the cold evening many of the boys wore nothing more warming than T-shirts, the better to display tattooed arms, and the girls had flimsy tops and ridiculously short dresses. Lack of inhibition gave vent to some raucous but good-natured singing and shouting. Steve felt a twinge of sadness that his early marriage, caring duties and night school had circumvented this stage of growing up. But his isolation had also fuelled his ambition, the hunger to succeed, that had lifted him above his contemporaries.

As he moved away from the centre he saw a group of young Asian men gathered on a street corner. Most were slumped inside oversize jackets, hoods up, hands in pockets, and there was an edginess and awkwardness quite different from their white contemporaries a few hundred yards away. Street lighting was poor and the darkness masked whatever it was they were doing. But something caught Steve's eye in a brief exposure to reflected light. The profile of one of the youths looked very familiar. The more he looked, the more he became convinced that he knew who it was.

Steve sternly reminded himself that there were tens of thousands of Asian men in the UK of roughly the same age and appearance and the probability of one of them appearing in the same city as him at the same time was slim. Unless, of course, it was not a coincidence. His mind raced with possibilities. An obvious one was that there were a lot of VIPs in town. But he prevaricated.

He wanted to talk to Shaida about the episode but then realised that there was little concrete to go on. A half-baked story about, maybe, sighting her brother would simply agitate her without helping. He hovered, watching the group from a distance. He was tempted to go across and present himself. Then the young men broke up, embracing each other before departing in different directions. The object of Steve's attention slipped away into the darkness of a side street. But his suspicions hardened into near certainty when he saw a characteristic hand gesture in the seconds before the youths disappeared into the gloom.

Who should he contact? He realised that he had other options apart from Shaida. In his phone he had the number Kate Thompson had given him in the Commons. He decided to ring. He was surprised to discover that she was in the same city for the same reason, albeit in the rather more comfortable Marriott. In explaining the call, he introduced a sufficient number of caveats to make her irritated.

'Is this an emergency or not?' she said tersely. 'If you are asking me to alert the security guys, I need to be clear that this is serious. Yes, or no?'

'Yes.'

'In that case I will alert the people who need to know.'

Until she was interrupted by the telephone call, Kate had been preparing for an uneventful day as part of the supporting cast. She was there to represent her department and support the Secretary of State for Defence who was to visit the city and tour the naval base and to thank the navy, the base commander and his staff, the workforce, and the city fathers for their work in getting the base port ready on time for the arrival of the first of the carriers. And, no doubt, to tell local voters, through the national media, that the government should get the political credit.

Someone in Whitehall had joined up the dots and realised that a lot of senior overseas visitors would be in London for the biennial DSEI, the defence and security equipment exhibition. Wouldn't it be a good idea to show some of them around the naval base and some of the fighting ships in part? Make them feel important as esteemed guests of Her Majesty's Government?

Kate's mentor, Jim Chambers, let it be known that her presence would be expected in her capacity as Trade Envoy, since among the visiting VIPs was India's Dr Desai. She wasn't expected to do much as the Red Admiral would act as his chaperone. Kate's job was the usual: 'Smile sweetly and look pretty… not difficult, my girl. Just make the Indians feel at home.' And besides ('and very much for your ears only'), 'The PM has said that in the next reshuffle you will have a big job in the government. You are now one hundred per cent on board.' She let the blandishments wash over her; she had decided to go with the flow and not to think too deeply about the motives of the men who were, for the moment, inclined to give her a helping hand.

Had she been fully briefed on Desai's recent activities she might have found a good excuse not to be there; but the ripples hadn't yet reached her. Following her visit, the Indian Prime Minister had asked Desai to carry out a wide ranging review of India's defence procurement practices, and this responsibility further pricked the interest of the UK High Commissioner in Delhi and the MOD and Department of Business back in London. They made sure that the grand tour of major prospective suppliers – the US, Russia, France – had a good slot reserved for the UK and, fortuitously, the dates coincided with this splendid opportunity to show off the best of the British navy, along with a shopping trip at the defence exhibition.

Mr Desai started his tour with the USA and, while there, agreed to speak at a seminar at America First, the new think-tank close to the Administration, and sponsored by his associates from Global. The subject was 'The Military and Political Threat of Islam' and fellow speakers included the President's Director of Strategy, who predictably scooped the headlines by letting the audience know what the President really thought about Muslims. Almost as much attention was given to an Israeli Cabinet minister from an extreme settlers' party who had advocated requiring all Muslims, including Israeli citizens, to wear green crescent badges at all times to identify them for security purposes.

The British broadsheets picked up on both stories and reported them with suitably outraged comment.

Much less attention was paid to the speech of an unknown Indian functionary who made a largely impenetrable presentation around a series of demographic projections that purported to show, for those who could follow, the convergence of the populations of Hindus and Muslims in India. Later in his speech he referred favourably to an aspect of Mrs Gandhi's emergency in the 1970s when her son Sanjay had embarked upon a campaign of mass sterilisation, voluntary in theory but often compulsory in practice. The programme had been concentrated on poorer people (who had larger families) including Muslims, and the potential of such a programme for 'stabilising India's demographic profile' was explored by the speaker and what was left of his audience. One listener, a young Muslim journalist who had got into the seminar under an assumed name, was paying particularly close attention and he ensured, through social media, that the speech was promptly reported in the subcontinent. Before long the reports, which had bypassed the British press, were reflected back into the diaspora communities in the UK.

The outraged response might well have burnt itself out had an alert junior diplomat in the Pakistani High Commission in London not spotted that the British government's list of official visitors included the self-same Desai. Questions were put down in parliament, predictably, by the Member for Islamabad East. The ethnic press became excited even if the mainstream press didn't, and for militant Islamists this became yet further evidence of the complicity of the British state with Islamophobes. Something would have to be done. But, except for a few boffins in the security services tracking political noise on the internet, there was little sense of threat.

※※※※※※※※※※※※※※

The Portsmouth visit got under way smoothly. The Secretary of State for Defence was on time for a 9am start. Security checks were heavy but the cluster of senior officials, naval officers and VIPs, including the delegation from India, were waved through and headed for the ships at anchor. The crisp early autumn morning, with a cloudless sky, was a perfect backcloth to a modern naval pageant. Everyone expressed themselves massively impressed by the carrier whose grey bulk loomed over them: the largest naval vessel by far that the Royal Navy had ever operated.

The VIPs were feeling peckish by 10.30 and the procession was directed to the gardens at the rear of the base commander's residence where a marquee had been erected for morning refreshments, and a microphone gave warning of speeches and thank-yous to come. The group spread out over the lawn, soaking up the morning sun and finding, in companionable conversation over coffee and cakes, some relief from the barrage of facts and figures directed at them during the tour. There was an armed security presence in the background but it was unobtrusive and modest.

After exchanging Oxbridge banter with Dr Desai, Kate did the rounds of Sheikhs and African generals and a group of suited, dapper, Asians who she discovered, through a translator, were from the Vietnamese politburo. She then found herself in conversation with the Lib Dem council leader who introduced her to his husband and she reflected how far the country had travelled in recent years so that such encounters were perfectly normal and drained of prurient interest. Desai was at the centre of a group of industrialists who were unsubtly peddling their wares, while the guardian Admiral was trying to moderate their shameless pitch for business. The Secretary of State moved towards the microphone and extracted his speaking notes before addressing the small crowd.

After an eternity spent clearing his throat and tapping the microphone, the Defence Secretary began his speech and the platitudes reserved for such occasions poured out in thick profusion. Then there was a loud bang and a scream from the back of the refreshments tent. Within a split second a security detail dragged the politician off the microphone, while soldiers in battle fatigues appeared from nowhere and pushed the distinguished visitors to the floor. Kate and the Lib Dem council leader managed a synchronised dive. Then a group of commandos advanced on the rear of the tent, guns poised. When they rounded the corner, ready to fire, they encountered two naval ratings flat on the floor. One of them had managed to knock over a pile of metal containers causing the apparent sound of detonation that had caused the panic.

When order was restored, the VIPs required some reassuring that this was a false alarm. The story quickly spread among the visitors that they had been rescued from a terrorist attack by a brilliant, rapid-reflex response from the UK military security. They were grateful and impressed and Kate for one was happy to allow the fiction to settle.

As Steve left he saw Kate standing next to Liam, his presence a product of Steve's phone call the evening before, and an officer who appeared to be responsible for the security operation. 'Mr Grant, I assume?' the officer said. 'I believe we have you to thank for the tip-off. As you see, we countered the terror threat.' The officer had a perfectly straight face but Steve sensed that the joke was on him.

'We are all indebted to your men and women for their vigilance,' he replied, chastened. 'I'm sorry but I can't explain the sighting yesterday evening.'

'I think I can. Overnight we checked out the ISIL operatives you identified, using local witnesses and CCTV footage. It turns out that they were a local five-a-side football team, celebrating in town after a tournament.'

Deepak Parrikar decided to launch his entry into high-level politics with a symbolic event. He would commemorate the death of his protégé, the unfortunate Patel, by launching his father's Parrikar Foundation on the site where the body had been found. The Foundation would commit to a scheme of community development in the baasti: improved sanitation, a primary school, a health clinic. Those who harboured doubts about the political colours Deepak now stood under would be reassured that he was a force for enlightenment, committed to helping the poor regardless of caste or religion.

When the big day came, the Maidan in the centre of the baasti was transformed. A stage had been erected and decorated with gaudy bunting. The stage was packed with chairs for the VIPs, sheltering from the sun under a canopy. The VIPs threatened to outnumber the slum dwellers: they included the Parrikar family, relatives of the murdered Patel, the local politicians from the council and the state assembly, a police delegation led by Superintendent Mankad, various functionaries from the city council who (for a small consideration) would ensure that the promised improvements would be made, and assorted businessmen who had decided to match-fund the Parrikar Foundation, judging that this was a politically significant new force they would do well to join.

Deepak had succeeded in persuading his father and mother to forsake the seclusion of their home in order to celebrate the Foundation launch, and even Rose, on one of her rare visits to Mumbai, had agreed to come, concealing her distaste behind her largest sunglasses. The real organisational triumph, however, had been the intense diplomacy that had resulted in the frail, tottering Sheikh to arrive, supported by his old friend. His freshly dyed beard and white robes advertised his religious identity, and few of those present were aware of his colourful CV.

The slum dwellers initially numbered around fifty and the elected council man, who had been instructed to ensure maximum attendance, was beginning to feel rather uncomfortable. His trusted local representative, the slumlord, would have some explaining to do. But the crowd swelled as it became clear that the police were not here to make arrests or launch a tax collection, and the whiff of cooked food started to drift across the encampment. Tables were set out with savouries and sweetmeats that the slum dwellers encountered, if at all, only on special occasions like weddings or as leftovers scrounged or stolen from local hotels. As the more adventurous, or hungrier, residents tucked into the feast it soon became clear that the organisers had miscalculated. Those at the front of the queue positioned themselves to return for several helpings and scooped as much food as possible into their clothes to ensure that their families could eat well for the coming week. The late arrivals at the back of the queue seemed likely to miss out and scuffles broke out. Sergeant Ghokale had to deploy his two constables to restore order and calm was re-established with a loudspeaker announcement that more food was on its way; there would be enough for everyone.

After fresh consignments of food arrived from a nearby shopping centre and all had had their fill, a troupe of dancers and musicians performed for the crowd, which was now in an altogether happier and less suspicious mood. Unfortunately, Deepak Parrikar had chosen the performers who reflected his classical tastes. The Bollywood hits the crowd had been waiting for failed to make an appearance. Before long the refined rhythms and delicate phrasing of the ragas could be heard only in the best seats and the crowd was again becoming restive.

Deepak was advised by the organiser to proceed at once with the speeches and dedication and after much fiddling with the sound system he was able to begin, but only following a lengthy introduction from the council man. He expressed deep gratitude for the generosity of the Parrikars in terms of such obsequiousness that even those familiar with the style of such occasions winced inwardly. Deepak was used to public speaking in English but decided to speak in Marathi, the language of the state that he judged to be the lingua franca of the crowd. He noticed that his clap lines elicited applause from the authority figures on the platform but most of the crowd simply looked puzzled. In this polyglot community five or six different languages were spoken, and for those recently arrived from impoverished villages in other parts of India, Hindi, Telugu or Tamil would have been more accessible.

Even if the crowd had fully taken on board the sweep and scale of the urban transformation Deepak envisaged, they would not have been easily impressed. The community already boasted the disused shell of a primary school promised after a visitation by a Scandinavian aid agency: the community worker left to supervise the project had pocketed the funds required to run it and disappeared. At the last general election, a new latrine had been promised in return for votes, had been half-dug and then abandoned. The Parrikars were made of sterner stuff but the crowd did not yet know that.

The climax was to be a ceremonial digging of the ground to lay the foundation stone of the promised new school with a blessing from a Hindu priest, accompanied by the release of helium balloons that had been distributed among the children, who then howled with anguish when their new toys had to be released into the sky. Ravi, the now forgotten hero who had discovered Patel's body, took the precaution of holding on firmly to his new red plaything.

Then there were fireworks, which spread delight and terror in equal measure. Superintendent Mankad instinctively reached for his revolver as the firecrackers exploded around him. He was nervously watching the three goondas in dark glasses standing by the hut on the hillock nearby where the murder was committed and where his rescue of Deepak Parrikar had been effected. Following Deepak's political baptism, the Trishul gang and its political mentors had achieved a state of coexistence with their improbable new ally. But the Superintendent knew the difference between a truce and a peace and was taking no chances. Deepak and the leading VIPs were bundled into a van and driven off to greater safety.

As they drove back into downtown Mumbai, Deepak reflected on the awkwardness of the occasion: the many things he needed to learn before he could call himself 'a man of the people'. He contrasted the discomfort he felt among his own people – he had almost thrown up on the platform, nauseated by the stench of the slum – with the easy, warm familiarity he enjoyed with his British lover who now seemed so very far away.

He needn't have worried. The High Command in the ruling party were delighted with their new recruit and the media exposure he generated. *Bharat Bombay*'s coverage, like that of other popular papers, focused on national and family unity and the generosity of the Foundation. No one noticed, or was inclined to point out, the half-completed latrine, the disused shell of a school, the scramble for food and the unsavoury gang of goondas watching from the hillside nearby. Together with other occasions around the country featuring India's eclectic mix of colours, castes and creeds, the Prime Minister's slogan for the forthcoming election – Inclusive India – took shape. It tested well with focus groups. It remained only to arrange, through intermediaries, a gesture of reconciliation with Pakistan, which would calm down worrying talk of war and enable him to proclaim: Blessed are the Peacemakers.

CHAPTER 17

THE EXHIBITION

Statement by the Metropolitan Police Commissioner, 1 October 2019:

A group of suspected recruits to an Islamic terrorist group is active in the UK. They are of Pakistani origin and may be seeking targets with an Indian connection in the light of recent confrontation and riots in the subcontinent. Extra guards have been placed around the Indian High Commission in London, offices of Air India and major temple complexes in Southall, Slough and Neasden.

Shaida's missing brother was nearer than either of them realised. His group arrived at its destination in the early hours of the morning. The van slowly made its way up a dark alley and moved quickly and quietly through a yard at the back of a three storey terraced house.

The group split up once inside the house. Each was given a room and told to wash, change and prepare himself for a briefing shortly after dawn. There were only a few dimmed lights in the room Mo occupied, but it seemed to be a child's bedroom, with a few soft toys piled beside the bed and a scooter in the corner. A reassuring, familiar smell of Asian cooking seeped through from the kitchen below.

He lay on the bed and tried to sleep. His brain, however, was in overdrive with memories flashing past: his parents, his brothers and sister in episodes of his generally happy childhood; the embarrassing, awkward, unfulfilling encounters he had had with girls; the horrific images he had seen of Muslim suffering around the world; the day when he had been allowed time off school to go to Buckingham Palace to see his father receive a medal – when his parents glowed with pride and happiness; then the demonstration and the look of hatred in the eyes of the racist thug in the seconds before his face felt the force of the man's blow. He felt mounting excitement and anticipation but also fear and a nagging, sinking feeling of doubt that he could not, despite his best efforts, totally suppress. In his semi-conscious state he could still hear every sound in the house: a snore from somewhere; a whispered, animated conversation somewhere else.

When the first signs of morning light appeared he forced himself to follow the routine he had been given. He washed and changed into the clothes that were waiting for him: what seemed to be a waiter's suit, which fitted almost perfectly. He tiptoed downstairs past the open door of a room inside which one of his group was kneeling and whispering his prayers. The lounge gradually filled and there was fruit juice and bread to break the fast. Tariq Ahmed stood at the back and left the floor to a burly man in black T-shirt and jeans who stood before them with a large chart taped to the wall. Mo noticed that one of their number was not present and he broke the silence by asking about him. The man was brusque and clearly didn't wish to discuss the matter: 'He has been allocated to another task.' He then took the group carefully through the morning's programme and the instructions they were to follow once they had been delivered to their – unspecified – destination up to the point that they were to open fire on their target: a group of mainly American businessmen who were supplying arms to the enemies of Islam. The rest of the group seemed drugged – with sleep or some sort of hypnosis – and did not share Mo's curiosity to know more. After being rebuffed several times, he was unable to pluck up the courage to ask the question nagging at him: what do we do after the shooting? The instructor read his thoughts but was studiously vague: 'Allah will protect us. You will be shown the way out of the building and return to continue our struggle.'

The weapons on which they had trained were distributed and checked. Then the group made its way back through the yard to the van. Mo was surrounded by his fellow warriors and two of the instructors who eyed him much as they would have done a prisoner in custody. If he had any second thoughts, it was too late. In the van he sat next to the African from his hometown whom he had wanted to get to know better but had never had the chance. The African smiled at him, an open, almost loving, smile, put his arm around him and said: 'You'll be fine, son.'

<hr />

The top floor of the tower in Canary Wharf provided a good vantage point overlooking Docklands. Tariq Ahmed had come up here with the help of a sleeper from his organisation to understand better the distribution of security around the exhibition.

What was unfolding in front of him amazed and delighted him. There were flashing blue lights and police sirens everywhere. In front of him, on the roof of the O2, a group of nocturnal protesters had painted, in large luminescent orange letters, 'STOP THE ARMS TRADE'. He could just make out a cluster of people on the public steps to the top of the building gesticulating, no doubt working out how to conceal this embarrassing welcome to the world's largest and best-attended defence equipment exhibition.

At the nearby City Airport, police helicopters hovered over the runway and there were scores of ambulances and police cars. According to the radio commentary, a group of twenty to thirty protesters were lying down on the runway having adopted the successful technique from their road blockage of the previous DSEI event in 2017. It would take several hours to clear them – perhaps longer since another group had apparently landed by dinghy from the waterway alongside the airport. In the air, a growing number of aircraft were circulating and a leading member of the Saudi Royal Family had already been diverted to Stansted, with his London-based entourage fighting their way through the traffic to get to the M11 in order to greet him.

The Metropolitan Police were expecting trouble. Thousands of extra officers were on duty. With forty thousand visitors expected, including delegations from some of the world's least savoury regimes, the attraction for protesters was obvious. And unlike at previous DSEI events, where protests had been small and limited to dedicated pacifist and human rights groups, this time there was plenty of advance publicity. Television programmes featured torture equipment, cluster bombs and landmines allegedly being sold, illegally, on British soil, in a privately run exhibition heavily patronised by the British government as part of its global export drive.

Moderate opinion was outraged. The kind of people who marched against the Iraq war but generally disdained public protests started to say 'something must be done', and those within travelling distance headed off to join hastily assembled demonstrations. Docklands does not have the public gathering places like Trafalgar and Parliament squares through which protest could be channelled, and policed. So the impact was chaotic. The DLR became dangerously overcrowded and had to be suspended. Key access routes, through the Blackwall Tunnel and Thames Gateway, became hopelessly blocked preventing emergency vehicles getting through. At the ExCeL entrance itself, a long thin blue line held at bay thousands of protesters, and delegates struggled to get through.

All of this was witnessed with mounting satisfaction by the watcher in the tower. He had played no part in organising the chaos below but it made his own job easier. He had long admired the self-restraint, discipline and humour of Britain's peaceful mass protesters and had seen the same techniques used with good effect in the subcontinent. But they lacked the impact of violence: the shock, the terror that even a few people could create. Personal experience, as well as theory, had led him into this, more brutal, kind of politics. And like moths drawn to a flame, the media would always amplify the violence and ignore the worthy and well intentioned.

Today was the biggest venture he had attempted. The arms exhibition was a perfect target. And meeting the African, now a committed recruit to the cause, had given him the idea of concentrating the attack on the Global operation. The propaganda value of taking on a company with links to rabidly anti-Muslim forces was potentially huge… if the attack was a success.

Success today did not depend on the tens of thousands of protesters but the team of young men who had been well prepared for their task. Their first big obstacle had been the security screen around the exhibition centre. But the obstacle proved to be scalable. The scrutiny devoted to searching the bags of visitors did not extend to the comings and goings of staff serving Michelin Star meals to VIPs and VVIPs, nor to their food containers. It had not been unduly difficult to find a willing helper who was able to obtain a set of security passes for a chef and a serving team, doctored to accommodate new faces and names. The only anxiety was whether the congestion below would prevent certain guests arriving.

Tariq Ahmed need not have worried. A block booking at the O2 InterContinental, near the exhibition, had secured penthouse suites and a comfortable, secure business meeting room for the board of Global. The evening before the exhibition opened, all were comfortably ensconced and unaware that they were the object of so much interest. The company had a prominent display to advertise its arrival in the big league of weapons makers and distributors and a list of potential customers or partners had been drawn up for board members to cultivate. It was also an opportunity for the board to meet, to hear the Chairman set out his strategic vision and, hopefully, discover that their services would continue to be very well rewarded.

The Chairman convened a meeting of directors and was in good form. Since their last meeting in London the Chairman had secured a one-to-one meeting at Trump Tower and had been given the names of key people in the Pentagon who the President guaranteed would be helpful. Not only that: the British acquisition had come through – well done, Admiral! – though it was a pity about the unhelpful publicity. Desai, for once, was on the defensive explaining the complex politics of India; but it would be sorted. A pity Orlov couldn't be here; the British had refused his visa: 'tiresome Cold War politics'.

The Chairman was, however, in an expansive mood. The heightened tension in East Asia over North Korea and China's increasing assertiveness was creating a big market for Global's products and services in South Korea, Japan and, above all, Vietnam. Global's new Vice-Chairman, ex-Pentagon Colonel Ted Schwarz – would lead that work. 'I will ask Ted to say a few words in a minute. He has just come back from Ho Chi Minh City, which he last saw as a teenage marine.'

He then explained his next big play: the opportunities that had opened up as a result of meetings Orlov had arranged in the Kremlin. Russia would pay very well indeed for access to the most sophisticated Western military technology that wasn't available through conventional channels. The White House had been kept informed and wouldn't make a fuss. Once Desai had cleared away 'obstructions', the Pulsar/Parrikar Avionics partnership would be the main conduit for equipment officially exported to India, but then diverted to other lucrative destinations, including Russia. Board colleagues, he concluded, could look forward to a 'bumper Christmas bonus'.

Elsewhere in the same hotel a couple of old adversaries met for their regular exchange of information. The mere fact of their meeting would, were it known, lead to demands for their court martials and exemplary execution. In fact, they were both passing to their mutual enemy information on nuclear missile deployment that no ordinary spy could have obtained. Yet they were not traitors or spies but deeply patriotic – indeed, nationalistic – soldiers whose loyalty could never be doubted. One was General Rashid, the architect of the 2008 Mumbai raid and the more recent, and less successful, adventure at Parrikar Avionics. The other was General Balbir Singh, known as the Snowman for his exploits fighting on the Siachen Glacier where extreme cold rather than Pakistani bullets had claimed several fingers and toes.

They were not friends exactly. Indeed, they spent much of their time working out how to destabilise each other's countries through disinformation, terror raids and military action short of outright war. Their family histories during Partition matched each other in horror. Neither had ever visited the other's country, though they shared a common language and history. But their acquaintanceship had engendered camaraderie and they exchanged presents: Cuban cigars for the Snowman; the best Glenlivet for Rashid who was obliged to curtail his drinking habits back home. And they both had a soldier's contempt for their respective politicians: venal, self-serving, lying hypocrites whose endless pandering to popular prejudices had, more than once, taken their countries perilously close to a nuclear exchange.

The events of the last few weeks had underlined just how important it was to be able to control these idiots in an emergency. And each could speak with confidence knowing that in a safe back home there were letters from their chiefs of staff, and Prime Ministers, authorising the meeting. At the end of it, they had exchanged enough information to be sure that nuclear war could not start by accident – or misunderstanding – and without trip wires to ensure that the politicians on both sides had a clear, unambiguous understanding about what Mutually Assured Destruction could mean.

When the business was complete they settled down to a companionable drink and an exchange of news about their families. Then they wished each other well and looked forward to a good day shopping for 'toys' in the exhibition.

Steve was on his way to London, to the exhibition for which he had been given a pass and time off for 'union duties'. He didn't much like the idea of an arms fair but he could no more disown it than a fisherman could reject the sea. The union expected him to be there, visiting the stands of Rolls-Royce, BAE Systems, Westland and the rest, including Pulsar, for a photo and reassuring words with the bosses and their prospective customers.

When he reached the underground he saw the signs advising that the DLR to ExCeL was closed, for reasons unspecified. Chatter on the station platform established that public and private transport was immobile. No problem: it was early; he would walk. He hadn't realised quite how far it was. But there was the entertainment, and mounting excitement, of endless flashing blue lights from police motorbikes, helicopters overhead and crowds moving in his direction.

It then took an age to get through the crowds milling at the entrance, the pass check and then the bag check. Either the organisers were utterly incompetent or there was something seriously untoward going on. Overheard conversation from people glued to their phones filled in the story: the demonstrations; the sit-in at the airport; the protesters' message on the O2. He could see that at the next Labour Party meeting Ms Cook's friends would have plenty to say when they discovered that he had been abetting the sale of weapons to a miscellany of visiting tyrants.

Once through security he headed for the main hall. He had a list of company stands to visit but his first port of call wasn't the exciting new drone at BAE as the list suggested but to attend to the woman he loved. Shaida was greeting guests at the entrance to an impressive, expensively designed marquee devoted to the products of Global and its various subsidiaries, of which there were many after the recent spurt of acquisitions. Today she was not the Asian princess he so admired but an impeccably smart woman in a fitted, perfectly tailored navy blue suit, white blouse, stiletto heels and glossy coiled hair. It was a style he hadn't seen before but had clearly caught the eye of the line of men waiting patiently for her to introduce them to the world of laser-bearing missiles.

When she saw Steve in the background she gave him one of her most welcoming smiles and asked him to come back in the lunch break. 'As you see, I am auditioning to be an air hostess. Company dress code. Suits only. No hijabs here. It should be quiet when the VIP guests are eating.' What she didn't tell him was that this was how she liked to dress on her private trysts in London. They were getting closer, more comfortable. But she didn't want to assume too much too soon.

The last twenty-four hours had opened Shaida's eyes to the kind of company she now worked for. The firm wanted her to be available to lubricate the socialisation of top management. Duty No. 1 was to be present at a drinks party after the board meeting the previous evening. She was one of two young women in addition to the waitresses and when she entered the room she sensed that more was expected of her than looking pretty and making small talk.

She gradually fitted names to faces. The Chairman was a larger-than-life, fleshy man – over twenty stone she reckoned – with a garish mustard suit and uncoordinated tie. His loud Deep South drawl could be heard above every conversation introducing his new 'catch': a top Pentagon official, recently retired. She could also see that his eyes were not fixed on the man from the Pentagon but on her or, at least, her body. Having heard the gossip about his reputation, rather similar to that of his friend and sometime business associate Donald Trump, she kept her distance and avoided eye contact. She experienced a brief moment of panic when she was introduced to the Israeli director who bore a striking similarity to her old flame; but it wasn't him.

By carefully avoiding the eyes and arms of the Chairman, she found herself embraced by the tentacles of another octopus: the Red Admiral, rather the worse for wear after several glasses of rum. When she disentangled herself she was struck by his handsome, weather-beaten face, the intense blue – if somewhat bloodshot – eyes and the rich, baritone voice. She could have warmed to him but his intentions were so crudely obvious that she made her excuses and headed for the other Asian in the room: a silent, stone cold sober Indian sipping apple juice in the corner. This was presumably the Desai she had heard about and seen reference to in the communications she had been channelling to Kate.

Although he was no conversationalist, she managed to extract from him the information that he had been badly shaken by a 'security incident' in Portsmouth earlier in the week. He was travelling back as soon as a flight could be found and would miss the rest of the exhibition. That provided Shaida with an excuse to leave, 'to help our Indian colleague with his travel'.

But that last conversation and in particular the description of the 'security incident' reminded her what she was trying to blot out of her consciousness: her missing brother.

※※※※※※※※※※※※

Liam sat in front of his computer screen, puzzled and worried. He looked around the room for inspiration, at the several dozen bowed heads absorbed in their own unresolved puzzles and at the silent screens on the wall offering a variety of news channels. The owners of the bowed heads, like him, had once thought of themselves as incarnations of Bond; but that was not how the Service worked. It had headed off attacks since 7/7 through meticulous intelligence gathering and data analysis. Boring. Sedentary. Necessary. No one wanted to be the person who missed something.

Liam's problem was that his intelligence sources had dried up. Mo had disappeared from the face of the earth, seemingly, as had other young men from around the country known to have an anti-Indian agenda. Mo's sister had been as helpful as she could and his friends were convinced he was still in the country. Nothing else. The consensus among Liam's colleagues was that 'something big' was being planned, by people who were well organised and had unusually secure communications.

A couple of days ago the mystery seemed to have been solved: the call from the Tory MP and Trade Envoy passing on what seemed to be strong intelligence based on a sighting in Portsmouth. His bosses trusted his judgement and mobilised help. Then, the farcical 'terrorist attack'. Sniggering all round. Liam's five-a-side triumph. His colleagues spent their lives hunting for needles in haystacks and weren't impressed by people who became overexcited at the first sighting of a shiny object.

The screens on the wall were showing the enveloping chaos in the Docklands area. Liam got up from his seat for a closer look: the drama at City Airport filmed from a helicopter hovering above; the lengthening queues and restless crowds at the ExCeL; the static traffic for miles around.

Shaida had already told him that she would be there representing Pulsar. Thinking of Shaida prompted other thoughts. The company board. They and a lot of other VIPs from pretty unsavoury places. A controversial industry bash that some highly motivated people found threatening or offensive. An obvious target. But the Met were all over it. Months of risk assessment and contingency planning. Judging by the unfolding drama on the screens, there were risks and contingencies the clever boys and girls at Scotland Yard hadn't factored in. The company Global?

He wanted to be on the safe side. So he rang the number he had been given of the officer in charge of security at the exhibition. Assistant Commissioner Maggie Brown. He didn't know her, but she was highly regarded. She ranked well above him but would listen to someone from the Service. She answered immediately: calmness personified. He explained his concerns about the suspected terrorist cell: 'Sorry, nothing more concrete. Just a hunch. May need some extra security.' She wasn't fazed: 'You can see we have our hands full. But we will check it out. American company; Global, you say? Consider it done.'

<hr />

The cavernous halls of the ExCeL were packed with stands advertising every conceivable mechanism for killing, maiming or hurting fellow human beings that our species' ingenuity could devise. The professionals, the military men and their civilian masters or servants eyed up the potential on offer and tried to match it to their budgets. Businesses from the biggest to the smallest practised their sales pitch. The halls gradually filled up as the police cleared a way through the demonstrators outside and celebrity spotters could identify the President of the DRC, the Saudi Defence Minister – a regular spender but reportedly short of cash this year – a couple of UAE ruling heads, and large posses of Chinese, Japanese, Koreans and Vietnamese preparing for mutual hostilities. The demonstrators outside would also have been alarmed to see how many delegations spent time among the stalls of the ingenious entrepreneurs offering a variety of novel techniques for disrupting demonstrations. Undoubtedly the stars of the first morning were the Presidents of Egypt and Nigeria who had each arrived with a long and expensive shopping list, albeit without a clear indication of who would pay for them.

The Global stand faced stiff competition but the beautiful Asian woman welcoming visitors was a pull for the overwhelmingly male delegates. At noon the Chairman was due to give an address, according to the programme, to an enclosure of invited guests, in a space set aside within the area of the stand. He would speak alongside the Secretary of State for Business. The defence correspondents of *The Times*, the *Telegraph* and the BBC had been invited to ensure that an announcement on the latest dollop of public spending on the Defence Industrial Strategy was given appropriate coverage. Then the guests would settle down to a sumptuous lunch provided by the catering arm of a top London restaurant, no expense spared. Board members would each host a handpicked table at which conversation would flow in the direction of Global's latest offerings. Apart from a couple of security guards with walkie-talkies and bulging pockets, this was to be a relaxed, convivial, corporate event that could as easily have been transplanted to the Chelsea Flower Show or the hospitality suite before an international at Twickenham. As noon approached, however, it was becoming clear that all was not going to plan.

<hr />

Kate Thompson could see from the rolling news on her office TV that something untoward was happening at the ExCeL where she was due for lunch with her Secretary of State and the board of Global. After the excitement and false alarm at Portsmouth she wasn't sure whether to be concerned or amused by the drama on the screen. She expected the event to be cancelled in any case since traffic was at a stand-still and Jim Chambers would never dream of using public transport. But after she settled to her files, Susan came in to say that she had just received instructions to take Kate to the helicopter pad on the MOD roof. It was late but they could still make the lunch.

The two women quickly made their way to Whitehall and Kate was in a cheerful mood; this was much more fun than being a rebellious back bencher. Chambers was waiting for them in the helicopter with Caroline, his principal private secretary, and he was altogether less cheery. 'Bloody anarchists,' he grumbled. 'Time we sorted them out. Britain can't be "open for business" when a few troublemakers can hold the capital city to ransom, like this.' Kate tuned out of his rant as the helicopter revved up and headed off across London. This was her first time in a helicopter and she was totally absorbed in the scenery and, as they approached their destination, the signs of chaos on the ground. The rude welcoming message on the O2 triggered another burst of indignation from the Secretary of State above the crackle of the intercom; but Kate was full of admiration for the protesters' nerve and creativity, and exchanged conspiratorial smiles with Susan. There was, however, a reality check as they landed next to the ExCeL: a serious warning from the security services. Should they go back? No. Just be careful.

Led by a couple of security staff, the ministerial group made their way through the exhibition hall, late but just in time for lunch. They went straight through the crowds of delegates to the Global stand and Kate noticed Shaida, stunning in unfamiliar Western dress, receiving guests at the entrance. They arrived just as the Chairman was about to launch into a welcome speech, looking greatly relieved that his chief guest had made it with his entourage to fill some of the embarrassing number of empty chairs.

Kate was struck by the Chairman's appearance: a rather gross man with remarkable coiffed hair in the style of his soulmate Trump. He was dressed in what Susan called, in a whisper, 'cowboy chic' missing only the Stetson hat. Kate recognised his accent, from the Mississippi delta in Louisiana, but his warm words scarcely disguised his irritation that British 'communists' were depleting his audience and delaying lunch. She had expected someone thoroughly sinister but found his folksy manner and cartoon-like appearance rather endearing. The Secretary of State responded with an off-the-cuff, charming and witty speech of the kind he had perfected on the Tory rubber-chicken circuit but with a few scripted lines for the journalists.

Lunch commenced. Kate was seated alongside a taciturn American, Colonel Schwarz, who had a military bearing, cold grey eyes and a severe crew-cut. He didn't do small talk and her attention wandered to the rest of the gathering. She recognised the Red Admiral entertaining what sounded like East European or Russian businessmen and he winked when he saw her looking in his direction. She had been told to expect a group of Indians, including Desai, but there were empty seats where they should have been. She couldn't help noticing the waiters, mostly Asian, who seemed remarkably awkward and inexpert as if they were serving a meal for the first time.

Shaida was watching events from the back of the stand, irritated that it hadn't occurred to Global's organisers that the woman who had charmed dozens of visitors to the stand might merit a lunch. Nonetheless, she was able to locate Steve and they found a good vantage point where they could see and not be seen. They had a laugh at the mannerisms of the strange American they now worked for. But, then, they noticed that there were more disturbing oddities.

A group of armed men silently filled the back of the stand around them and one of them indicated to them to stay where they were and remain silent. Then they noticed the strange behaviour of the waiters whose clumsy unprofessionalism was in marked contrast to the sophisticated food they were serving. One of them managed to spill a soup bowl over one of the guests. Next, Shaida saw that one of the waiters looked familiar: an African; she knew she had seen him before. Then, to her shock, she saw her brother. Instinctively she stepped forward, out of the shadows, towards him. He didn't see her. But a moment later one of the waiters dropped a tray of glasses and, as everyone looked at the offender, the other waiters drew weapons from under their jackets.

Firing started. There were screams and shouts. Mo raised his weapon but then froze when he saw his sister in front of him. They stared at each other, fixed to the spot. Then he crumbled under a fusillade of bullets.

The firing stopped almost as quickly as it had begun, though the screams and cries for help continued along with a fire alarm that someone had activated. Shaida's first thought was for the body in front of her. She embraced her brother, whispering words of hope and encouragement. Steve rushed to join her to try to revive Mo, who was clearly critically injured and bleeding from the mouth. But it was hopeless. As more security men, police, medics and voyeurs descended on the scene, Steve led her away, shaking and too stunned to speak.

The carnage was, however, less serious than initially suspected. Kate and most of the other guests had found refuge under the tables, though several appeared to be injured and at least one, a Korean, was dead. A passer-by, a waitress at a neighbouring hospitality event, had been hit in the head by a stray bullet and was also dead.

One of the assassins had failed to fire a shot after his weapon had jammed and he was pinioned to the floor by a scrum that included Jim Chambers and the Red Admiral. Another, described as African in appearance, managed to flee in the mayhem leaving his white jacket and gun behind. Two others, one a white convert, were unambiguously dead. And the fifth was found, mortally wounded, being cradled by his sister. There was one other body: Chairman Le Fevre. His corpse was unscathed, however; he had died of a heart attack.

As the news channels and, later, the newspapers sought to interpret these events, the initial focus was inevitably on another terrorist outrage in parallel with those on the Continent and in the USA. Several terror groups claimed credit – not that there was much credit to claim. The biggest peaceful demonstration in recent years, and its cause, largely disappeared from the news. As the journalists hunted for a human interest angle, the first target was the waitress, an innocent bystander. But she turned out to be an illegal migrant from Moldova; no one knew her backstory; even her name, Irma, was probably false. The image that dominated the story was the photo taken from a mobile phone and distributed on social media, of the beautiful young woman holding her dying brother. Divided family; divided allegiances; here was a modern parable for the country to debate.

The funeral took place several days later in the corner of the municipal cemetery where the town's Muslims buried their dead. It had taken a few days to get Mo's body back from the authorities, while they investigated the plot. It was a cold wet day: the first real sign of coming winter. Steve had come to join the mourners, but he soon realised that he was the only non-Muslim in the gathering crowd and judged from facial reactions that he was unwelcome. So he retreated to a copse of trees and watched from a distance. Even there he was caught up in the mood of the ceremony. At the sight of Shaida, in the front row of women relatives cradling her mother, he felt, for the first time in years, warm tears running down his cheeks and he sobbed to himself quietly. He was distracted from his grief by the sound of several men moving through the trees behind him and when he turned he recognised Liam among them. He assumed that they were here to watch the mourners rather than to mourn.

After the funeral crowd dispersed, he waited and then stepped forward bearing the red carnations that he judged were suitable. He placed them on the freshly dug soil covering the grave and then stood for a long time contemplating. Not since the death of his mother had he been to a funeral and that was a rather antiseptic, badly attended event in a crematorium, drained of emotion. He was more profoundly moved by this young man in the earth in front of him, who had shown little beyond hostility but who had helped to send his own life in a new direction. He was at the point of leaving when he heard a rustle of clothes behind him and then felt a hand slip under his arm. It stayed there and a head rested against his shoulder.

A week later Deepak Parrikar passed through London on his way to the USA. There was a joyful reunion with Kate in his hotel. They had both survived near-death experiences and had much to share. Kate and he knew that their paths were diverging but they were reconciled to the reality and were able to savour each other's company as it came, for the moment, as if each encounter were to be the last. They had not been truly alone together for weeks, and longed to express their passion for each other. At last, their physical desires satisfied, they lay entwined and talked in the warm glow of shared contentment through much of the night with an easy fluency and depth of understanding that neither had ever had with anyone else.

They explained to each other how they managed their roles as accidental politicians whose family circumstances and events had moulded them rather than career and ambition. They shared, too, their awkwardness as outsiders; not part of the tribe; not anchored by rigid ideology; used by but also learning how to use the system. Neither was a saint nor even particularly idealistic but both had a basic sense of decency and a nose for detecting evil. They marvelled at the fact that the dividing lines between them of convention, colour and country mattered so little.

As Kate prepared for an early morning departure she took a folder from her briefcase and gave it to Deepak. She explained the role played by the unlikely couple: the British trade unionist and Labour MP in waiting and his courageous and beautiful friend (she had never established what precisely the relationship was). Shaida's researches had established a trail of nefarious activity across several continents. The folder compiled by Shaida detailed Desai's activities within Global. There was almost certainly enough – the offshore accounts, the lavish tax-free payments, the involvement with political figures on the American extreme right – to have Desai ejected from the inner circles of government, and from Parrikar Avionics. The Indian ruling party valued the appearance, at least, of probity and the threat of bad publicity was a powerful inducement with an election approaching.

<hr />

When the drama of the terror attack had passed, Kate organised an appointment to see the Secretary of State. She arrived with a fat folder.

'Well, Kate, I hope you are none the worse for our little adventure. Terrible business. I hope it will silence all those hopeless, wishy-washy liberals who want to go soft on Muslim terrorism.'

'I guess we owe a big debt to Liam and the security people. They were ready and casualties were minimised. Your rugby tackle helped too!'

Jim guffawed. 'I was just doing my bit for UK plc. A pity we didn't have more time at the exhibition. It was a superb, professional, show. Inevitably we lost some business in all that fuss, but I am told by the defence sales chaps that we still had record turnover. But let's get down to business. The Prime Minister has asked me to confirm that the job we have promised you is coming through in a reshuffle in a few weeks' time. Have to keep it under wraps, but probably a big job at the Treasury. Next step the Cabinet! And he also wants you to take on an inter-ministerial task force on diversity as someone who has empathy for our ethnic minorities, as well as being a champion of women.'

Kate smiled in acknowledgement. 'Actually, I wanted to talk to you about something else. Global. The Red Admiral.'

'He's fine. Tough as old boots.'

'He isn't fine. He's a crook.'

'Oh Kate, really. Not that again. I do hope you haven't been encouraging the Overheads to tell tales out of school.'

'Nothing to do with the civil servants.' She put down her folder on Jim's desk. 'This file is made up of documentation from inside the company. If you want to look at the sections I have highlighted, it points to the fact that he has been involved in illegal arms smuggling, corrupt payments to officials in overseas governments, tax evasion, sanctions busting and unhealthily close links with a Russian associate whose enemies have a habit of disappearing. Liam and the permanent secretary will confirm what I am telling you.'

The Secretary of State maintained his composure remarkably well. 'That's quite a charge sheet. If you leave the file with me, I will consider what can be done.'

'I should say, Jim, that there are several copies. I think you should ask the Red Admiral to clear his desk immediately and pass the papers to the police. Otherwise I may not be able to restrain the people who gave me this material from going straight to the press.'

For the first time since she had known him he was totally lost for words. Eventually he recovered enough to speak. 'Well, Kate, I take my hat off to you. You have learnt how to survive in the political jungle, and more. I can see that I shall have to ditch my old friend the Admiral. Pity. Basically a good man fallen into bad company.'

'That isn't quite all, Jim. There is one very large payment that looks as if it could only be to one person. You. You should check if the bank details correspond to your own. If they don't, I apologise for jumping to conclusions.'

She was taking a risk. In fact, she had no proof, merely a suspicion. If he called her bluff, she would be in difficulty.

He looked at her for a long time, calculating the odds, she thought. 'Actually, you are right. It is me. But the money went to the party. I didn't keep a penny.'

'I suppose you think that makes it OK. Sorry, Jim. No go.'

With that she left the room.

⬛⬛⬛⬛⬛⬛⬛⬛

The Sloane Square flat felt bigger and emptier than he could ever remember. He looked again at that photo with his men, taken before they set off for the Falklands. The open, trusting, confident smiles. That picture often produced tears. But tonight the tears were of self-pity.

The two policemen had been quietly and respectfully spoken: almost gentle in their questioning. But it was painfully clear where they were leading: the lucrative, undeclared, conflicts of interest; the secret accounts; the national secrets passed on for a financial consideration. When it was clear that he could not save himself he tried not to implicate others like the Secretary of State but the officers knew too much already and he finished up dragging his friends down with him under the waves.

When it was all over he picked up the phone to speak to the only people he had left. But Louisiana didn't want to take the call. The acting Chairman, Colonel Schwarz, was busy. An underling, a new voice, told him that an exit payment was being arranged to his Caymans account. The acting Chairman had decided that, in view of terrorism risk, lax security, embarrassing publicity and the police interest, Britain was no longer a good place to do business. There were big opportunities opening up elsewhere. European operations would be handled in future out of Paris by retired General de Massigny, formerly of the French Defence Ministry and Dassault.

He tried St Petersburg but it was very late, even for an old friend in distress. Orlov yawned: 'Sorry, Comrade.'

He remembered that he had kept his service revolver locked in the desk drawer.

Author's Note and Acknowledgements

My biggest debt is to my wife Rachel, who acted as literary critic, moral support and typist in the early stages of the book and who also suggested the title.

Joan Bennett did a large amount of work typing and amending the manuscript.

I am grateful too to friends like Pippa Morgan and the Oakeshott family who read early drafts and gave me both encouragement and the benefits of constructive criticism.

Those sections describing British political life, and the civil service, draw on my own experience of politics, parliament and my years in the Cabinet. But any similarity between the characters in this book and real people is entirely accidental.

The sections on India draw on over half a century of visits to that country, and to Mumbai in particular, as part of the extended family which had my late wife, Olympia, at its heart. I also had many professional visits, of which several were as a minister promoting British exports, including arms.

The scenes depicting slum life in Mumbai rely not just on personal observations but on fictional and non-fictional accounts as in Suketu Mehta's *Maximum City*; Katherine Boo's *Behind the Beautiful Forevers*; Gregory David *Roberts' Shantaram*; and Vikram Chandra's *Sacred Games*.

The book can be traced back to my first serious experience of British politics as a Glasgow city councillor, over four decades ago, and the conflicting demands of jobs for Clyde-side workers, political idealism and the requirements of the arms trade. I then found myself in the Diplomatic service for a period, charged, among other things, with promoting British arms exports to Latin America. In opposition I challenged the corruption involved in some of our arms exports business. And then, as Secretary of State, I had ministerial responsibility for arms export licensing. The companies and individuals described in this book are however wholly fictitious.

The particular contract I describe, related to the creation of a shield against a nuclear strike, is based on what is publicly known about Indian and Pakistani defence policy. I am grateful for advice I received from Professor Michael Clarke at the Royal United Services Institute.

The book was made possible by the excellent team at Atlantic Books: Will Atkinson, Karen Duffy, Susannah Hamilton, Sara O'Keeffe and Margaret Stead. And, as ever, I benefitted enormously from the encouragement and advice of my literary agent, Georgina Capel.